RUNNING WILD NOVELLA ANTHOLOGY

VOLUME 7, BOOK 2

EDITED BY LISA DIANE KASTNER

RUNNING
Wild
PRESS

Running Wild Novella Anthology, Volume 7 Book 2

Published in North America and Europe by Running Wild Press. Visit Running Wild Press at www.runningwildpress.com Educators, librarians, book clubs (as well as the eternally curious), go to ww.runningwildpress.com for teaching tools.

ISBN (pbk) 978-1-955062-67-1

ISBN (ebook) 978-1-955062-78-7

CONTENTS

FRIENDLY GHOST

BY STEPHANIE WEBER

ONE

There's a ghost at the end of the hall.

I can't believe it really looks like that. Grayish, whitish, and see-through. A mix of not quite. Not quite any color. Not quite any consistency. Not quite a person.

"Hello," I say.

The ghost stares. Does it really see me? Is it staring into the distance or is it looking at me? It's hard for me to tell where the vacant, not-quite-black eyes are focusing on. I don't want it to come near me or feel threatened by me. I'm leaving anyway.

"You can stay here," I tell it.

The ghost nods. "So can you," it tells me. Its voice is both present and faraway. Like a whisper in my ear despite being three feet from me.

I'm surprised by what it tells me. The audacity of it. I pay rent here, pal. But, of course, it was here first. It was already living in this place.

I want to say more. I want to ask questions. *What is your name? Why are you here? For how long? Do you like my decor? Is it okay that I moved in? Did you die on purpose?*

Instead I tell it, "I have to go to work."

It nods.

It disappears like it was never there.

I leave and lock the door behind me even though the ghost can neither leave nor enter. I leave it behind like a house guest or a pet. I go to work and don't think much about it for the rest of the day.

TWO

It hits me midway through the day that ghost is technically in my job title. I'm a ghost, too, in that way. A ghostwriter for romance novels. I work at Raven's Nest Publishing, an online publishing company that specializes in romance novels. None of the titles are published under my name which is a good thing. My name isn't very sexy anyway. Gladys Alvarez. Everyone calls me Gladdy. Erotica doesn't get written by someone named Gladdy.

Instead I work with a team of people to write under the pseudonym Virginia Southgate. Even that name. How do people not know it was fake?

It didn't matter. The company is small, consisting of only about eight people, and we work on about two or three different novels at a time. The goal is to churn out as much sexy erotica as online publishing can handle. I work with two other people to write Virginia's sultry sex scenes and scintillating romance.

Sometimes it is fun. Sometimes it is hot. Most of the time it feels silly and even more than that it feels like work, like any other job. We sit at desks, typing away and casually chatting about everyone's weekend plans.

The company mostly consists of men in their twenties and thirties. It is owned by a former scientist named Brandon who saw the romance novel industry as his ticket to success. I suppose I do, too, now.

Only two women work here: me and Betty Trujillo who feels like my opposite in a lot of ways. She's a funky person with vibrant clothes and vintage glasses. She has dyed pink hair that she touches up regularly, so it rarely fades too much which keeps her head bright like a highlighter. She likes to wear red lipstick, too. She is a walking pop of color.

I wear a lot of brown.

Betty is also a lot louder than me and with a much more vibrant sex life that she pulls inspiration from. She talks about tying people up and using toys and techniques with a lot of expertise. I talk about it like I'm sharing a dirty rumor and don't want my parents to hear me say anything.

It's not that I'm inexperienced. I'm simply not that adventurous and sex makes me shy. Most things make me shy. I never know if I'm doing anything right. Usually when I'm having sex, I'm wondering if it's actually satisfying for the other person. Am I being as sexy as a pornstar or a girl in a movie? Am I as good as the last girl? Am I better than being alone tonight?

I was in a long term relationship for almost three years and we lived together. It was fine. Until it wasn't, but even then it wasn't a disaster. If anything, I was the disaster which no one would expect by looking at me. I was the one who blew everything up and I still feel guilty about it.

My boss Brandon comes up to my table. He's an extremely gruff guy who is very bad at social cues and general politeness. I chalk it up to his former life as a chemical engineer before he discovered that romance novels were lucrative and not nearly as difficult. He's not a compassionate person. He sees romance novels as a paint-by-numbers operation, not a creative writing one. He only sees formulas and bottom lines.

"You have to write a seduction scene today," he tells me. "Make it playful. Use some of that cute humor you have."

I smile. "Cute?"

"Yeah, whatever. Base the character around you a little. Kind of a dweeb, but can be sexy when she takes her glasses off. That trope."

I nod. Is that what he thinks of me? Is that what everyone thinks of me? The 'before' girl in a romantic comedy?

I look over and lock eyes with our art designer, Jon. He designs all the covers, does some marketing. He's the artist here among writers and as such he seems edgier than all of us. He has long, messy hair. He wears a lot of black T-shirts with the names of bands I've never heard of. He comes in later than the rest of us and often looks like he's recovering from last night's parties. There's a tattoo of black shaded tree branches reaching up his left forearm. I wonder what other tattoos are under his clothes.

He smiles at me.

Maybe they all did think of me that way.

"Not too cutesy," Brandon warns. "She IS a drummer. Read the outlines and the notes."

"I know," I say. I was in the meeting that developed this story of a female drummer who gets swept into a hot rockstar's band.

"Can you make sure you work on that this week?" Brandon asks to make sure I get him loud and clear.

"Absolutely," I say with the enthusiasm of a Girl Scout. I was never in Girl Scouts. I wanted to be, but I was too shy to ask my parents to sign me up. Instead I would read in my room after school. My parents would brag to their friends about how much I read. *She's reading Shakespeare and she's only 12. Yes, she understands it! Gladdy, come here. Summarize A Midsummer Night's Dream for Mr. Anderson.*

A seduction scene is tough because a lot of the action in the book hinges on that scene. It comes relatively early in the book because it brings the attraction out. It pushes the rest of the romance along. It's the memory the character comes back to: the thing that makes them fall for each other. It is important and, most importantly, sexy.

The book we had been writing as a team effort - like all of our books - was the story of a rockstar named Ash who had to replace his drummer with a hot shot female who didn't really like his music right away. But then she came around to his music, and him. It became Ash who kept the beat in her heart.

I stare at the page. The beat in her heart. It's so cheesy. And It's so hard to write romance and seduction when I feel like my heart has been hollowed out. My insides were scooped like a jack-o-lantern leaving stringy guts and seeds never to be planted. I have to write about falling in love when I threw my love away.

Even my thoughts feel like bad creative writing. It's going to be a very long day.

THREE

As I unlock my front door, I remember that there was a ghost there this morning. I wonder if the ghost will be standing there on the other side when I open the door. I wonder if it will ask me how my day went. I wonder if it will say 'where have you been?' I wonder if it already knows what I do all day, if it follows me.

I open the door very carefully and peak my head through first.

"Hello?" I call.

I don't get an answer. No ghost.

I walk in and turn the hallway light on. I'm not sure if lights matter to the ghost. They probably do. That makes me think. What are the ghost rules?

I put my keys on the designated hook next to the door. I put my purse on its designated hook hung up in the hallway. Everything has a place in my new apartment even if not everything is unpacked yet.

When I walk into the living room, I am faced with that very reminder. There are boxes. These are boxes with contents that need to be put in places. But do they? I live by myself now for the first time in my life. Who do I have to impress with order or cleanliness? Who do I even have to invite over for company?

I consider texting my ex-boyfriend Jacob. I want to ask someone for help and company. Why not him? Would I still have a place in my heart? I look at my phone. I don't think he'd want to hear from me. It might be hurtful, but I'm hurting right now. Loneliness hurts.

Did I make a mistake?

A glimmer hits the corner of my eye. The hallway light flickers on and off.

"Hello...?" I ask.

The lights go all the way off.

The ghost appears in the hallway again.

"Hello," Ghost says.

I look at it for a moment, still amazed that it's kind of see-through. And also somewhat not. Like pantyhose.

"Did you need me?" Ghost asks.

I shake my head. Did I?

"I don't think so," I say. "Why do you ask?"

"I got a feeling."

"Oh. No, I'm okay." I am lying, but I don't know what the ghost can do for me.

"Okay," Ghost says. Ghost then walks with its feet not really touching the ground. Ghost walks toward the bedroom and then vanishes.

"Hello?" I say to see. Is it gone?

I rush to my bedroom door and look inside the room. I see nothing in the dark, so I flip the lightswitch on. In the yellow light, there's nothing there. There's my lonely bed and nightstand. There's no ghost in this room.

Maybe there's no ghost in this house.

I open a living room box that is filled with books and start piling them on the living room floor. I have to take out every book so that I know what I have. It's so easy to forget what your own possessions are. I want to organize them in some fun way like lifestyle bloggers do. They organize them by color, making rainbows of book bindings that seem broken when one or more books are taken off the shelves. I realize I don't have enough brightly colored books to do this. Instead I try to figure out which books I like the most and organize them on the shelf from the best to the worst. The best and worst according to me, the person who has read them. An arbitrary list.

I'm embarrassed by the ones I haven't read. I wonder if I will ever read them. Now that I'm alone, there might be time. There might be too much time. It strikes me that reading, while lovely, is such a solitary activity. The more well-read you are, the more time you've spent alone.

I do this for two hours until I forget the ghost enough to go to bed.

FOUR

I have a few questions about ghost mechanics and they are these:

Can it go through walls?
Can it SEE through walls?
Does it see at all?
Does it know what day it is?
Can it feel?
Can it go through me?
Why did it stay here?
What is special about this place?
Does it have unfinished business?
Does it need help?
Does it need me?

FIVE

Okay, a seduction scene. I can do this. I can write about the rockstar Ash and his female drummer Jamie. I can write about how they come together. I can write their seduction. I can do this.

I peak above my desk to my boss Brandon's office. He's staring at his own computer screen, angrily typing something. Everything he did seemed angry which was so silly because we were in the business of romance.

I go back to my work and hope that I can get into a really good groove if he does end up looking up. That way he can see how hard I work. I never see anyone look at me though - except sometimes the graphic designer Jon.

I interlace my fingers and stretch them above my head as if stretching my fingers really helped them type faster or helped the creativity flow from brain to finger. I look at the blank Word document in front of me and I start to write. Sometimes I just have to start. The only way out is through, so I have to write to get through the blocks in my brain that might prevent the seduction from happening.

I began:

Things seemed to come easy to Ash Beckham. Stardom. Rock music. Navigating his adoring female fans who drooled at the sight of his chiseled chest. It was admirable in a way. Now if only his music would come easy to Jamie.

She had been practicing for hours, messing up the tempo on his most famous song "Kamikaze Love Machine". She just couldn't hit it right, so she finally thought that she might be able to if she actually tried to connect to the song lyrically. What was he trying to say? Perhaps if she could get the essence of his feelings, then she could feel her way through the song. But what did Ash feel? Did he feel anything through that thick head of jet black hair? Could anything penetrate his heart through those muscular, tattooed pecs?

She was banging through the chorus with his lyrics in mind: "Baby, love bomb me. Kamikaze love machine. Give it to me like I knew you would. Give it to me like I didn't know you could."

Jamie actually starting to get the hang of this. She started singing to herself: "Give it to me like I knew you would. Give it to me like I didn't know you could."

A familiar voice suddenly joined her:

"Give it to me like I knew you would. Give it to me like I didn't know you could."

Jamie looked up. Ash. Standing there in the doorway, casually leaning on the frame like he owned the rehearsal studio. She was so startled that she missed a step in her drumming and one of the sticks flew out of her hand instead of flying hard onto the cymbals. It flung across the room straight toward Ash who caught it in his left hand, standing cool as a cucumber.

"Ash!" she exclaimed.

"Trying to kill me with a drumstick?" he asked slyly with his luscious lips forming a flirtatious smirk. "I gotta admit. That's

not how I saw myself going out. Overdose. Accident. Sure. But drums? Didn't see that one coming."

She blushed. Why am I blushing? *It was just Ash and his mindless music that was all about screwing your brains out. Although watching him walk into the room in those tight jeans and black tank top that scooped low enough to show off a smattering of chest fuzz, Jamie started to understand his lyrics a little better. Or at least, she wanted to understand them.*

"I'm sorry," she said. "I thought I was alone."

"Do you want to be?" he asked.

She shrugged. "I'm trying to get better at this song."

"You gotta feel it. You're the drummer. You hold everything down!"

"I know. That's why--"

"Hey, I'm just teasing you," he said. He was so cool. He walked over to her and took a seat on an amp, spreading his legs and drawing her eyes to the bulge between his legs. "I feel like we got off on the wrong foot."

He can say that again, *she thought.*

"Tell me about yourself." He said.

It's hard to offer information when I don't know what exactly it is that he wants. *Demanding she tells him about herself hardly felt genuine. She wasn't sure if she could trust this guy who is so beloved around the world for his killer voice and toned biceps.*

Jamie boldly decided to toss the ball back into his court. "What do you want to know?"

"I want to know...everything."

Smooth move, *she thought. His green eyes blazed at her, filled with what might be curiosity. He also seems amused, perhaps more at himself than at her. He was that kind of guy, always amused at himself more than anyone else in the room.*

He knows he's charming, *she thought.* He knows he's irresistible. And yet...here I am resisting him.

"You first," she said.

"I'm from Akron, Ohio," he said as he swept his hair to one side.

I'm resisting him, but just barely.

"Really? I'm from Columbus."

"Two Midwesterners making it big in the band. How about that?"

"I'm hardly making it big," She told him with her cheeks catching fire from his flattery. She shrugged and looked down at her scuffed up shoes. "I'm just your drummer."

"You're my heartbeat."

She looked up at him. Gazing deep into his soft green eyes, she realized that he might actually be sincere in trying to get to know her. I should try to do the same. *After all, she wouldn't mind getting to know him further - perhaps under his clothes.*

"And you?" He asked with a pout, drawing her eyes to his lower lip. There was a flutter in her pants as she found herself wanting to suck on that lip.

"Me?"

"Yeah. You haven't told me anything about you yet. Who are you? Who's Jamie?"

I step back from my laptop for a moment.

Who's Jamie? Who is she? What else can I write about the rockstar named Ash and his female drummer Jamie? Jamie, a girl who grew up a tomboy and is now in the male dominated world of rock music. She's not like other girls. She's a girl who can hang. She's a girl who drinks beer and bangs the drums.

She's a girl that I'm not.

I'm the kind of girl with needs that she's afraid to say. I'm the kind of girl who wears thrift store skirts from the 70s and sweaters that don't fit me quite right. I'm the kind of girl who likes to drink a bedtime tea. I'm the kind of girl who is actually a 30-year-old woman, so the girldom has all but faded. The cuteness is subsiding. This is who I am. This is the adult woman I am who will only get older and watch herself disappear from public viewing as men take their gazes off of her and move them to younger women in shorter skirts and tighter sweaters. I'm a woman who might fade into obscurity. Unlike Jamie. Unlike Jamie who will drum onstage in stadiums around the country and enjoy the perks of rock-n-roll success without being hounded by recognizable celebrity. Her life is constantly thrilling. Her life is late night rum and green room privileges, drunk texts and exciting sex. Mine is going to bed around 10:30 and waking up in the morning to not a single text message.

I'm nothing like her, this character I have to write for. How can I access her voice and seem believable? How could anyone get turned on by the absolutely sexless me?

I close my laptop, pack up my bag, and dip out of work thirty minutes early.

SIX

Back at my apartment, I open a box that has a beautiful mid-century lampshade in it. It's a pink color and a sort of trapezoid shape the way that fifties shapes tended to look like they were trying to burst out of their own confines and fly into space. My ex-boyfriend Jacob and I bought this lamp together.

I admire the lamp and remember what it was like to find it at the vintage store. I remember our excitement over talking about its shape and imagining outloud where we'd put it. Such a small, mundane domestic task made us feel legitimate. A real couple with real things to do together.

I shook it up and threw it away.

When we had what I would call our final conversation, I tried to hug him. He brushed me off, holding up his hands to block my advances. He told me that I didn't get to break his heart and comfort him at the same time. He was right. That was cruel of me.

Instead I watched his hands carry his head in his lap, taking my place as the one who could offer solace. He would have to get used to it because this was going to be it. This would be our end.

"I don't want to be mean, but if you're going, you have to go," Jacob said to me. He didn't mean it literally. He meant it emotionally. He didn't want me to be halfway out the door, but I wasn't sure yet if I wanted to actually leave. I told him I wanted to try something else. I told him I wasn't really there. I finally told him the hardest truth of all: that I didn't think I loved him anymore.

The operative word was "think". I had been doing so much thinking. So much. He would never understand that. It wasn't the snap decision that he thought it was. It lived in my mind for so long. He was mad I didn't keep him in those conversations with myself, but how could I? How do you begin to talk about something like that?

By the time I tried, I was already elsewhere in my mind.

He was upset that I didn't include him in all of those conversations that I had with myself. He was upset that I made decisions for us by myself. He was upset with me.

When I first told him, he stayed somewhere else. He took a couple of things and he stayed at a friend's place. He would take more and more things here and there until little by little our lives started to peel away.

With each picture taken off the wall, each knick-knack or tube of shaving cream that got hidden away in his new space for refuge, the story faded out. The isolated incidents of unhappiness transformed into a dreamlike state where I no longer knew what was real.

Did we really do that? This life together? Did we really share this space? Were we ever really here?

Can it ever actually come back?

Part of me honestly thought it would. I thought maybe I

just needed to say these things out loud. After all, why would I *want* to leave Jacob? *He was so nice.*

Well, to me he was. When we were together. Afterwards, he became hard and cruel as he closed himself off to me. It felt like having sunshine everyday and then it was suddenly cloudy. The warmth was taken away. It hurt so bad, but I told myself it couldn't hurt me more than I had already hurt him. Hurt people hurt people. It was all necessary. I understand that, but it doesn't make it easier.

In a lot of ways, I thought I deserved his cruelty. How could I expect or want anything different after breaking his heart? I'm trying to come to terms with how we ended and to tell myself that there aren't good guys and bad guys. Just people. But it's hard to believe that. Really hard. It's hard not to be in bed alone at night and consider all the bad karma I put out into the world, analyzing the ways in which it is or isn't yet coming back to me.

At least that's been my super chill night time routine ever since our split.

There was no hard-and-fast reason to leave which makes leaving harder. If he had only done something wrong, then it would be so clear. If I did something wrong, then he would want to leave. Instead we were in this gray area where things weren't wrong, but they simply weren't right. Or at least they weren't with me.

He was fine. He was happy. He wanted to buy us a condo and live peacefully. He wanted us to have Christmases with his family and Thanksgivings with mine. He wanted us to live out our days watching one another grow older, doing it together, watching our favorite TV shows as a pair from time to time.

I simply didn't and I couldn't figure out why.

I didn't see myself walking down an aisle. Not with him. When I pictured my future, he didn't seem like he was there. The future felt blurry for me anyway, so how could I really know what I wanted either way? I went back and forth constantly.

He wanted to marry me and I felt that as a thirty-year-old woman I was supposed to do it, as if it were now or never. To be a single woman in her thirties was to be the butt of all desperate, single lady jokes. Did I really want to volunteer to enter into that category?

And yet the thought of marrying him - of a wedding with our families - filled me with panic. I wanted to claw my way out of the restrictive wedding dress in my dreams and smash the cake as I ran naked away from all the pageantry, fleeing to my freedom.

I read a horoscope for myself the week it was really over. It said, "Don't be sorry. We all have our reasons to leave." That became my mantra.

Finally, he came back to our shared apartment. We talked about the state of things, but things had been broken that were hard to repair. I wasn't sure I wanted to. He told me to go. If I wanted to end things, I had to be the one to go. This time he was asking me to physically leave. He said he was going to repaint the place and make it more his own.

I agreed.

We no longer lived together. We no longer really talked. Instead I lived alone with a ghost.

I look up and see Ghost staring at me. Was his sadness magnifying my own? Or reflecting it? I put the lamp back in the box and go to bed. I don't know if I want to actually unpack it yet.

SEVEN

Before I go to work, Ghost appears again. This time Ghost shows up in my kitchen as I make myself tea in the morning. I make myself a cup of English breakfast tea every morning as I eat breakfast - usually toast with peanut butter - and scroll through my phone. It's a simple, quiet morning ritual.

As I take the tea kettle off the stove, I turn and see Ghost there. It scares me. So much so that I almost drop the kettle of boiling water. I reach out with my other hand to stop the fall and recoil in pain. It's hot. Boiling hot. Of course it is. What's wrong with me?!

"You scared me!" I shout.

I think my voice surprises both of us because he seems to wince. Can a ghost wince? He certainly appears to have done so.

"I'm sorry," he says.

It's an odd feeling to get an apology from a ghost. It almost feels like a child apologizing to you. You don't want to be mad at them and you know they definitely didn't mean any harm.

"It's okay," I murmur as I pour the water into my brown

mug. It looks like a mug from an old homey diner. In fact, it might be. I can't remember where I got it and I have a feeling I may have stolen it to prove I could be wild and edgy. Who was I proving that to? I can't remember.

I don't know how to act when Ghost is hovering around in the kitchen. Ask him how his day is going? Talk about the weather? Ignore Ghost entirely?

"I'm going to eat breakfast," I say.

"Okay."

I take my toast and tea and sit down at the table. Ghost is still there, watching me. It's a very eerie feeling. It never feels good for someone to watch you eat, let alone something supernatural.

I look up, finally. It's far too awkward to just sit there munching loudly on crunchy toast.

"How are you?"

"Fine, thank you."

"I have to go to work soon," I say.

"I know."

He knows. He claims to know...everything. In that way, Ghost is like most middle-aged men that I know. Maybe that doesn't change in death.

"So...um...what do you do during the day? Like when I'm at work?"

"Oh," Ghost pauses and considers this. It's funny to me that the ghost has to think of an answer. "I go here and there. I wander around. Here and there."

I don't know what that means. If it means pacing around my apartment, then that sounds painfully boring. I don't want to think of how boring it is, especially when I'm at work. It would only make me feel bad. I might be compelled to come home and entertain Ghost like a pet.

"That's nice," I say because I don't know what else to say.

I chug the rest of my tea. The shot of hot black tea directly into my insides doesn't feel great and I worry that the surge of caffeine will give me a weird headache. I place my dishes in my sink and let Ghost know that I have to go.

"I know," Ghost says again.

"I'll see you later," I say.

"Yes."

Yes. A definitive yes. I wonder if here and there could possibly mean outside of this place. Outside of here to haunt someone else.

When I get to work Betty is having an animated conversation with Jon by the coffee pot. He is laughing a lot at what she's saying. I can't tell what they're talking about, but it seems like fun. I feel a twinge of jealousy. I want to make Jon laugh. I want to hear Betty's stories.

When their conversation dies down into dwindling trails of laughter, Betty sits back down next to me. She seems satisfied like that coffee break fueled her. She doesn't say anything to me. I want to have a good conversation, too.

But how exactly?

I think about my conversation with Ghost this morning. If that could count as a conversation. What exactly was that? And why? I should've asked him why. Or maybe that's the exact kind of thing that could spark a conversation. The ghost!

I have to blurt it out. I have to tell someone about the ghost. I pay a therapist to talk to, but there is no way she'll really believe me. She might prescribe me some kind of medication to get rid of the "hallucinations". But it isn't something I'm hallucinating. I know what I see.

Telling Betty might be a great idea. I can get it off my chest and start a stimulating conversation. This is what people like to talk about, right? Ghosts? I'll find out.

"I think my apartment is haunted," I tell Betty who has only just begun to start typing at her desk.

She pulls away from her desk, the wheels rolling on the hardwood floor to face me.

"Tell it to leave," she says plainly.

"What?"

"My mom was a medium and that's what she would do. You can tell them to leave. Sometimes they don't know they can. They think they're stuck. They don't know they can move on."

"Does that really work?" I ask.

"Sometimes," she says. She thinks for a minute, looking a little far away as if remembering something and seeing it so clearly in front of her that's blocking my face. She returns. "Sometimes the spirits don't want to leave. Usually those are the bad spirits."

"How do you know if a spirit is bad?"

"Negative energy. You can feel it...is yours negative?"

I shake my head. "I don't think so. It seems very passive."

She nods as if she knows exactly what kind of spirit I'm talking about. "That's good. That spirit will probably leave if you tell it to."

"For good?"

"Hard to say. Sometimes they can't."

"Then where do they go?"

Betty shakes her head. "Oh, dear, I don't know the answer to that. If I did, I probably wouldn't be here right now. I'd be a millionaire!" She cackles as if this is true, as if people are clamoring for the answer to the question: where do ghosts go when you tell them to leave?

Maybe they are. What did I know? I was the one asking the questions.

"Betty," I say again to get her attention. "Have you ever seen a ghost?"

She shakes her head sadly. "No, I don't have the gift. I wish I did. My mom, she said she would look at a person and see all their spirits around them. All your dead friends and family. I tell you, if I could do that, I wouldn't be here right now. I'd be too busy talking to all my dead friends and family."

Betty laughs again before wheeling herself to her desk. I don't think that's how it works. She said her mom saw other people's dead friends and family...could she also see her own? And why wouldn't she be here? There was a ghost in my house. I can guarantee that the dead don't make good companions. They aren't that engaging.

I don't tell her this. I let her believe. It feels nicer that way.

It reminds me of being the only girl in my class who knew that Santa Claus wasn't real. My parents were straightforward with me. They didn't want to lie to their child, but they didn't realize they would be taking away the magic of Christmas to a child in public school where December parties were filled with lists to Santa and stories of reindeer on the roof. My mother was aware, however, that my knowledge might ruin the magic for other kids. She insisted I respect that and not tell anyone.

I abided.

In second grade, a particularly snarky boy bragged that he knew Santa Claus wasn't real. We cut pieces of construction paper in snowflakes and listened. He whittled down his paper with ease into an intricate pattern that was devoid of Christmas magic. It held only logic. My classmates were really listening and some of them believed him.

"It's your parents," he said. "You can tell because they leave the price tags on the gifts."

Having never had a Christmas where I believed in Santa, I didn't know if leaving price tags on gifts was part of the tradition. It felt like negligence on his parents' part, but other seven-year-olds nodded in agreement. Maybe they had price-tagged gifts from Santa as well as if Santa had a toy store he shopped at for every child around the world.

Everyone nodded except for one pretty blonde girl with a big green bow in her hair. She pushed back and told him that she knew it was Santa Claus and that he was only saying this because he didn't believe. Looking back it all has a vaguely apocalyptic tint to it: believe and be saved! Repent, non-believer! Repent and unwrap gifts on Christmas morn!

They argued back and forth. I had been silent. Finally, I was dragged into the fight. The little girl looked at me and said, "You believe in Santa. Right, Gladdy?"

Her crystal blue eyes batted at me, on the verge of drawing water from their wells. It stirred me. It stirred me the way I'm sure her adorable blue eyes would stir people for the rest of her charmed life. I don't mean that in a bad way. She was an adorable little girl who surely grew to be an adorable woman - especially if she continued to believe in magic.

"Yes, I do," I said. "Santa is real."

She smiled and went back to cutting snowflakes. That was all the reassurance she needed. I learned then that sometimes it's nice to let people believe in things. There's no harm in that. Not all lies cause harm.

I like for Betty to believe what she believes. I go back to my work and open up the seduction scene I'm supposed to be writing. It does feel a little like lying to be a heartbroken writer for romance novels. I'm not sure what I believe in right now. This will make people happy even if it hurts me.

A little lying can be okay.

EIGHT

I'm trying to hammer away at this seduction scene again, but I feel so lost. It's hard to want to have sex - yet alone write about it - when you feel as if you've just emptied your heart. But it's my job. I'm on the clock. I have to *try*.

(But wasn't I always trying?)

I've stared straight ahead of me for too long. Brandon has noticed in his office with the open door that lets him spy on us. He grimaces at me from his desk. I turn away filled with shame for not working on this seduction scene. A hilarious thing to be ashamed of, but it's shameful nonetheless. I turn to the screen, hoping words will magically appear. But they don't. They never do.

Now it's the keys' turn. *O, keys, please guide my hands.* I wait. I thought maybe since I'm seeing a ghost on the regular that I might be some kind of supernatural or have telekinetic powers. I don't. The keys don't guide me. My hands just sit there, lifeless and idea-less. I place my hands in proper typing positions and force the fingers to tap away:

. . .

"And you?" He asked with a pout, drawing her eyes to his lower lip. There was a flutter in her pants as she found herself wanting to suck on that lip.

"Me?"

"Yeah. You haven't told me anything about you yet. Who are you? Who's Jamie?"

Who's Jamie? She asks herself. Not even I know the answer to that question, *she thought to herself.* All I know is that I'm the drummer. I make things move. I pound rhythms. I'm the backbone and he's the frontman. We're so different, but maybe music is the only thing we have in common.

"I'm a musician," She told him in a lowered voice that made him cock his head toward her. "I'm the drummer."

"Well, I know that." He got up from the amp and looked like he was about to leave because she shut down his curiosity. She didn't mean to. In fact, she was more curious than ever about him, especially when he turned around in those tight jeans.

"Why do you do this?" She asked to get his attention again. "Music. Why this career?"

He turned around and swept the hair out of his hunky eyes.

"It's my calling," he said. "My dick doesn't get hard for much else."

Ugh. Ew. Did I just write that? Jesus Christ.

At the end of the day, my brain feels drained. I thought I would love a full time writing job, but it winds up leaving little room for creativity for me outside of work. During the final minutes of the day, I alternate between rubbing my wrists and rubbing my temples. There is so much rubbing to do until 5pm.

Brandon leaves his office in a hurry. He makes a production of locking his office door. Something must be up.

"Hey, Gladdy," he says to me as he passes my desk. I look up. It's just me, him, and the graphic designer Jon who is bent over his desk. Jon keeps to himself mostly, but he has a very warm spirit. He has tan skin and round brown eyes that feel like they've seen the world. His long hair is tucked behind his ear. It skirts the outline of his sharp jaw. It frames his oval face. It makes him look like Jesus.

But Brandon isn't like Jon. Brandon is a doughy guy with the anger and energy of a bulldozer with a lot to smash that day.

"Are you done with that scene?"

"Oh, yes, almost I mean."

"So...no?"

"Oh, no, but almost."

"It's a yes or no."

"She said she's almost done, Brandon. Chill." That was Jon.

Brandon nods. Brandon listened to him. Maybe he was always mad at me for being a woman. Or maybe I was annoying and legitimately worth being mad at. I couldn't tell.

"Like he said, I'm almost done." I smile at Jon. He looks back down at his work, but I think he's smiling. This is the most I've interacted with him since I started at this job.

Even Brandon smirks. I decide to take this inch and go the mile.

"Hey, Brandon, when you go home at the end of the day do you watch a bunch of monster truck rallies?"

Jon looks up. He's grinning. There's such a lightness in his eyes.

"No, I go home and read more romance novels and so should you."

Brandon zips up his computer bag with an intensity that feels undeserved. Why am I getting this aggression? I thought I was being playful. That's what I get for trying to joke around at work.

He whisks past me, leaving the office for the night.

I turn around and see it's just me and Jon there.

"That was funny," he says. "What you said to Brandon. I didn't know you were funny."

"We've never really talked before," I say. Then I feel bad because I'm presuming that I am funny. I'm not really.

"My bad," he says. He's smiling though. It's such a nice, slightly crooked smile. A smile with edge and warmth. A smile that means it. "Look at us remedying that right now."

"Yeah, I didn't mean anything by it. I mean we barely have any reason to interact."

"I'm going to make a point to talk to you now, Gladdy. Every day. You'll get so sick of me and I'll love it."

"Can't wait."

I'm blushing. I know I am. I hope he doesn't notice.

"Do you..." I start to ask him and realize he probably does. I was going to ask if he knows how to lock up the office because I don't. Maybe he could show me. Maybe we could do it together. But that's okay. He's busy. He probably doesn't want me to bother him right now.

"Do I what?"

"Nothing," I say. "Have a good night."

"Well, wait," he says. "I'm just finishing up. Were you trying to see if I know how to close up the office?"

I nod. "You caught me," I say to make it cute.

He smiles. "I do. I can show you if you hang out for a second."

I hesitate. He takes the hesitation to be an answer.

"You don't have to either. I'd ask you to have a drink with me after work, but you're probably busy."

I am not busy.

"Another time?" I say.

Why? Why am I saying this? He's a nice, cute guy at work. We'd just be going together as coworkers to get to know each other and unwind after a long day at work. But I can't say yes. I can't let myself have fun. I'm already kicking myself for this.

He nods and looks back down at his work, but before he does that he gives me a soft smile. He is very sweet. I want to take back what I just said, but I had already put it out there. Now I feel terribly awkward. Part of me wants to ask again about doing it another time. *How's Thursday? Or tomorrow even? I'm more available than you think!*

"I'll close up," he says. "Goodnight, Gladdy."

"Goodnight, Jon."

I leave. Alone.

NINE

A lot of people nowadays have standbys. Standbys are people you can call or text to hook up with if you are feeling particularly desperate. You know your standby will come over if you call or that they will be interested in you when you put it out into the universe.

Because I turned down the opportunity for a potential date - and really I'm not sure that it would have been a date or if it is a good idea for coworkers at a very small company to do that kind of thing - I am starting to feel very alone and anxious about being alone. I should have said yes. I should have went for it. What did I have to lose? Some awkward silences? Oh, but those awkward silences can give up so much of myself. My budding work crush could burn out and then I would have nothing.

Maybe I'll text Kevin, an old friend-of-a-friend who wanted to date me before Jacob and I started up.

I sort of want to text Jacob, but I don't think he'd like that at all. I don't know what the point of that would ultimately be. We hadn't talked or hooked up or anything since we broke up and it was going okay.

It's so hard to be alone.

Three hours later, Kevin and I are having sex. I texted him and I barely had to text him anything at all before he offered to come over with a pack of Whiteclaw. Ugh. Sure. He did and after two drinks each we made our way to my bed. We barely chatted before this. It was clear this was his M.O. from the moment I opened the door and I don't mind it too much. It feels okay - good even - to be wanted after the last few months I've had.

I'm underneath him and he's grunting on top of me. We slightly fumbled with each other's bodies in place of foreplay, but it wasn't that electric. I wasn't that turned on. I decide midway through this that I'm not sure if I want to do it again, but I don't mind doing it right now. It's okay and it's okay to have okay sex.

I see Ghost looking in the corner of the room. Mouth downturned. Sadness.

I give Ghost a look. *Do you mind?*

But I don't think Ghost can read human expressions. I can't tell. That's still something about ghost mechanics that I don't understand. Ghost continues watching for some time. I finally turn away in disgust, but I can still feel Ghost there. I worry Ghost will say something and scare this guy away. Would he even be able to hear Ghost? Is it only me that can?

Thinking these things is making it impossible for me to be in the moment. I look up and see Kevin is somewhere else. His eyes are closed and his face is upturned. Who is he seeing? Where is his brain? As my tits bounce on my chest, I can't help but wonder what the boobs in the ceiling look like. Or whatever it is he's envisioning.

When he finishes in a climax of quick, sweaty breaths, he

dismounts and lays next to me. I glance over again, but Ghost is gone. I wonder when Ghost vanished. I wonder when it had had enough.

Kevin falls asleep surprisingly quickly. I didn't want him to fall asleep with me. I didn't want him to stay the night. That was never discussed beforehand. But now he is sleeping and I'm left to deal with it. I deal with it by staring at the ceiling for some time.

I look over and there is no Ghost. Maybe Ghost really left.

I get up and reach for my shirt which I slip on. This wakes Kevin up.

"Hey," I say in a cute voice bordering on sexy. Why am I even trying?

"Did I fall asleep?"

I nod.

"You're putting on your shirt?"

"Yeah," I say. "I might take a shower."

"Oh." He says. He seems disappointed by that and he gets up, his body kind of slumped over with sleep. He silently grabs his clothes and puts them on. Suddenly, I'm not sure that I want him to go. If he goes, then I'll be alone. The idea of loneliness was creeping up on me and making me anxious.

"You don't have to go," I say.

"It's fine. I'll talk to you soon."

It's fine. What is fine? I don't understand what is happening. He got upset with me for putting clothes on like I was giving him silent commands to get out of my bed. Although, I suppose I did want that.

He put on his shoes and opened my bedroom door to leave. He opened the door and I saw Ghost standing at the end of the hall. Ghost had a slightly different energy. The room was a little cold. I let out a frightened gasp.

"What's wrong?" he says.

Ghost vanishes. Warmth comes back in.

"Nothing," I say. ".The dark."

"Aw, you're scared of the dark." He kisses me on the cheek. I wonder if his masculine desire to protect a frightened young damsel like myself will kick in and make him want to stay. It doesn't.

"I'll talk to you soon," he says and then opens the door to leave.

What is soon, I wonder. It's not even that I want *him* around. I just want *someone* around. Ghost must sense that because Ghost comes back.

When the door shuts behind him, I see Ghost. I'm mad. I'm mad that Ghost didn't let itself be fully known. I wanted to point at Ghost and say, "Look!" I wanted Kevin to see it, too. I wanted to bond over it and to feel less insane.

"Why were you watching me?" I ask Ghost.

"I couldn't look away."

That's perverted, I think. I say nothing. I'm disgusted by Ghost at the moment.

"You don't like him," Ghost said.

I shrug. "I'm lonely. It's been a while since Jacob."

"But you said you wanted to be alone."

I turn to the ghost. "How do you know that?"

"Did you really want to be alone or did you just not want to be with him?"

I storm off. I rage into my bedroom and slam the door behind me like a petulant child. Of course, Ghost is not a mother that I can run away from. Ghost is not a roommate. Ghost went through the door. Ghost appeared behind me in my bedroom.

"Leave."

"Wait," Ghost whimpers.

"Go. Away!"

And with that Ghost vanishes, just like Betty said.

I'm left alone for the time being with no disappointing lover in my bed and no ghost in my room.

TEN

Here are some possible places I think Ghost goes to when he goes away:

- Purgatory
- The closet
- His former life
- The other room
- Another dimension
- Another timeline
- The apartment next door
- In the body of a cat
- The DMV
- The ocean
- Inside my TV
- My mirror's reflection
- Heaven
- Hell

ELEVEN

I'm in therapy the next day and the whole thing with Ghost and Kevin is fresh in my head, but I don't feel like I can explain it. I haven't told my therapist anything about Ghost. It sounds...crazy.

I wasn't sure if Ghost had left me for sure, but that morning I called out to him.

"Hello?" I said to the empty apartment. I did this three times before Ghost appeared just as before.

"Hello," Ghost said to me.

"You're back."

"Yes," Ghost said. "I live here."

I live here, too. We shared a moment where we both existed in the hallway together, looking at one another. I think we were both grateful to be there. It felt like having a friend. Being haunted made me feel less alone. I wasn't sure if I should apologize to him or not. I didn't. Instead I said that I had to go to an appointment.

Now that I'm sitting across from my therapist, I want to tell her all about this. I want to ask her if I should apologize to

Ghost. Is Ghost my friend? Should I treat him differently? Should I be concerned that I'm hallucinating? What does it all *mean?*

Instead of ranting about my apartment haunting and sounding like I'm spiraling out of control, I figure out how to couch these concerns in other things. I focus on a feeling of being unsure if I'm doing the right thing because, honestly, that is how I felt in that moment. I didn't know whether Ghost was projecting those questions on me or if his very presence made me consider the weight of my decisions. It was all unclear. All I know is that I felt a tugging at my heart that asked: *is any of this worth your time?*

"I don't know what's wrong with me," I tell her. "But something is. I'm not right."

My therapist squirms in her seat. She always does this. She's a very slight woman who is in incredible shape for her late middle age. I wonder if part of that is because she burns calories throughout the session fidgeting and squirming in her seat across from me. Sometimes she sprawls out on the armchair like it's a chaise lounge. Other times she crosses her legs like a pretzel in the chair. Today she tries arching her back in a stretch, keeping her legs seated like a normal person.

"You're much more well-adjusted than you think you are," she tells me with a stern look through her purple-framed glasses. I hate being told this because I don't think it's true. I'm living in my head and sometimes it's hard to live here. Other people seem to have it so easy. They don't seem so alone and they don't set fire to their house to ensure they are *absolutely* alone.

"Then why did I leave everything behind with Jacob?"

"You weren't happy."

"He was perfectly nice. *So* nice. Everyone thought so."

She looks to one side and kind of bobs her head. She isn't

buying this. One thing I can use as reassurance of my actions is the fact that my therapist doesn't think I didn't do anything wrong. She doesn't think Jacob is a saint.

"But was he? Was he really that nice to you? That attentive to your needs?"

I shake my head. I admit defeat. "I never felt like he understood me."

"I know," she said. "I don't know him from Adam, but I don't think he did either."

"He didn't know Adam?" I know what she means, but a little deflection goes a long way.

"No, he didn't know you."

"But then why was I there for so long? We lived together. Was I just lying?"

She pauses. She repeats the word lying to herself.

"No, that's not lying. Relationships are just...complicated. Trust me, this is all so common."

I almost feel bad for being so common. I want to be unique and have problems that feel like a puzzle. Instead, it's old hat for her. At least she's attentive, perhaps more than Jacob was when I told him how I was feeling. She earns her $20 co-pay well.

"You're not a flawed individual," my therapist tells me as she crosses her ankles. "There might be some faulty wiring along the way, but that's just something to pay attention to. That doesn't indicate you're somehow bad or inferior or anything else you're worried about."

"I'm worried I'm going to be alone forever," I tell her as if I'm blurting out a big secret. "Not out of an inability to meet people, but because...I don't know...maybe I don't know how to really love."

"Love means a million things and I don't disbelieve that you love people well. Everyone just has different needs and wants. It's all a balancing act."

"How do you know what to do? How much of this is feelings and how much is a choice?"

She laughs and gives me a look that says 'who knows'.

"If I knew that, I wouldn't be doing this. I'd be on a yacht somewhere thriving off my riches from cracking the code to human emotion."

"Ah," I say. I consider that she's the second person in recent memory to tell me she'd be rich if she had the answer to my question. Who are all these people willing to pay millions for answers?

"What if I'm, like, haunted?" I ask, considering out loud that Ghost is some kind of cosmic punishment sent to weigh over me until I decide to take it all back and return to my humdrum relationship. Then I quickly cover it by saying: "By my bad decisions. What if they follow me for life? These...ripple effects?"

She sat up. "Let me level with you. Not so much as your therapist, but as a human. I've been happily married for 20 years and I like my life. It's a good life, but I know that I could have married ten other men I dated and about half of those would have been good lives, too. I chose to marry my husband at a time I wanted to get married and he did, too. That's how it went. Timing. Choice. Love. But it could have gone differently and that would have been okay, too."

The alarm on her phone goes off to indicate we're done for the day. We schedule our next appointment and I leave to go the apartment I live in without the man who wanted to be my fiance.

TWELVE

"Why do you do this?" she asked to get his attention. "Music. Why this career?"

He turned around and swept the hair out of his hunky eyes.

"It's my calling," he said. "My dick doesn't get hard for much else."

Ugh. Gross. What the hell was I thinking?

"How's the ghost coming?"

I startle as if a ghost just came up behind me. Not my ghost, he's friendly. A different, scarier ghost. A more traditional ghost. I turn around and see it's only Betty. She's grinning to herself with fuschia lipstick on her lips and she wears a kitschy dress that looks like it was originally a tablecloth from the 1950s.

"You scared me!"

"*I* scared you? You're the one with the haunting!"

"Yeah, he's still there."

She takes a seat at her desk next to me and asks in the same tone as my therapist trying to get to the bottom of a neurosis: "Do you know why?"

"No...I didn't really think about it." I hadn't. I don't. I never really questioned it. It felt like his place that I was coming into. I never asked questions and he never told me anything. Should we be talking more? Should my relationship with the ghost in my apartment be the same as other relationships? A give and take of personal information and feelings.

"You don't wonder why?" she asks, surprised.

"I don't know. I mean I think, but mostly I kind of get along with him. I don't know. I don't mind him there. I think I like it."

"You've come to the other side, I see."

"I don't know about that. I'm not a medium or anything."

"Gladdy, you see a ghost every day. That's some medium shit."

I smile. I don't know anything about the supernatural or ghosts or anything. I'm Cuban and I barely know what Santeria is other than my abuela had to wear white for a year to become a priestess or whatever it was that she was "training" for. I'm still not sure.

"I see him every day because he's there. How could I not see him?"

"Ghosts don't make themselves known to everyone. They open themselves up to people who are open to them."

"That can't be true," I say thinking of all the screaming ghost stories I've heard.

"Well, they think these people will be open like we might think someone is interested in us and ask them on a date, but they say no. We still thought we had a shot. Ghosts are like that."

I nod. It makes sense. Or I don't know. I don't know what to think.

"Well, I don't mind him there. I kind of like it."

"You like being haunted?"

"Yeah. I'm less alone. Someone's home."

"Honey, that's a roommate."

"Yeah," I shrug. She's right. That IS a roommate, but this roommate never makes a mess and never plays music too loud at 4 in the morning. "I live with a ghost."

She shakes her head, smiling to herself. "If you ever want help with it, let me know. We could conduct a seance and see what his unfinished business might be. Maybe we can help get him over to the other side."

"Maybe," I say, but I don't really want to entertain it. "But not right now."

"Suit your haunted self."

After work again, Jon and I are left in the office. It feels purposeful. Was he waiting for me? Am I waiting for him? All I know is that this seduction scene is not coming easy and he's there. He seems like he could be used as inspiration. If only I were brave enough.

Well why not? Why not be brave?

"It's just us," I finally say. The words don't feel real coming out of my mouth, like I can see them getting away from me and I want to pull them all back in. *What are your words doing? Where are you going?*

Jon, casual and sweet as always, looks up and smiles. He has a very warm, jagged-toothed smile that instantly makes me feel calm. Why was I worried about saying anything at all?

"Time to party," he says. "If only they had alcohol here."

"Doesn't Brandon?" I ask as I gesture to his office.

"You bad girl! You wouldn't."

I want him to think I'm cool and bad and tough like him or like Jamie, the character I've been writing for this dumb rockstar-meets-drummer story. I wanted to be like her, taking no shit and attracting cool guys in the process. I wanted to be effortless. I don't feel effortless at all.

I stand up defiantly. I wouldn't? Well...I don't know if I would. But I was about to prove to both of us that I could.

I walk over to Brandon's office door and turn the knob. Damnit. The office is unlocked. Part of me hoped it would be locked so that I wouldn't have to go any further, but alas. I open the door and step inside. Are there cameras in here? I have no idea. Brandon seems like he would have a camera. I look to my left and spy a filing cabinet. To my right is his desk. There are drawers there! Bosses in TV shows and movies usually keep their alcohol in --

"Let's go get a drink," Jon says suddenly.

I turn around. I was so prepared to risk my job to rummage through my boss's office. Maybe that risk was enough to prove I *could* be *somewhat* of a bad girl.

"Now?"

"Well, yeah. Let's get out of here."

"Okay!"

Jon and I take a short walk to a dark cocktail bar around the corner. At first I feel shy around him out of nowhere as if I've never talked to this guy before, but he starts complaining about work and there's something about that that loosens me up. He feels comfortable complaining around me. Being negative and positive. I want to hear his frustrations and likes and dislikes. I want to know about his good and bad days. I find myself starting to want him in all the worst ways.

We walk inside the small bar that looks closed from the outside, but inside it's all dark and redlit like a mix between a dive bar and a brothel. We both look - and feel - impossibly sexy in this lighting.

We sidle up to the bar and each order a cocktail. I order a vodka soda and he orders a rum and coke. To my surprise, he pays for it. He insists.

"Where do you want to sit?" he asks.

I look around. I want to be casual and easy. At the bar feels casual, like we're just two buddies, but I also want to look at him. Would sliding into a red vinyl booth together be too intimate?

"I can do whatever," I start to say.

"Booth," he interrupts. He was thinking that same thing I was thinking. I make a mental note of that and remind myself to just fucking speak up next time. Say what I want. Put it out there. He'll probably agree. We slide into the round booth, but sit across from each other even though the vinyl seats go all the way around. We could easily slide toward the middle. It's such an alluring danger! Aware of this, I put my purse in between us to ensure we don't somehow end up closer than we've ever been.

"So we've never talked about this," he instantly begins. "But what are we doing at this romance novel publishing company? How did we become monkeys for Virginia Southgate?"

I shake my head with a smile. It's a ridiculous place to work, but I also really don't mind it. I don't mind it at all.

"I wonder that some days. But other days? It's a really nice writing job."

"Yeah those are hard to come by, right?"

"Very."

"What is it that you want to write?"

I shrug. It's been a long time since I wrote for myself. I wanted to be a journalist or an essayist or both or everything - it didn't matter really. I just love to write and I saw avenues for myself with those things. But this? This works.

"Anything and everything," I tell him. "I guess that's why I like the job. At the end of the day, I want people to read my writing and feel good. We provide that, bizarrely enough."

He nods and looks like he's honestly considering it as he takes a sip of his drink.

"That's what I tell myself, too. There's no harm in making some horny women happy."

I blush. Oh, no. I hope he didn't notice. I hide my face in my drink.

"But is this all you want to do?"

"I don't know. It's hard for me to look much ahead--"

"Why? That's what dreams are."

"No, dreams are like...I am floating in a river of chocolate and my mom is not my mom but she looks like my mom."

He laughs. I like that. It distracts me from the fact that I feel like I'm being boring by saying I don't have dreams. That's not true exactly. I've had dreams, but dreams get dashed. Dreams get taken away. I don't want to live in misery anymore.

Maybe I'm just depressed.

"I don't like talking about dreams," I say. "Dreams don't seem achievable. You're talking about goals."

"Okay, yeah."

I can't think of any goals (true love and success maybe?), so I flip the question his way: "Do you have goals?"

"Yes and no," he admits. "I like my job. I like that I can create outside art. Like I have other clients, but then I also make things for me. I've been sketching a friend's graphic novel idea for a while."

"That sounds awesome."

"Yeah, I really like that...so if you ever have an idea."

"We could do an erotic graphic novel."

We both smile. It's a wildly flirtatious smile shared between us.

"I just want to make art forever. That's a happy life, you know?"

I nod, admiring the sincerity in his eyes.

"So what's your idea of a happy life, Gladdy? Writing romance with other people under someone else's name forever?"

"For a lot of people romance is the meaning of life!"

"Of one's *own* life. You're...well, I guess you are helping other people by infusing romance into their lives."

"See?!"

"Okay, but what about *your* life? Your life, not Virginia Southgate's life."

"It's the same as everyone, right? To love and be loved."

"That's a good one!" He lifts his drink like cheersing me.

"Is it so important to have goals and dreams and all that anyway?" I say this thinking of Ghost. Did Ghost have dreams? Is Ghost here because of his unfinished goals? Or maybe living in the future has doomed him to my present for eternity. Would my unaccomplished life lead to some kind of hell on Earth? I didn't want to think about that, but I also couldn't let Jon know any of those thoughts without sounding absolutely insane. So instead I posit this question: "What if looking toward the future and setting goals or dreaming actually takes us out of living in the moment?"

"Dreams propel us forward! Otherwise we'd all be stuck in the same place."

"What if we could trust the moment to take us forward?"

He doesn't look convinced. So I ask him:

"So then what's the meaning of life?"

He smiles and his eyes move over me like he's thirsty. "Good cheese and a good lady."

I start laughing uncontrollably, but he doesn't get offended or embarrassed. He laughs with me. He knows he's somewhat ridiculous and that's refreshing, but I also think he believes what he says. And? I don't think he's wrong. It's just *such* a line - a line that feels like he and his "old lady" should mount their Harley and bike into the sunset.

"I think I'm feeling this drink," I giggle.

"I could do one more."

"Same, well..." I trail off. I don't want to admit that I think one more drink will make me feel drunk and cause me to embarrassingly stumble out of this booth while telling him how cute his nose is. I have a thing for a distinct nose like his, but then again I'm starting to have a thing for everything about him.

"What if we split one?" he suggests, like he could read my thoughts.

"Okay," I say.

"Order what you were drinking. I'll let you get this one."

I get out of the booth and he calls after me. I turn around to see him holding up two fingers.

"Gladdy! Two straws."

I order a vodka soda with two straws like we're two kids in the 1950s sharing a milkshake. It's adorable and innocent. It's salacious. It's presumably what two people on a date would do. I suddenly wonder if this is a date. If it wasn't a date at first, it's certainly slid into that territory.

When I return with one drink and two neon green straws, we're both giddy. We act like we're the only two people in the world to do something cute and unspoken. I wait for him to sip first.

"I never make the first move," he says with a smirk.

"Never?"

He shakes his head. There's a twinkle in his eye.

"You're the one who suggested two straws. I'd say that's a move."

He laughs and concedes. "Okay. Your move next."

I blush and all at once everything feels like too much or like I don't deserve it. He's talking to me like we're in one of the seduction scenes I have to write.

Oh my god...these lines...they should be in the book.

"What?" he asks. "You just got this weird look in your eye."

"Oh. Nothing. I just - work stuff."

"Do you have to go?"

I shrug. I don't want to, but I feel like I should. I always feel like there are things I should be doing - things that take me away from having fun. We were having a wonderful time and a voice in the back of my head was reminding me that I don't do that. I don't have fun.

"We can start walking out," I suggest.

We leave the bar and he walks with me. I intend to walk home which is about a mile and a half away, maybe two miles, but I like to walk. It clears my head and it lets me see my city. Jon keeps walking with me up the busy street until I finally ask him where he has to be.

"Just home," he says. "I can walk you to yours."

"It's kind of far," I say.

"Okay. How about I walk with you until I get tired?"

It turns out that Jon doesn't tire easily. The two of us walk all the way up Milwaukee Avenue, past Damen and past Western and almost to California Avenue where I live. We're talking so much about absolutely anything that we're losing track of time as the cool spring night gets progressively darker and darker. I get cold, too, but it doesn't bother me that much. We're laughing too hard for me to worry.

I eventually notice we're getting *very* close to my apartment. I'm nervous about what to do then. Do I invite him up? Does he want me to? Swift scenes of what might happen when we're alone together in my apartment play through my head. Talking, laughing, drinking the half-open bottle of wine I have left, fumbling on the couch, clothes half-on and half-off, drifting into the bedroom, trying to figure out the positions to sleep comfortably in with each other's bodies, leaving together in the morning for work.

It all plays in my head and it all makes me scared as a deer on the highway.

"You should go home," I blurt out.

He looks at me for a second with slight embarrassment. Did I humiliate him just now?

"Okay, goodnight," he says and just like that he turns around. I can't believe it. He did exactly what I said.

I turn over my shoulder and see if he is looking behind his shoulder back at me. He isn't.

I start to feel bad that I asked him to turn around. He was being so sweet and traditional, walking me home like he was courting me. I walk only a minute, not even, when I get a text. It's Jon. We've only texted once or twice before. The text says:

That was so fun. I totally lost track of time. That doesn't happen to me often.

I smiled, hugging the phone to my chest like it was his hand or something. I felt the same way. The very same way. So I wrote back:

Same.

Oh, god. That's too flippant. Why be coy? Why be cool? I should tell him how I'm feeling and how I'm feeling is absolutely buzzing. I feel like doing backflips. I feel like skipping home. My cheeks are red and my smile is wide and everything looks like it's in technicolor. So I text him when I'm right outside of my brick apartment building.

Thank you for tonight. Let's do it again sometime.

My phone almost immediately buzzes. He already texted me back?! I look at my phone and see that he had written: "**definitely**". Definitely. It feels so good to be on the same page as someone and to not have to play a game about waiting twenty minutes to text someone back.

I open my door and practically feel like singing. Although, part of that might be the alcohol. I feel buzzed for sure. I plop down on my brown leather couch and let my dizzy head rest. My head feels like a cartoon carousel is winding around, joyfully chaotic, and with no choice but to enjoy the ride.

Ghost appears. "What's going on?" he asks.

"Oh, hello!" Ghost is across from me, not his usual position in the hallway. He's in my living room in front of me like he's made himself right at home. He's getting much more comfortable.

"I had a really nice night."

"Good! You deserve it."

I smile. Maybe I do.

"We all do," I suggest. I'm drunk enough to say, "You do too."

"I wish I could."

"Can't you?"

Ghost is silent.

"Ghost, can you leave here? Can we leave? Go out on the town and do...I don't know...anything? I mean you can go through walls! You can go anywhere! Right?"

Ghost is silent.

"Talk to me here. Can you?"

Nothing.

"I know I'm kind of buzzed, but I mean it. I want to know. I want to help you. Help both of us! You just said I deserve a good night. Well! So do you!"

Finally, he says: "That's for you to enjoy. I can't anymore."

Ghost exits, vanishing into thin air.

I try not to let that bother me. Instead, I focus on recalling the details of Jon's face as he smiled across from me in that red lit room. I dream of him that night. Literally dream.

THIRTEEN

The next morning at work, I can't wait for Jon to come in. He's occupying all the possible space in my brain. I keep peeking over at his desk to see when he'll sit down right there. I hope no one else notices how much I'm looking over there, but I can't help it. If I even think I hear the door open, my eyes dart over to see him. But he hasn't come in yet.

Usually he comes in late which I always associated with some kind of cool rockstar lifestyle he must lead outside of work. He must stay out all night going to concerts, drinking, hitting on girls, and taking beautiful photographs to work on later. Maybe he stays out with many beautiful women.

That's not really the case as I've come to find. He's a social guy, but he doesn't seem to have women around and he isn't much of a rockstar. He's much more together than I thought, but somehow more exciting.

This crush is keeping me burning inside and at the very least, it's giving me things to write about. I have the seduction scene open and I start railing away at my keyboard:

. . .

"It's my calling," he said. "It's the only thing I'm passionate about."

"The only thing?" she asked.

"Well, maybe it's one of three things. I'm partial to good cheese and a good lady."

She was blushing and she couldn't help it. He was being so corny and so hot with it. That's what made him so sexy. He was able to say sort of corny things with the confidence of a rockstar. No wonder women quiver and scream when they see him melting faces onstage. He was absolutely melting her panties.

"We have two out of the three right here," she said flirtatiously.

"That makes you the good lady?"

"Well, I'm not always good."

He knowingly smirked.

"How about you come back to my place? There's a smoked gouda you have to try."

A cup of coffee appears on my desk from the coffee shop down the street. I look up and see Jon, placing it there.

"You take it black, right?"

I grab the cup and smile. He bought this on his way to the office - nice, locally-roasted coffee that is a million times better than the wasteful Keurig that the office uses.

"How did you know?"

"I notice what you do," he says as if it were obvious. He sits back down at his desk and gives me some raised eyebrows before he turns to his screen. He notices what I do. I feel so touched and interesting. He watches me? He notices me? ME?

I look down at my outfit. A mustard blouse tucked into a brown skirt. How can he notice me in these clothes? He wears torn black jeans and a striped shirt like he's a hipster mime. I look like a secretary. I look over at him again and catch him actually glancing at me. Maybe there's something special to me after all.

That's part of the fun of a crush. For as much as you feel fantastic about them, they make you feel good about yourself. He makes me feel like I might just be worth crushing on.

I take those feelings and I turn to this scene. Time to spice it way up.

FOURTEEN

For once after work I feel powerful. Sexy, even. I take this power home and feel it slowly deflate a little as I realize that once again I am alone. Since I'm alone I should unpack the rest of the boxes in my apartment. There aren't that many, but there are still enough that make me feel like I'm not fully at home yet.

I sit down with one and open it to find small knick-knacks. Pictures of my family and friends flood this box as do different things I've hung on the walls in other places like a cross-stitch my grandmother did of an orange blossom that I could swear smells like the real thing. I look fondly at all of these. I want to hang them up again, but that requires unpacking the box that has the tools necessary to do that. I look around. How are there still boxes? How do I still not know where my things are?

I wish I had someone to help me or anything else to do to distract me from this.

There are no friends to hang out with, no hobbies I engage with, and no man to spend a nice evening with. I want more than anything to spend an evening with a man. I want to feel wanted. I want to touch and be touched. I want to see Jon, but I don't know if that's appropriate.

I open another box. It's the pink lampshade. I close the box.

Might as well text Kevin.

Once again, it takes Kevin no time at all to get there. The downside is that he arrived drunk. I wasn't sure if I wanted him there when I opened the door to his cross-eyed face, wobbling from side to side ever so slightly as if he was standing on a boat. We weren't even going to pretend to have a nice drink and get to that place together? What was I doing? Wasn't I having fun flirting with someone else? But so what? I shouldn't put all my eggs in that basket. I had no idea how Jon felt about me or maybe things would still work out with Jacob. Maybe I was making mistake after mistake. But why worry? Why worry about any of that? Kevin was here ready to slobber over my half-naked body - since he'd likely be too drunk to care if I were fully naked - and leave when it was done.

What was affection if not just warm bodies getting close to one another? Sure, I want intimacy, but I no longer know if I deserve it.

Kevin is drunk because he had a date with a woman who didn't want to sleep together that night. He said this to me like I "get it". Like I'm the kind of girl that would sleep with him any place, any time, without conditions.

"She has morals or whatever," he says. "Remember those?"

He forgets that I also didn't sleep with him right away, but apparently I no longer am seen as someone with morals or class. I'm a girl to fuck and fuck over.

"You texted me right on time!" He trips over his own shoes as he slips them off. He doesn't untie his laces. He just kicks them off like they were slippers. They are not. It's a struggle. I'm embarrassed for him. He should just leave.

Instead he reaches his hands forward. One hand latches onto my left boob.

"Honk!" he says like a child. Then he laughs. I'm a bit appalled. He can be a childish dick, but this is a lot right now.

"Bedroom?" He asks like he's the one offering. It's my bedroom. It's my apartment.

Ghost appears behind him. It's like he arrived just in time to ask 'is there a problem here, miss?' He hovers in the hallway corner and watches the fumbling. I'm not ready to go into my bedroom and I don't know if I want to at all - but how do I get out of this?

"Let me get you some water." I slide past him, but he grabs one of my arms. He pulls me, harder than I'm sure he intended.

"No, Gladdy, come on! We know the drill."

"You're really drunk."

"No, not really. I'm okay. Come on."

He plants a kiss on me that bares so much whiskey that it almost stings. I'm inhaling what he drank, making me feel drunk in the process. I just want him to leave. I want to push him off me, but I don't want to become physical with him. That's not really my nature. Still, his grasp on me is really hard. I wonder if it'll bruise.

I yank my arm away. "Sit down in the living room for a moment --"

"Girl, what are you trying to do? You invited me over here for a reason. Am I wrong?"

"Yes, but now --"

"What? You change your mind? We know the drill, Gladdy. This is what this is."

"I know, I just --"

"This is bullshit. I came all this way for you."

Am I supposed to feel bad? All I want is to get out of this, but now I feel like I owe him something. He did come all this way.

Then the lights go black. They're extinguished like a candle.

"Did your power just go out?"

Ghost!

A gust of wind blows through the room so hard that it knocks Kevin over.

"What the --" He struggles to get up, tripping over himself. Another gust of wind blows him over a second time. A laugh sputters out of me, but I try to contain it. He catches my face in the dark. I'm sure I look like the Cheshire Cat grinning at his misfortune.

"Are you smiling? What the fuck? Help me."

He reaches out his hand and then to my surprise Ghost appears in front of him. Ghost reaches out and swipes the hand away.

Kevin shouts.

"What the fuck?! Someone just touched me."

"Touched you? No way," I say and I know that I am smiling. I'm trying to stifle it, but I can't. I laugh a little. Ghost shows up behind him and taps him on the shoulder. Kevin turns around and sees nothing. I laugh like I'm watching Kevin as Donald Duck in a Halloween cartoon.

Kevin doesn't think any of this is as funny as I do. He finally gets up and reaches for the lightswitch to turn the lights back on, but when he touches the switch there's a spark. That scares me. Is Ghost going to electrocute him? I definitely don't want that on my hands. He can scare him, not hurt him.

"This is fucked up, dude," Kevin says. Is there anything less sexual than a man calling you 'dude'? I definitely want him gone and thankfully Ghost is on my side. I don't know why exactly Ghost decided to shoo him out, but I'm grateful.

"Oh, I never told you?" I say, feeling suddenly like I'm a cool chick in a horror film like I'm a witch in *The Craft* and I'm about to unleash a deadly spell with cool special effects. "My apartment is haunted."

"No, you never told me that. Why the hell are we here? I'll get a Lyft and we can go to mine."

"No, that's okay."

"Come on, Gladdy. Hasn't this horror stuff made you *a little* horny?"

Ghost is behind him and the energy is bad. I've never felt this from Ghost before, but his usual demeanor is completely changing and with that his color. He turns a dark, shadowy color and a feeling of desperate rage fills my apartment.

"Let's get out of here," Kevin says. "I've got a bad feeling." He looks over his shoulder and that's when we both see Ghost in his new shape. He's grown taller than the ceiling, an overgrown shadow cast on the wall and all the way up to the ceiling. It's like looking at an 8-foot tall man, but he's completely made of shadow. It's scary even to me even though I trust Ghost. This negative energy is not directed at me.

Then, to my surprise, Ghost *bellows* with a voice that feels like it's coming from underground.

"GET OUT!"

"WHAT THE -?!" Kevin is so startled that he falls back against the wall, staring up at Ghost's towering frame. Ghost snarls - SNARLS - back at him like a beast from the beyond.

"OUT!" Ghost commands.

Kevin looks at it with wide eyes that have been drained of the drunkenness he came here with. He's terrified, pale and ready to leave.

It makes me laugh.

"You look like you just saw a ghost," I say between hearty laughs. Each laugh feels like I'm releasing him from my life entirely.

"You're fucking crazy, Gladdy," he says which is a meaningless insult.

He isn't gone fast enough for Ghost. Ghost comes up behind him, crowding him and snarling again. Kevin opens the door and Ghost actually pushes him out. When the door slams, the lights slowly flicker back on and Ghost lets out an exhausted sigh. With that sigh he deflates from a tall shadow man back to his original self. His color crawls back and soon enough he's the Ghost I always see: a short, chalky-white, transparent, floating embodiment of a man.

I can't believe any of that happened. I'm smiling, wild from the excitement. I want to leap around the room and celebrate, but it's clear that Ghost wouldn't match that feeling. Even though the negative energy is gone I can still feel that Ghost doesn't have his full energy back. The room feels fatigued.

"I had no idea you could do any of that," I say.

Ghost nods. "I've only done it once or twice. I used it to scare former tenants here."

"Really?!"

"The people before you. I didn't like them at all."

No one mentioned to me that the former renters were scared out of this apartment. I certainly wouldn't have taken it had I known that, but I'm glad I did. I'm extremely glad.

"Thank you," I say.

Ghost bows his head a little. He seems so low energy now. Can a supernatural energy *be* low energy?

"Are you okay?" I ask.

"Yes, just so so tired. That takes a lot."

"You feel tired? I didn't know ghosts could feel."

"I'm only energy now," he explains. "Negative energy takes a lot out of me. It's hard for me to harness."

I feel a slight guilt that he had to harness that for me, but I realize he isn't trying to make me feel bad. He's just telling me. That's okay, right? It's okay to accept his kindness.

"Thank you," I reiterate.

I think about my conversation with Jon earlier and about dreams and goals. I want to know more about Ghost's life, but I'm scared to ask. What if it hurts him?

"Ghost, did you like being alive?"

"Not then. But now that I'm dead? I realize I liked it oh so much and I wish I had liked it more."

I look at my phone. A text...from Jon? It said:

I ordered a milkshake tonight and almost got two straws, but you weren't there. They would have thought I was drinking with a ghost.

So I write:

I drink with a ghost a lot. It's cool.

He sends back a smiley face. There's no way he knows what I mean. Then:

Will you be at work tomorrow?

Of course.

Want to take a coffee break with me?

It was the first step to asking me to do...anything. I had thought about asking him to have lunch with me someday. The more time we spent together, the more obvious that move seemed. But coffee? That was a cute first step and I was thrilled that he made that first move. So I texted back:

I'd love it!

Ghost is in the room. He's been there, watching me because he is still in his protective mode. He feels like my dad in the room, watching over his little girl.

"You're smiling," he says.

"Yeah. I'm texting with this guy at work that I like."

He's genuinely happy. "That's great. Don't waste your time on people who don't make you smile."

He's right. Sometimes I forget that he lived a whole life before he was a ghost. He's filled with life experience, wisdom, and advice to give. I should use him more often.

"I feel like I'm floating," I tell Ghost.

Ghost seems amused which is surprising. He suddenly feels different. The air doesn't feel as cold and empty. The energy coming off of him is warm like fresh baked chocolate chip cookies. I feel surrounded by coziness all of the sudden.

"Would you like to float?"

"Huh?"

"Stand up."

I stand from the couch and stare at Ghost whose hollowed eyes feel like they are smiling. My stomach drops all of a sudden, but in that good way it drops on a rollercoaster when the ride starts. I feel like I'm going up the hill! My body is no longer planted on the ground and it feels so strange. I can feel my roots being pulled up from the ground as my head gets lighter and higher in the air. I'm ascending higher and higher and with each inch I feel the weight of Earth fall off of me. I'm now zero pounds. I can now fly in my apartment. I can soar out the window if I wanted to! There is, however, a ceiling to my apartment. My hands stop my head from hitting the ceiling. I curl up into it like I could crawl on it.

"I can't believe this!" I exclaim. "Is this real?!"

"Yes!" Ghost laughs. "I thought you'd like it."

I plant my feet on the ceiling. I could crawl around like Spiderman if I wanted to!

"Okay, I'm going to lower you," he warns.

"Wait! Will I crash?!"

"No, it'll be just as slow on the way down."

Ghost wasn't exaggerating. I descend so slowly that I barely notice. When I almost hit the ground, I fetl my gravity come back to my body. I am once again a person on the ground whose feet sometimes feel heavy. My head is the last thing to come back to feeling normal. I savor the lightness until it all goes away. What an incredible feeling. Who knew that hauntings could provide experiences that rival psychedelics!

"Remember this feeling and remember you can float any time you want. You can be weightless."

With that sage advice, he disappears and I'm left dreaming of this date tomorrow. I go to sleep clutching my phone to my heart like it's him. I wake up before my alarm, excited about our coffee date.

I look at my closet to find a pop of color. I have a blazing red-orange cardigan that looks like it could help a plane land. *Let's take a risk. Let's do it!*

I put it on with jeans and head out the door, looking forward to a fifteen minute coffee date as if it were going to change my life.

FIFTEEN

Every month we have a creative meeting at work where we pitch ideas, outline stories, and discuss what books are being worked on. Sometimes they tell us about sales, but not always. This is mostly for the creatives to be creative. It's one of the rare times we all talk to each other and see our faces. Most of the day is spent with our eyes glued to laptops as we try to make magic happen in these campy, kitschy, sultry stories.

We all sit around a table in the break room that doubles as a conference room. The entire office isn't that big or that fancy. There's a bowl of pretzels on the table, but I doubt that Brandon left that out for all of us. I'm sure it was left there from someone having a snack the day before.

People go around the room and excitedly pitch ideas. I rarely have ideas and I rarely pitch. I'm not seen as an "ideas person" at work. I fill everything in as if I worked in a coloring book.

However, this meeting is different. A few ideas for a new book that 2-3 people would work on were tossed out, but nothing really caught Brandon's eye. In an absolute first, he turns his attention to me.

"Gladdy, you did a really good job on that seduction scene last time," Brandon says. A compliment? To me? In front of...everyone? This wasn't typical Brandon. "We're readying that book for publication, so do you have any new pitches?"

I bite my lip. I do, but I'm nervous. I don't usually pitch ideas. Everyone looks at me. Betty has her list of ideas out as do the other two men who usually write sex scenes with more enthusiasm than I can ever muster. They're all so much better at this than I am. Jon has his notepad out, but he doesn't contribute editorial ideas. He's there to get the inspiration needed for the covers and marketing. When I look at him, he smiles shyly. I want him to smile confidently. I want him to bask affection toward me. That's what we all want.

"I do," I finally say. "It's a kind of supernatural romance."

"Perfect for Halloween," Betty chimes in.

"A woman moves into a house that an artist used to live in. He was a handsome man, a sculptor maybe so something that used his hands --"

"How very *Ghost* of you," one of the other writers snarkily says. I ignore it.

"Anyway, he was an artist. A creative type. Incredibly hunky and sensitive. She feels she's not alone there. It's scary at first, but then she likes it. She gets used to his energy. They get to know each other. It's very sensual."

"Will there be ghost sex?" Brandon asks, very matter-of-factly. It's business as usual.

"There can be," I say.

"There should be," he responds.

"But why is he a ghost?" one of the other writers asks, a guy who seems to specialize in S&M stories. He's always pushing for handcuffs to make an appearance.

I shrug. I'm not 100% certain. Luckily - and surprisingly - Jon comes to my assistance.

"That can be part of the story. He doesn't know why he has unfinished business and she helps him. Maybe he was married and his ex-wife's death was so tragic that when he died he continued haunting that place, but Gladdy - er, this woman - helps him to move on."

I smile close-mouthed at him. He's blushing back at me before he averts his gaze and pretends to doodle in his notebook.

"But when he moves on will he stop haunting the place?" Brandon asks.

There is a silence as we all consider that tragic factor. A love found that instantly becomes a love lost.

"No," I say definitively even if I'm not actually sure what I'm about to say next. "Maybe there's a way to bring him back to life...or bring her to the other side."

"That's dark," Betty says. "But I like it."

"I like it, too," Brandon says. "The bones of this idea, anyway. Let's outline it. Congratulations, Gladdy. You're going to run your first story."

I look up from my notepad where I was scribbling all of these ideas. Is this for real? My idea is approved and I get to outline and run the story. I can assign chapters and ultimately make creative decisions for it. I'm no longer relegated to telling other people's stories. It's going to be my story this time. Well, not literally. It's an idea I have, but still.

When the meeting is over and everyone stands up I turn excitedly to Jon. He puts his hand on my arm. It feels electric.

"Thank you so much," is the first thing I tell him.

"Why are you thanking me?"

"You had my back in there."

"Always." He smiles. I blush. "Besides, it's a cool idea...and an artist, huh? I wonder if that artist is going to be inspired by any artists you know in real life."

"Maybe," I say coyly. I want to kiss him so badly, but we're at work. "He might be a cool guy with long dark hair and a nose I want to trace with my fingertips."

"And a huge cock," he says.

"Oh my god!" I exclaim. That joke took me by surprise. I burst into laughter and he slowly follows me.

"You were being so nice," he says. "I had to break the tension with a cock joke."

I'm grateful for the break in tension. It's almost embarrassing for me to be so complimentary of him. I am used to keeping my affection to my chest, but he makes it pour out of me. He makes me feel like that's *okay*. It might even be encouraged. Even if it makes him feel the need to make a joke. That makes it all even better like we're in an R-rated screwball comedy.

Plus I'm still riding a high from being successful at work for once. So I take that confidence and sling a barb back at him:

"Ah, so you're familiar with my work."

We're *flirting*! My god, it's so much fun! What a joy to live in this little world where there is excitement and romance at work and it can just feed directly into my world. I would have never guessed this would happen. I simultaneously want to mount him and run away all at once. I want to live in these little moments forever where my whole body feels like it's smiling.

"Oh! And he never makes the first move," I say with a smile. Two flirts at the end of this interaction? A score for me. His face says it all.

Triumphantly, I return to my desk and start to work on my new story about new love and ghosts.

SIXTEEN

I had been eyeing Jon for about thirty minutes while everyone else in our office got up to leave. I used to leave promptly at 5 o'clock, but I started to stay later and later. I want to leave when he leaves because that means we walk and talk together and sometimes we hang out more after that. I want to feel buzzy again. I want him to almost walk me home again. I want him to actually walk me home.

I have been fantasizing about kissing him and telling him that I want to kiss him and more - so much more. I had a dream the night before that his long dark hair was between my legs. I woke up and instantly masturbated, praying Ghost wouldn't come in and catch me like a parent walking in on their tween watching porn. Ghost left me alone, but I'm sure he knows. JUST like a parent.

"Staying late again?" Jon asks me finally. It's just me and him.

I pretend I don't notice and that this isn't on purpose. "Looks like it."

"Hopefully not too late, so I can walk out with you."

"Yeah?"

"Yeah. Want to leave now? You can walk me to my next class."

It's impossible not to smile. He's always so smooth. Impossibly smooth. So smooth that he feels written, but he's not. He's real. He's real and I really want to kiss him.

We close up the office together and I start to feel nervous. There's a tingling, jumping feeling in my stomach when I'm close to him. I feel like I might explode and word vomit all of my thoughts into a puddle on the floor and I simultaneously want to hide in the bathroom and make him leave before me. It's confusing and tumultuous and beautiful and makes me feel like a teenage girl all over again.

We start walking and I find myself having trouble thinking of things to say. I laugh too much - nervous giggles only - and feel my mouth getting dry. I keep swallowing hard and I feel like I'm in desperate need of water. We're not even talking about anything important - just work - and I feel all of these symptoms. Why do I suddenly feel this way? We were effortlessly flirting earlier in the safety and boredom of the office, but in the freedom of the great urban outdoors I feel like a baby deer.

In the middle of complaining about Brandon's ridiculous demands in the office, Jon stops and looks at me.

"You're being weird," he says.

"No..."

"Don't do that. It's fine. Let's just talk about it."

Talk about it?! That's the first *and* last thing I want to do. It's all I want to do and all I don't want to do. To say how I feel out loud could potentially move us forward and closer to realizing my wet dreams from the night before or it could make everything explode. We're living in a fun, flirty bubble. Popping the bubble could have all kinds of disastrous effects. Or! It could be lovely.

I wasn't sure if we were ready either way.

He knows. There's no way he doesn't know. I think this because he then says:

"I want to talk."

I nod. I take a deep breath. He smirks.

"You want to go first?"

As much as I want to hear what he has to say or what he thinks this is about, I will be brave. I still want to impress him after all and I want to do this for myself. I want to put myself out there. I don't want to wind up calling old shitty flames to come over for sex. I want something real.

"Okay," I say in a breath. "I think I'm feeling a little weird and nervous right now because..." I consider kissing him right then and there. Maybe all of my feelings will go away if I just kiss him? I take another deep breath. My throat feels like it's swelling and ready to swallow my words to keep them from coming out. "I have real feelings for you. I feel like we're flirting and having fun and I don't know what's going on, but I like it. I like it."

We keep walking slowly down the street. He takes a second to think about that and it's a terrifying second for me. *What have I done?!*

"Well, Gladdy," he says. He's looking down, but I can see him smiling. "You're not alone."

"Yeah?"

"Yeah. I like this too. But I can't keep flirting with you everyday. I want to actually see you outside of work."

"Really?"

"Yeah. Let's go on a real date. Let's be real."

"Why didn't you say something?"

He laughed. "I'm saying something now...plus I thought you had a boyfriend for the longest time."

"I did," I sheepishly say, afraid of Jon thinking it was too soon for me to date. People make up all kinds of terms and rules for getting over someone else. I did feel over it - very over it. I felt over it when I was in it, but that didn't mean that he'd be comfortable with that.

"And you don't now?"

I shake my head.

"Well. We're both single. We like hanging out. These are great things."

We stop walking just outside a small park that is sparkling green, the sun filtered through the fully grown trees. I look at him, smiling. I can't believe this is happening. He puts his hands in his pockets and waits for me to say something, so I do.

"I like you," I tell him.

"I like you, too."

I need to know what it's like to kiss him. I need to know if it's sparks and fireworks or if it will be a bad, sloppy first kiss that erases all of these feelings that take me back to being seventeen with a crush. We are walking outside of a park with the sun hitting his face in a wonderful golden way. Hair peeks out of the black beanie he's wearing. His eyes fall on me. I need to know what it's like to kiss him.

"Can I kiss you?" I ask, surprising even me.

"Okay," he says and his lips spread into a smile.

I go in close to him, not sure exactly how to start this dance, but he takes the lead. I tilt my head to his lips. He very lightly brings a finger to my chin and assists as our lips meet. Our lips meet, warm and soft, and press one on another like a lock and key. I felt everything I thought I'd feel and more. Of course, there is a spark. There is such a spark that it lit a fire. We kiss softly at first, but we keep kissing. He put a hand on my lower back. I put an arm around his neck. We press into one another and kiss with abandon. We kiss like we had been waiting to kiss, excitedly training for this moment like athletes going for the gold. He introduces his tongue into my mouth and it's most welcome. That's when I know that he wants all of this, too.

We kiss outside of a park that is filled with children, dogs, and families. It's broad daylight. I don't remember having many first kisses in broad daylight. I had them at the ends-of-nights with drinks and expectations for something saucier. This? This was sober, daylight passion and it meant so much more. Kiss me in broad daylight. Show me you are unafraid. Here we are, so unafraid and so filled with feeling.

I back away finally and state the obvious, "We're getting too intense for all of these children."

He barely glances at the park. It's clearly the last thing on his mind. "So? Let them learn."

"Would you want to hang out together tonight?"

"I thought that's what I was saying," he laughs.

"How about you walk me all the way home?"

"Going all the way? Too soon, Gladdy."

I blush. He smiles. He kisses me again. This feels like a dream.

Then he says, "Oh by the way - I read your seduction scene. This rockstar guy kind of talks like me, huh?"

"What do you mean?" I ask. I'm trying to remember what I wrote, but my brain is still replaying the first kisses we just shared. It's really hard to concentrate when he's talking to me with those same lips.

"He said something I said to you...like word for word."

"Really? Oh no, I'm sorry. I --"

He kisses me again, interrupting the torrent of apologies that was about to inarticulately flow out of my mouth.

"It's okay. I kind of like being a muse."

"I guess I was inspired."

"Me too. I have a good lady right here. So do you have any cheese?"

After a warm walk home - and a stop at a grocery store for a brick of Wisconsin cheddar - Jon stands with me outside of my apartment door. I pause. He looks at me with a question in his eyes. I don't want him to think I have second thoughts about him. That's not it. It's the ghost.

"I should tell you: my apartment is haunted."

"Is it a friendly ghost?"

"Actually, yeah."

Jon investigates. He steps inside ahead of me gingerly with his toes barely touching the ground. He walks like he's sniffing the air. I let him do this like he's doing his job, closing the door gently behind me. It's a wonder to watch him here in my space.

"There isn't a negative energy here," he says. "But it is a sad energy."

He looks at me full of concern. "Is that coming from you or the ghost?"

I brush past him and put my keys in their proper spot.

"Do you want water or --"

"You didn't answer me," he says.

"Oh. I didn't know you were seriously asking."

He shrugs. "Yeah, if you want to talk about it." He loves to talk. It's refreshing.

"I'm not sure," I say.

He nods.

"I mean I'm not sure what happened to the ghost. I don't know why he's a ghost."

"Do you think the ghost is sad?"

"Sometimes. I feel like the ghost is kind of...parental.

Watching me. It doesn't mean any harm if that's what you're asking."

"I guess. I just feel an energy. I don't know. I can't tell where it's coming from."

He inspects me. There are deep layers in those soft brown eyes.

There is a lump in my throat. "Things have been...hard," I say. "I just moved here. I left my boyfriend a little bit ago."

"Oh." He says. Jon looks around again and this time takes stock of the boxes. "How long ago is a little bit?"

"Didn't you know this?"

"Yeah, I knew you had a boyfriend you lived with. I mean I had heard as much when I asked about you --"

"You asked about me?"

He smiles. "Well, yeah. I like you."

"I like you, too."

"And I'd like for you to live in a place that you actually lived in."

"Huh?"

"These boxes."

"Oh," I'm not sure what to say. I've lived here for a few months now. Was everyone always immediately unpacked? Some chores take a long time to get to.

"I can help you," he says.

"You really don't have to."

"I know. I want to. I want to help you."

I blush.

"But we don't have to do that right now," he says. His hands are in his pockets. He looks absolutely adorable, eyes shy with vulnerable and overflowing with requited feelings all at once. His hair tucked behind his ears. His growing grin.

"Can I kiss you again?" I ask.

"You don't have to keep asking."

I thought he would say yes, but I wanted to be sure. I wanted to make sure I'm reading him correctly and so far all of his cues have told me: yes, yes, please and yes!

He takes me in, wrapping his arms around me. Our kiss feels like breathing in together. For a moment I am able to forget everything outside of our mouths, but after a few more inhales I am worried about being too swept up in this or that he will get bored of it. Either way, I get worried despite the euphoria and the rust of warmth I feel all over my body. The wetness I feel in between my legs. I feel the way the romance novels tell people to. I feel the way I write.

I pull away and look into his eyes. He kisses me again. Then we hug. He breathes in, smells me. Our hug feels like the most intimate part of the evening.

I peek around him to the space in the hallway that Ghost usually occupies, but Ghost isn't there. I don't feel Ghost's presence at all. We're alone.

"Come with me," I say.

I take his hand and pull him into my bedroom. It's the most daring I've been in a long time. I feel strong, brave and sexy. I feel desired. I feel like a goddess.

He takes this goddess into his arms on my bed. He opens my legs and tastes me. I feel heaven in my thighs.

Sleeping with someone for the first time is so intimate and difficult. Actually sleeping. There's so much negotiation. Bodies need to be learned, positions need to be tried, and breaths have to get into a rhythm. It gets too cold and too hot. Covers can be an issue.

Are we naked or are we clothed? Are you awake? Are you sleeping?

He falls asleep rather quickly. I didn't expect it. He also

snores. It's very loud. It is not a light snore. It's deep and cartoonish. It's kind of cute because I'd never expect it from him.

I have to go to the bathroom, so I slip away from his balmy grasp and walk out in the hallway. Ghost is standing there. I gasp quietly. It still scares me sometimes.

"I didn't expect you," I say.

"You were having fun."

"Yeah...you left us alone?"

"You needed some alone time."

"So you like him more than Kevin?"

"I like a real love."

"Oh, we're not --"

"Or a beautiful thing, rather. Whatever you want to call what it is you're doing. I can see it. I can feel it."

"Do you feel love?"

Ghost pauses.

"I feel the absence of feelings I once had. That's how I know they're there."

I don't know what that means. I want to ask questions. I want to ask more about Ghost - the things I never thought to ask before - but I really have to pee. I excuse myself and slip past Ghost into the bathroom. Ghost never goes into the bathroom, always respecting my privacy. I've convinced myself that maybe bathrooms aren't haunted, but I know that's not true. So many horror movies have a scary bathtub scene where a ghoul's hand comes up from the water.

For now, I don't feel a spirit. I feel like I'm alone. Ghost described the absence of feelings. That's sort of what I feel about Ghost. I can feel when he *isn't* there.

SEVENTEEN

Things I know that Ghosts feels:

- Sadness
- Warmth
- Positive energy
- Negative energy
- My presence
- Love
- My happiness, my feelings, etc.
- Anger
- Loss
- Absence

EIGHTEEN

At work the next day we share glances. We steal smirks. Our looks tell stories and secrets. No one else knows. We thrive in that secret.

We went to work together and didn't make any kind of show about really hiding anything. We didn't do that trope where we walk in separately, one person waiting a few seconds to go in after the other. We walked in together, but no one noticed because that's life. Everyone is too busy doing their own thing.

That's the most freeing realization of adulthood: no one really cares what you are doing and that's so marvelous and so depressing all at once. That's why it's nice to find a partner because they care. It's part of their job description to care.

Jon has plans after work, so I'm unable to hang out with him again even though that's all I want to do. I want to immediately see him and hug him and fuck him and cuddle and have the sweetest pillow talk. But that can all wait. It's nice to have patience and to take things slowly. It's nice to nurture it and let us grow naturally as much as I want to jump into being a couple that has been together for months and months. I have to wait. It will come with sweet rewards.

On my way home from work, I leave my excitement for Jon behind. It isn't right to spend so much time together. Probably. There should be space. I think. We should have some time apart, the time in between, to make the time together sweeter. ...right?

As I unlock my front door, I remember the night before. It already feels too long ago. It's hard to believe that just the day before he came up with me and we shared a beautiful evening together. Our bodies made secrets.

When I'm actually inside my apartment, however, my focus shifts.

I can't stop thinking about Jon's read of Ghost and the sad energy in my apartment. I want to clear the air, but I know burning twigs of sage isn't going to do it. Maybe it was time to see if Ghost had unfinished business, but to do that I have to actually know who Ghost is.

Quietly, I wait. I read in my living room as the sun goes down and am careful not to leave too much light. It is very hard to read as the light fades from the living room. I don't want to turn on the harsh overhead light. I look at the few remaining boxes in the room.

That pink lampshade could be put to use.

At the very least, I can plug in the lamp itself. I take the lamp and place it on the table next to my couch. I plug it in. The lightbulb shines bright, filling the room with its strong yellow light. It could use some softening. It's time for the lampshade to be taken out of its box.

Just then the light flickers. Ghost wants to come in. I turn the lamp all the way off and creep into the hallway where Ghost is.

"Good evening," Ghost says to me.

"I've been waiting for you," I say.

"Oh. You can always ask for me. If I'm not busy, I'll come."

The idea of him being busy is funny to me. Busy doing what?

"Can I know who you are?" I ask.

"You really want to see?" Ghost asks me.

I don't understand the question fully. I say yes.

Ghost reaches out to me with arms outstretched like it wants to grab me, but Ghost ends up walking up to me and into me. I feel hands on my shoulders and the next thing I see is this apartment in different colors and lights.

It's the same layout, but everything is different and the time period is not the same. There is a lot of lace. A lot of wood. A steel lamp with an ornate shade. Soft yellow light coming from the bulb.

A sound comes from down the hall. Is it a horn playing? I don't know. It sounds like a horn in an old movie, sort of muffled and faraway. I walk down my short hallway and turn into the living room. It's my one-bedroom apartment, my living room, but everything is different. Everything looks like a set in the 1920s or 30s. It's hard to tell. Some things look even older, Victorian even. A gaslight is on the windowsill and it appears to be working. It's lit. I realize the horn is coming from a radio program playing music to slow dance to in a cocktail bar. It's music to rub your cheek against another person's cheek and sway to the sound of each other's heart beats.

I feel like I do know what year it is and I even know the day. It's October 21, 1933.

"There! That's everything," a woman says behind me. I turn around and see a woman in her twenties with a round face and deep red lipstick. In fact, the red lipstick is the brightest color in this place. She wears a belted blue dress that I can only describe as "smart". It is incredibly flattering on her figure and stops just above her ankles.

She looks right at me. Right into my eyes.

"Papa?" she asks. "Are you alright?"

I don't know how to respond to her. Am I alright? I don't know at all. I'm her father and yet I'm me. I look at my hands. They are a man's hands, thick and sturdy with callouses. I feel my chest and it is flat with a tummy below a brown sweater.

I nod.

"It'll be fine, Papa. Just fine, I promise." She turns around and starts down the hall again. She is still talking, but I can't hear the words. I don't know what she's saying, but that's partially because I feel so disoriented. Who is she? Who am I in this moment?

She comes back into the room.

"Oh, I thought you were right behind me, Papa!" she laughs. Her laugh is delicate like a chime.

"I'll be back to visit, you know," she says. "I'll be back sooner than you think! Well, hopefully not too soon. I want to make it big."

A blaring car horn is heard outside. It's the loudest squawk I've ever heard a car make. Jesus old cars were loud.

"Oh, there's my ride!" She leans forward and kisses me on the cheek. I hope it made a cherry red mark. She looks at me with concern again. This time there is worry that fills me. A worry I cannot describe. What is this feeling? This dreadful, dreadful feeling.

"Are you certain you can't come to the train station?"

I feel overcome with the idea that I will never see this beautiful young lady again. My daughter.

"Papa, I worry about you. I don't want your agoraphobia to worsen while I'm gone."

It will. It will get worse. Oh, god, it will get so much worse.

"Promise me you'll ring friends and neighbors to visit you at least. I hate the thought of you being alone here."

Alone. Yes. I am alone and I will be so alone. When my only daughter leaves, my whole heart will go with her.

"I'll be back so soon."

And when she dies in an accident shortly after this goodbye, so will my heart.

The part of me that is me wants to gasp at air and cry, but I cannot. I'm him and as him I can feel his feelings and hear his thoughts. I'd rather claw my way out of his ghastly skin than feel this cavernous pain. The pain of something digging itself out of you. The pain of loss.

She kisses my cheek again. I feel that kiss stronger than the other one. My heart flutters with a fervor of excitement for her and everything she could accomplish if her future was not cut short. *Oh, how she has no idea. None at all.* My head pounds like a timpani trying to warn her, but I don't say anything. I don't say anything because I know that when this happened for real, he didn't know it would be the last time. He was just feeling scared to leave the house, as if leaving would take so much effort and he told himself she'd be back soon. She'd visit her father so soon, just like she said.

She shuts the door behind her which turned the room black. Dark, pitch black. It's terrifying and cold, like we're in space. I open my mouth to scream, but nothing comes out. I try to scream a full bodied, animalistic scream, but there's simply no sound. I'm desperate for the sound. I want to scream harder and louder. I want to keep screaming until the sound leaks out of my throat, no matter how small it croaks.

I bend over in the black with a hollow feeling in my stomach. I grip my stomach and see that these are my own hands again. I look to my right and I see Ghost in a way I've never seen him: a stout, middle-aged father who knew so much loss.

First his wife, then his daughter. He spent his days - his decades - in this very apartment afraid to go out into the world and meet the kinds of gruesome ends his girls did.

I don't know exactly what happened to his wife, but I could feel that he had experienced that loss. I felt that he viewed everything about his daughter - his hope, his pride, his concern - through that lens.

It's him standing there, too. He isn't see-through or floating. He stands with feet planted and looks at me with the same emotion that I often get when he is in his ghostly visage. Why is he different now? What is this place we're in? I don't feel fully a person here. I don't feel like I exist.

This place is horrible. Everything is black. I know that we have souls because I felt the absence of one. The absence of a soul is in that room.

I feel the pain of loss. I feel the pain of nothingness.

Ghost, the real man or whatever he is now, seems relieved that I see him for who he really is in this terrible place. It's the least amount of pure sadness I've ever felt from him.

The sound of the door slamming shut is heard and we are back in my hallway. I'm no longer in the cold in-between world and I'm not in his yellow-lit memory with faded edges and soft jazz playing. I'm in my barely decorated apartment with boxes still unpacked and a hook for my keys and purse next to the door. Ghost looks like Ghost. Faded and white, but now that I know what Ghost actually looked like, I can make out his features a little better. I do see his face. I see his eyes sharper than before. I can recognize his worry. He gives me the same looks that he gave his daughter.

Tears hit my eyelids before any words come to my mouth. I simply don't know what to say to him. My life and loss pales in comparison. I did what...leave a long term partner? He lost his wife and daughter. What could I possibly say to him that doesn't sound childish and small?

"I'm so sorry," I tell Ghost.

Ghost does something that he hasn't yet. Ghost smiles. He's been warm and tender - like when he let me float - but he hasn't smiled. It's odd to describe. The smile is very faint on his face. More than anything, it's a feeling. It's the glowing feeling of being smiled at. That feeling that brims with sweetness. I think he likes that I attempted to know him. He feels like someone sees him, finally, after all these years trapped in this place.

"You experienced so much loss," I say.

"Yes," Ghost says. "But who hasn't? Life is about love and loss and the longer you live, the more you lose. I know that now. Now that I'm no longer living."

"Do you want to leave here?" I ask. "Do you need me to help, I don't know, free you?"

Ghost shakes his head.

"No," he says. "I can't imagine another home." Then he says, "But I do like living with you here, for what it's worth. You remind me of her."

"What was her name?"

"Rebecca," he says. The name falls out of him. He hasn't said it in so long.

"Rebecca was lovely," I say.

He smiles again and this time he fades away. I still don't know where he goes when he's not here. I hope it isn't that cold, dark place. I hope it's a warmer alternative to here with color and light and music. And I hope he isn't gone for good.

NINETEEN

I lay on my stomach in bed. Jon is laying behind me, tracing my body with his hands. I have my mismatched bra and underwear on, but he treats me like I'm naked. He traces my shape delicately with his fingertips.

"You're so beautiful," he says.

"Aw, Jon," I coo. I'm never sure how to respond. Thank you? You too? That's sweet? Of course, I mean all of these things. I mean them so profoundly.

Then he says, "I wish I could forget what you looked like so I can see you all over again."

That's simply the hottest line I've ever heard.

I'm overcome. I want him - no, I *need* him. I've never felt sexier in my life as I reach over and kiss him. We embrace and kiss and french and lick and touch and touch and touch and whoop! We roll over. I unhook my bra and let him see what he's already seen before, what I hope he hasn't yet forgotten.

He's below me and he looks at me with wonder in his eyes. But I don't know. I don't think I know how he feels. Sure, I can *feel* it...I think...but I'm always second-guessing. His glances could mean anything, I suppose. Or maybe he gives them to everyone. Maybe I'm not the special one. Maybe I'm just another.

I get brave above him as he takes me in, devouring me with his eyes and mouth. I sit up with my legs still straddled around his.

I look into his eyes, the eyes that melt into puddles when looking back at me. It feels like we could go on staring for ages, our eyes flowing into each other like fucked up rivers of lust and affection.

"Can I ask you something?" I ask. "What do you want?"

He looks at me so softly that I feel almost embarrassed by his tenderness. He puts his hands on my cheeks and pulls me in, kissing me. With his face close to mine, he closes his eyes like he is tasting something too delicious for this world. Then he whispers with some of his words almost getting lost in my lips, "I want so much of you."

After a while of rolling around in bed, we fall asleep. It's one of those sleeps where you don't know what time you actually drift to sleep. A lamp gets left on and you wake up disoriented, realizing you have been asleep in a precarious position for hours but it somehow didn't really hurt. Our arms were tangled around each other and I carefully untangled them without waking him so that I could get up and turn off the lamp across the room.

When I got up, Ghost appeared. I'm always shocked when he appears outside of the hallway as if I forget that he can go anywhere he wants in this apartment.

"You almost scared me," I whisper. I look over to Jon, nervous he'll wake up and either see me talking to a ghost or see me talking to myself. Which one was worse really? I motion for Ghost to follow me out into the hallway. I tiptoe out the door with Ghost hovering behind me.

"He seems great for you," Ghost says when we are safely not in my bedroom where Jon can wake up and see him at any moment.

"I don't know. He's a little wild," I say. "Like he's this artist with cool stories and epic adventures and I'm -"

"A writer with cool stories and beautiful things to share." Ghost interrupts me, talking to me like a best girlfriend giving a pep talk.

"Thank you," I say. "I just get scared that maybe I'm not enough for him."

"You are or he wouldn't be here."

"He's not what I'm used to."

"That's okay," Ghost says. "That sounds like what you need right now."

"I just hope I'm enough."

"Try it and see."

I nod. "He says he wants me. He's around me. But it's hard to believe. It's really hard to believe. He's so optimistic."

"That's good!"

"I don't want to confuse optimism for promises."

Ghost frowns.

"He wants so much of me," I say. "It's too much."

Ghost looks at me sadly. There is a silence now. It's making me uncomfortable because I'm silent, I'm waiting, but I know Ghost is busy thinking. I know Ghost is thinking through something.

"What is it?" I finally ask.

Ghost sighs. Then says, "I think it isn't Rebecca you remind me of. It's me."

"What do you mean?" I ask. I still have a hard time seeing Ghost as anything other than what is in front of me.

"You're like me. You're so afraid."

"Afraid?"

"So afraid. Of all of it. When I was alive, I was so scared. The world felt so big and I was so small. Somedays all I could do was tremble thinking of the outside world, of its changes and risks. That's why I'm here. I'm stuck."

I had never put that together. I thought it was all the loss of his daughter, but was Ghost here because he was simply afraid to leave?

"I thought you wanted to be here."

Ghost shook his head. "I'm just afraid to go."

"Can you leave?"

"I think so," Ghost says.

"Do you want to?"

"I'm still scared."

I smirk. "The ghost who is afraid."

"Yeah," he says with a sad laugh. "You and me both."

I nod. I feel such sadness all of a sudden and it makes me defensive like I want to shield myself against any self reflection. I don't want to be like him.

"Do you think I'm really like you?"

"I don't want you to be."

That stings in a way I don't anticipate. It makes it sound like I'm tumbling down some kind of depressive spiral where I'll wake up one morning and be dead like him, existing in some kind of in-between world.

"Then you can say no," I tell him abrasively.

"How could I say that? I don't know for sure."

"It's just nice. It's a white lie. It's something friends do."

Ghost shakes his head. "Friends help each other. Friends tell the truth. The truth is that you seem to live in a world before this one."

"So do you!"

"Because I have to. You don't."

"Well, what about you?"

"You're alive! I'm not --"

"Can't you leave? Can't you be brave? Why are you putting this on me?"

Ghost looks at me with confusion. "I don't know why you're upset."

"You're accusing me or dragging me down to your - whatever this is."

"That's not what I'm saying--"

"I don't want to be haunted and sad. I don't want to be like that."

"Me neither," Ghost pleads with me. "You shouldn't be like me. You should live life. Say yes. Why not? What's the worst that can happen?"

I really don't have a good answer to that. It stops me in my tracks a little and calms down the red hot rage that was inexplicably burning up inside me.

"Rejection? Loss?"

"You get through it," Ghost says. "You get through it until you don't."

"See! Sometimes you don't."

"No, I mean, you get through it until you don't. Because you die."

"The only escape is death?"

"You have nothing to escape from. When you're alive, the only way out is through. You're going through right now! You left your old heartache behind and you have opened yourself up for new love and opportunities. That's living. That's the opposite of me."

"What if I fuck it all up? Then what?"

Ghost is silent.

"Then what?!"

"I don't know. I never lived enough to know that."

"Exactly. You're just a coward."

Ghost is quiet again, but it's not for a lack of anything to say. I hurt him.

"You think you're doomed to be here forever, but you're not. You're just here because you're a coward. You're a coward and I don't want to be like you."

Ghost gets quiet as if he physically were smaller. His voice is a whimper when he says: "I don't want to either."

I've had it. I feel out of control. I don't understand my feelings. I'm upset, but why? Because he insinuated wanting to help me not be like him? His presence suddenly annoys me as if he were a little brother poking at my side, begging for attention. I wanted him to leave. So I said:

"Then leave!"

"No--"

"GET OUT!"

Ghost dissolves into the air like sugar in water, slipping into the other world. The world of black and cold. I stay in the warm apartment, but ever since I saw that world I think about it when Ghost isn't in front of me. I wonder if he gets cold.

His absence leaves me feeling the aftershocks of my emotions. I felt so wild and unstable and now he's gone. I immediately regret losing my cool like that.

I want to call him back, but I also have to think about what he said and why it made me so angry. I didn't think I was scared.

I don't want to be scared.

TWENTY

The next morning I whisper for ghost to come back. Before I leave for work, I put my hand on the doorknob and look over my shoulder. He isn't in his usual spot.

"Ghost?" I call quietly. He said I could call him any time. I try calling for him again a little louder. "Ghost?"

There is no response.

The rest of the day I feel guilty. Had I shooed him off for good? I remain very upset about my interaction with Ghost. It plays on repeat in my head like an argument with a lover. It feels like the kind of fight that gets out of hand because two people are determined to stand their ground, but wind up almost losing everything. The kind of fight that feels like things were said that can't be taken back. I wish I could go back and swallow my words. Just go to bed. Just shut up. Why did I have to yell at him?

After work I'm afraid to go back. I'm ashamed of what I said to him and scared that what he said was true about me. How do I apologize? Should I apologize?

So I ask Jon if I could come over to his place. To my delight, he gladly accepted.

When I am not with Jon, I can still feel him like our hearts are tethered on a string. I think of kissing him outside at the park. I think of playing with his lips. I think of folding into his side. I recall the pitches in his laugh. I think of him.

Of course, I see him often. Every day. At work.

Now we eat lunch together. We go on walks after work. Sometimes he walks me to the bus. I walk him to where he has to go next. He invites me along. I love the invitation. I love the way he makes me feel welcome to barge in on his life.

But this will be the first time I see how he lives. I haven't yet been to his apartment. He always comes over to mine. So this is the first time seeing his apartment which is also a favorite activity of mine for any person I'm getting to know.

This isn't a surprise, but his apartment is very cool, like a treasure you hope to find when you're searching for a place to live. It's a second floor apartment above a quiet stationary store. The layout is incredible, but it's his personal touches that fill me with wonder. He lives like a messy boy with photos and notes sprawled all over his desk and superhero action figures on the shelves. There was a table filled with sketches, doodles, and random art supplies. He's been spray painting a canvas for months, not exactly happy with how it is going and an entire corner of his kitchen is dedicated to that process with spray paint cans and crumpled up sketches surrounding the half-painted on canvas.

All over the place there were framed pictures of superheroes and action figures here and there. Those seemed like the most organized things in the apartment. It was adorable to see a grown man with so many toys and it made him seem less unapproachably cool to me. He seemed real. I asked him what he did with the toys and he shrugged.

"I like to look at them. I like things that remind me of fun.

Don't you?"

I do. That's why I like hanging out with him. He asked me why I didn't want to go home, but I was too afraid to tell him. I am still concerned that talking about Ghost makes me sound crazy. My eyes start to water when he asks me again. I didn't expect to get so emotional. I hate when that happens. My feelings betray me, making me feel like I've been caught, as they sneak attack upon my fragile eyes and give me away.

"I can't talk about it right now," I whimpered like a child. I felt pathetic.

He put his arm around me and assured me that it's okay. He kissed me on the forehead and told me he would hold me until I felt better. I ended up falling asleep peacefully in his arms. I don't remember moving once.

That was last night. Last beautiful night.

It's morning. I realize that I had successfully slept through the night this time. Not only that, but we are still holding each other. Our arms have figured out how to stay intertwined without creaking in pain. He's on his back with an arm still around me and I am curled into his side as if I'm seeking shelter. The light filters through the single window in his bedroom and I wake up to take a look at his sleeping face. This time he didn't snore. He slept without a sound. He looks the way he sounds, too. With his eyes shut, he looks so much like an angel. I love carefully inspecting his face as he sleeps, studying the lines that surround his mouth. There is a danger to this. He could flutter an eye open at any time and catch me ogling. I try hard to stare lightly, if there even is such a thing as that, so that he won't feel it and wake up.

He, of course, wakes up.

"Ah!" he says. Then he smiles. If he didn't smile - that soft, soft smile - I'd feel ashamed to be staring. But he did, so I don't.

"Watching me sleep?" he asks.

"Maybe," I say flirtatiously.

"Hope you like what you see." He rubs the sleep from his eyes. I wonder if I was being creepy. "You fell asleep before me, so we're even."

"You watched me?"

He nods. "You were super cute. You may have farted, but I wouldn't bet on it."

"What!"

"Haha, is that okay to say? You made fun of my snoring!"

"Our bodies make bizarre sounds."

He giggles. "I kind of like it. But, hey, I'm gross."

"I guess I can be, too."

"Let down your hair, Rapunzel."

"Hm?"

"Let down your guard, princess."

I didn't love being called a princess - even as a metaphor. But I did love being encouraged to be myself. He was strange like that. Jacob didn't actively encourage me to be that way. He assumed I already was.

"Jon?"

"Yeah?" There's still sleep in his eyes, but he still sees me.

"Last night...I was upset about Ghost."

"The ghost in your apartment?" There is no condescension in his voice. He asks it honestly. He doesn't think I'm stupid or crazy. He just wants clarity.

I nod. "We had a bit of a misunderstanding and I told him to leave, so he did. And he didn't come back."

"The ghost left?"

"Yeah."

"Isn't that...good?"

I don't know how to answer that. Not truthfully anyway. The thing about being haunted is that it meant I wasn't completely alone.

"You'd think so, but it made me kind of sad. Or scared."

"Scared? Of no ghost?"

"Scared of being by myself."

He hugs me, his arms squeezing me harder than I thought possible, but not hurting me. It's a beautiful blend of physical intimacy.

"Scared for him. Where does he go when he's not with me?" I ask that question out loud, but I know the answer. It's a horrible place. I've seen it and I don't want to see it again. "I asked him to show me and it was horrible. I don't want that for him."

Jon thinks for a minute, hopefully not about committing me to an asylum. I try to think of something rational to say to fill the silence, but he speaks before I can think to make up some story about a shoe sale or a recipe to try. Things that are not crazy. Things that are of this world.

"Betty mentioned doing a seance, right? Maybe we should do that for real. It might give us some answers or show him a way out."

"That's such a good idea," I say.

"Well, I have good ideas."

"I know he's not alive, but I want him to be okay. In whatever afterlife is."

"We should all be okay in whatever life we lead."

I pause. What exactly does it mean to live a life? How do you do it "right"?

"How do we live so that we don't end up like Ghost?"

Jon smiles and looks me up and down like I'm delicious. "You just have to enjoy the things in front of you. Good cheese and a nice lady."

"Oh my god, you're a cartoon."

"What? I think that's it. That's all I need anyway. And I got one of those things right here, so let's see about breakfast."

TWENTY-ONE

I stop at home later in the day to change my clothes before meeting up with Jon again. I know I can't keep doing this. I have to face Ghost. We have to talk this out.

But when I go home, he's nowhere to be found. He doesn't appear and I don't feel anything.

"Ghost?" I call out.

No response.

Maybe he just needs space. Or maybe the space needs a change.

I open another box that has an old radio in it. It was my mom's kitchen radio and I've held onto it ever since she tried to trash it in an attempt to modernize. I wanted to hold on to this piece of my childhood, remembering listening to it as I ate cereal in the mornings. I take it out and plug it into an outlet. I find a jazz station. I don't know anything about jazz, but I love the way the music sounds like it has to keep going or it will die. It's a great soundtrack to my determination to finally settle in.

I end up hanging two wall shelves in a corner and another one in my bedroom. I forgot I had these. When I successfully hang all of the shelves up, I empty my box of knick-knacks on them. Soon the rooms in my house are personalized with pictures and trinkets from vacations. I open up a box that contains makeup and nail polish. Had I really not been wearing makeup this entire time? I had a tube of red lipstick in my purse, but that was it. I organized all of those on my dresser and set my red nail polish aside. I wanted to paint my nails when I was done using my hands.

The books all go on a bookcase in the living room. A few DVD's line up underneath the TV on the TV stand. I place a candle in the middle of my coffee table. Who knew this place could look like an actual home in a few hours?

Lastly, I open the box with the pink lampshade and place it on the lamp. I screw it in place. I turn off the overhead light and turn on the lamp. Its soft glow makes my living room feel complete. I had avoided it for so long, but it was perfect. It gives the room warmth.

I feel proud of myself. I wonder if Ghost is proud of me, too.

"Ghost?" I want to see if Ghost can feel the difference here.

"Ghost?" I ask again. I leave the living room and peek out into the hallway. Nothing. I check the kitchen as if he's hiding somewhere.

Then. I feel a brush of cold air. That's all I get. It's enough to let me know he's there, but he never actually appears. Is this a ghost's version of the cold shoulder?

"I want to talk," I say.

I wait, but there's no response. It's still cold.

"Ghost, I'm sorry. I'm very sorry."

The cold leaves. Nothing.

I think it might be time to force him to come out and talk to me, for us both to get to the bottom of what's going on. It's time for a seance.

TWENTY-TWO

Jon and I have been curled up on the couch like two small kitties as we watch *Night of the Living Dead* - he had never seen it which is so hard to believe - when Betty arrives. Early. She's a pretty punctual person, but it turns out that a seance is so exciting that she'll arrive nearly forty minutes early for it.

"We haven't finished the movie yet," Jon said. Did he want us to start it from the beginning? Have Betty sit down and watch it with us? Betty remains excited to talk to the dead and is completely nonplussed by his complaint.

"You can finish if you want. I'll just set up."

Betty then stands in the doorway and looks at the TV for a while. I keep looking at her, but her eyes are glued to the TV like it's hypnotizing her.

"Sit down, Betty," I say after nearly two minutes of this.

"No, that's okay," she says. Then she keeps watching. "This movie is just so good. I mean. Romero knew that a zombie movie isn't really just about zombies, you know? It's about the fear of the other. It's so good."

"I haven't seen it," Jon says to ward off any spoilers.

"They're coming to get you, Jon!" Betty says with a laugh. "Get it, Jon?"

"Yeah, I saw that part already," he says flatly. His eyes are trained on the TV, but it doesn't look like he's watching it anymore.

I thought Jon and Betty got along really well, but he seems pretty annoyed with her in this moment. Maybe it's the movie or maybe he's scared of what we're about to do. I try to read the situation, but it's hard while the sounds of grunting zombies play in the background.

"Sit down, Betty." I sit up and scooch over, but she doesn't accept my invitation. She's here for business.

"No, I should get into the right mental state. Gladdy, where should we do this?" she finally asks.

"Follow me."

I take her into the kitchen and I can tell that Jon isn't sure if he should follow. I think it's adorable that he wants to finish the movie, but there will be plenty of time after the seance. I mean there's no way we'll be able to just go to sleep after. Who knows what will happen? I anticipate staying up all night and unpacking this.

Jon ends up following us and leans on the entryway of the kitchen like he's James Dean or something. He's so effortlessly cool all the time, even in the face of summoning the afterlife.

"And you know how to do this?" Jon asks Betty.

"Yes, I Googled it. There's actually a step-by-step guide."

"Cause that feels safe." He gives me a look that screams 'we shouldn't do this' which is confusing to me because he was encouraging it just a few days ago.

I've learned that I'm not as superstitious as he is and I'm not nearly as scared about this seance because I know Ghost. I've already seen and talked to Ghost. This is more for the two of them. I think. I'm actually starting to wonder why we're doing this at all.

I give him a look back that says: *it's okay. We can do this.*

Of course, Ghost has avoided me since the outburst we had. It's been strange in my apartment because I know that he isn't gone. I can often feel him hovering around me, but he hasn't made himself known to me. I think he knows what we're planning to do.

"Don't be doubtful," Betty warns. "The first step in the guide is to have people that are spirit-friendly! We have to be welcoming to the spirit."

"Ah, the spirit already knows me. I think this is a friendly group," I say. "Ghost has at least seen Jon before. You're the only one he doesn't know."

"Oh, in that case then I'm happy to introduce myself." Betty digs into her bag for awhile before she asks me if I have a lighter.

"Oh! Yes!" I exclaim. I'm excited because I recently unpacked that from a box of kitchen things and other useful objects like can openers, scissors, nail clippers and a thermometer. Of course, I can't remember exactly where the lighter is.

I dig through my kitchen drawers for a little bit. Jon leaves the room and comes back with the lighter.

"It was on the coffee table," he explains. "You lit the candle with it."

"Oh, let's blow out *that* candle just to be safe," Betty suggests. "We'll light the ones I brought instead."

I don't entirely understand that reasoning, but I'm putting all of my faith into her practice. Jon and I go into the living room where I blow out the candle. He turns off the lamp, but not before stopping to notice it.

"Was this always here?" He asks.

"It's been up for about a week," I say. "I unpacked everything."

"I noticed that," he says. He smiles at the lamp like it's a person. "I love this. It's really cute. It's very you."

I blush. It was an object I didn't think of as wholly mine before, but it is. It's mine.

We return to the kitchen where Betty lights four candles on my kitchen table. There are only three chairs. They are all chairs I dug up from alleys after my move. They're as eclectic as the three of us to the point that one's chosen chair felt indicative of their personality. It was like having a wand choose a wizard or a broom choose a witch. The chair meant something to our core power and it knew us.

We each quietly chose one. Betty sat in the robin's egg blue chair that was slightly taller than the rest. Jon sat in the metal folding chair with a cushion. I chose the creaky wooden one with a stately back.

"Should I light incense?" I ask.

"Oh, yes! That's going to add to the mood."

I quickly get up and grab a stick of incense to light. Betty checks her notes and realizes she forgot something: a glass of water. We nixed using anything like a Ouija Board because Jon felt that was too scary. It's kind of cute that he's afraid of that.

Betty fills a glass of water and I light incense to bring to another corner of the room. I don't want it on the table because nothing can disturb this process.

We all hold hands in the candlelit room. Jon's hands are familiar to me, but Betty's are new. Her hand is warmer and smaller than I expected.

It is 11:45. We read that seances are best when performed between 11:30 and midnight because spirits are friendly around then. Spirits are awake. We could text "u up?" to a spirit and they might appear.

"I'll start," Betty reminds us. "Have yes or no questions ready - or questions with simple answers - just anything we can throw out when he appears."

I wonder if Ghost is watching this set up and snickering somewhere. I could just ask nicely and he'd appear, I think.

"Do you know the ghost's name?" Betty asks me.

I shake my head. Ghost is Ghost.

She closes her eyes. I follow. I think Jon does, too, but I can't be certain because my eyes are closed.

"We gather here tonight hoping for a sign of your presence. We are a friendly circle, a safe space for you to join us whenever you feel ready. Please, spirit, join us tonight."

"How do we know he's here?" Jon asks.

"If any spirits are here, please make yourself known," Betty announces.

I look over to the corner of the room. Ghost is there. He feels different than usual. He's amused by this little game, as if he had just stumbled into a room of children playing pretend.

"He's here," I say.

"How do you know?" Betty asks, excited but perhaps miffed that she wasn't the one to feel his presence.

"I can see him. Over there." I point to the corner.

"...You can see him?" Betty asks as her eyes drift over there.

"She sees him," Jon explains. "But I never have."

"Spirit, can you make yourself seen to all of us?"

"I don't know how," Ghost says.

Betty almost jerks her hands away, but thinks better of it. Her eyes flutter around the room. Okay, so everyone can hear Ghost. Good to know.

"Oh my god! Where are you?"

"You don't have to do it like this," I say, pulling my hands away and gesturing to the candles. "He can talk to us."

Betty actually looks scared. This might be her first ghost

encounter. She takes a deep breath and says: "Okay, spirit, we can hear you."

"That's nice," Ghost says pleasantly.

"Is anyone with you?"

"No." And then Ghost says. "Should there be?"

I laugh. "No, we just want to talk to you."

"You know I'm the only one here."

Betty looks at me in total bewilderment. She seems absolutely shocked by our familiarity which fills me with a bizarre pride. She may be able to conduct a seance, but I'm friends with Ghost. I told her about Ghost! I told her! She didn't know what to expect, but this it.

"Spirit, we're going to ask you a few questions. Is that okay?"

"That's fine."

Betty directs her attention to the same corner of the room I'm looking in. I'm still unsure if she can see anything. I don't think she can.

"What is your name?"

"Howard."

"Howard!" I say. My smile grows from ear to ear. I can't help myself. I'm delighted to know him - to really know him. I can't believe I never asked. "You're Howard."

"Hello, Gladdy."

"How did you know my name?"

"It's everywhere," he says.

Jon raises his eyebrows. I can tell he thinks that's creepy and it certainly would be if Ghost - er, Howard - were alive. It's funny how the standards for creepiness change when you're dead.

"How did you die?" Jon asks.

"You're not supposed to ask that," Betty whispers.

"It's okay," Howard says. "Gladdy knows."

I nod. "He showed me."

"Showed you?" Betty asks.

"Yeah, in the other world. The one he's in."

"Can we go there, Howard?" Betty asks.

There is a pause. For a moment, I can tell Jon and Betty are worried he's gone. He's standing there, thinking.

"I think so, but I don't know if you should."

I look sadly at Howard, remembering what I saw and what I felt. Remembering that he said being dead is the absence of feeling. Remember what *that* felt like.

"It was painful," I tell them.

"Maybe we could help you if we saw it," Betty says.

Then Jon asks the question that all of us should be asking: "What exactly is it? Where are you?"

There is another pause.

"I've never been certain," Howard says. "When I'm not here, I'm there. I can relive my past or I can come here...or I can go to the other place. I don't like it there."

"What is the other place?" Jon asks.

"It's very cold," he says.

"And there's no sound," I say, remembering the scream.

"There's no...anything. Just me and a total absence."

"So what is it?" Jon asks more plainly.

"I...I don't know."

"Purgatory?" I suggest.

Howard hesitantly says, "I *hope* so. I'm afraid it might be final."

I had never considered that which I think is why I wanted this seance. I want to make sure that he finishes all unfinished business, but truthfully I have no idea what that unfinished business could possibly be. I saw his reasons for staying. What could make him go?

There must be something else. That can't be it. It simply can't be.

So I tell him that.

"There's no way that place is final," I say. I want to say his name over and over again like a lullaby. *Howard, oh, Howard, please don't worry.* "There must be something to move you on."

"On to where?"

We all pause. Heaven? Hell? Something *else?*

We have no answers for him. He is supposed to have the answers for us. We came prepared with questions. Yes or no questions. Simple answers. Here he is asking us things we have no way of knowing.

"Is there another place?" Jon asks. "Do you have a way of knowing that?"

"One question at a time," Betty warns as if the rules still apply when the ghost is in the room.

"I have no idea," Howard answers. "There's here and there's there."

"Why do you come here?"

"It's better than there."

"It's kind of bad there," I add. Howard and I exchange a sad glance. Maybe that's the sadness that Jon mentioned feeling. Maybe it was a shared energy between us, like a secret. The secret of the other place.

"Take us there," Betty says. She doesn't ask. She demands.

I'm not sure that's a good idea. Howard isn't either. We're silent. It feels like Jon has to be the deciding factor. Does he want to come with?

Jon looks at me. His eyes are so full of encouragement.

"Howard, can you show them what you showed me?"

Howard is so full of sorrow and slight defeat when he says, "I'll try."

A gust of wind pours through the windows, rolling through

with a mission. The candles blow out in one giant breath. The entire room goes dark - darker than before. It is so dark that only eyeballs glimmer in the pitch black. My eyes search for Jon's which glisten only slightly.

It suddenly became very, very cold.

I see Jon's eyes and then my own breath. Jon tries to open his mouth - I can tell by his white teeth in the blackness - but no sound comes out. We are there. We are in the place.

Then he appears: Howard. Howard is the only thing visible in the room. He is able to be seen as plain as day: a middle-aged man in his green pullover sweater and brown slacks like a small bush.

He slowly musters a smile. It's a welcome. Welcome to this world. But the smile can be interpreted as menacing because there is nothing in this world. Welcome to darkness. Welcome to the void. Welcome to hell.

How do we get out?

Last time there was a door. The door conveniently brought me back to my apartment. But this time there is no apparent trigger to get us back. I don't know what to interpret as an out.

Jon looks at me in the dark. Those eyes that are usually calm are filled with so much worry. He looks to me for guidance, for help. Betty turns to me, too. I don't know much more than what is in front of us. I look at Howard. I mouth his name.

He shakes his head.

I see Jon pointing out of the corner of my eye. He gestures behind us, but I'm afraid to look. Jon takes a step and I reach out to stop him. He grabs my hand. His hand is the only thing in this world that is warm. Suddenly, Howard is next to us. Howard puts his hand on Jon's shoulder to stop him. Jon looks at Howard and Howard shakes his head. A door slams. We can hear it. We then hear the wind pick up again - wind that brought us in but laid silent as if it were waiting to pick us up again. It howls at us to go back. Before we can even register what's happening we are all back in the kitchen.

Each of us gasps for breath like we were all drowning underwater. The air in my apartment is considerably colder than it was before and the candles are blown out. For a moment, I wonder if we are still in the other place or some new kind of nightmare.

"Was that place--?" Jon starts to ask.

"Yes," Howard the ghost says. He appears in his ghostly visage. His voice came first, making it seem like he was all around us and in another realm.

"We need to get him out of there," Jon says.

"I don't think he can leave," Betty says, finally finding her voice.

"No, that's not true," I say. "That place - that place isn't final. It can't be final."

"It might be."

I look over to see if I can find Howard, but he's gone. He's no longer there. Was it something we said?

"I should get going," Betty announces. She seems genuinely spooked by everything that went on tonight. I'm surprised considering it was all at her urging. She did say she hadn't actually seen a ghost before and she obviously had meant it. She looked like she might have wet her pants.

"Are you sure?" I ask her. "You can stay the night if you want to. You both can."

Jon smiles at me. I assumed he would spend the night in my bed, with me. Betty can take the couch.

She nods. "I really need to process all of this in a safe space." Then she stops like she just remembered something extremely urgent. "You have sage, right?"

No.

She opens her purse and hands me a plastic bag with loose sage leaves in it.

"I know it's not much, but it should be enough to sage your apartment. You definitely want to do this tonight. Then, Jon, sage your place when you get home just to make sure nothing followed you."

"I don't think Howard would follow me home --"

"You never know! Not just him - any spirit. Who knows what was in that other world? I just...I didn't like it. It didn't feel good."

She gets her things and leaves.

When I shut the door behind her, Jon leans in like he has a secret. For a second I think he's going in for a kiss, but it's bigger than that. It's serious.

"There's a way out," he says.

"What?"

"In that place. I think I saw a way out. That's what I was trying to tell you."

"Why didn't you say something earlier?!"

"Betty was really scared. She needed to go home and Howard...I don't know if Howard wants to leave."

"What do you mean?"

"When I pointed behind me - remember I was trying to get your attention - so then I turned to go toward the light and Howard stopped me."

"He stopped you?!"

"He must know."

"Well, what did you see?"

"There was a sliver of light behind me like a door was ajar. It was small, but I could see it behind all of us when I looked around. It seemed small and like it was a bit of a walk, but it was there. I saw it."

"And Howard saw it?"

Jon shrugged. "He saw me go towards it, anyway. But then he stopped me."

"Maybe it was someplace worse. Maybe he was helping you."

"Or maybe he doesn't want us to help him."

TWENTY-THREE

.Jon and I have been scheming both during and after work about how we are going to help Howard. We decide not to include Betty on the possibility of doing seance #2. She was so freaked out the first time that this wouldn't be helpful. Besides, Howard was comfortable with me and by this point he was comfortable with Jon, too. He likes Jon. I know he does! And I love that. It always feels wonderful when the people (and spirits) in your life approve of the person you choose to spend the most intimate time with.

After work we split a milkshake at a hamburger stand - two straws as an ode to the drink that made us fall dizzy in love over each other - and continue scheming.

"I'm nervous," I tell him as I swish the peanut butter chocolate shake around the cup with my straw.

"That it won't work?"

"No, not that. I don't know what will happen after."

"What do you mean?"

"Let's say this is his unfinished business --"

"Yeah, I'd say it is."

"Right. So what happens when it is finished? What then?"

"Then he...moves on. To whatever is next."

"But then..." I drift off. I look at the ribbons of peanut butter swirled together in the thick shake. He looks at me, eyes wide with waiting. I love the way he listens to me. "Then what. Like what for me? I'm just alone?"

"You're not alone," he scoffs.

"In that place, yeah."

"But you moved in there to live alone...right?"

I shrug. I did. But I liked Howard. Should I get roommates? Roommates leave messes and Howard doesn't.

"It's too soon, but..." Jon drifts off for a second.

I look up at him. *Oh my god. Finish that thought. Are you going to say...*

"We could move in together when your lease is up," Jon says with his eyes down, trained on the milkshake. He looks up after a sip and smiles out of the side of his mouth. "If this thing is still going strong."

A part of me wants him to put down that sly attitude. IF. But I decide not to focus on his if. I have to let go, let loose, take a risk. Yes, he's being cute so to not be so vulnerable. But, yes, it is a risk. It is an unknown. While we both want to say it's forever, there is no forever. Forever as we think we know it is just a word, but that won't stop me from hoping this thing goes on for a very long time. I can only hope he feels the same.

"I like that."

"Cool. Me too. We can talk about it more?"

"Definitely."

Together we finish the milkshake and I take comfort in this moment and knowing this moment can be revisited in the future. There will be many more milkshakes. I feel so confident about that.

We take a walk back to his apartment and pass a bookstore.

He suggests going in together where he looks for a photography book a friend suggested to him. I can't remember the name or what he's looking for exactly, but I wander off and find the scintillating romance novel section. I can't help myself. There's a secret thrill to finding a Virginia Southgate novel and knowing I had something to do with it. Sure enough, there's the book! The newest book! It's even sitting on the shelf with its cover facing the world, so that anyone can walk back and get titillated.

The rockstar has his shirt unbuttoned, sporting firm abs as a guitar sits in his hands. He holds it low and suggestively.

"Jon!" I call over to him.

He looks up from a Pablo Neruda book - which wasn't at all what he was looking for - and comes over to me. I hold it up for him: *Music to My Heart by Virginia Southgate.*

"Hey! You're famous, Gladdy!"

"That's Virginia to you!"

"Miss Southgate if you're nasty." He kisses my forehead as I flip through the pages. I look for my seduction section. Sure, I had already seen it a lot. I saw the mockup at work. I saw Jon's cover art already. I edited and re-edited my work, but seeing it on the page in my own hands was exciting.

I opened to the seduction scene I wrote with Jamie and Ash. Their banter, her confidence, his charm - it all filled with the early feelings that my crush with Jon brought me. That nervous excitement that feels like it comes out of your fingertips. The crushing feeling that yearning brings and the fire that comes with desire. I look up and see him smiling at me. I almost can't believe it all worked out this way.

"Are you staring at me?"

"Yeah, this is cute," he says. Then he holds up his book. "Do you know Pablo Neruda poetry? That feels like something you'd know well."

"Kind of," I sheepishly admit. I don't want to disappoint

him with my glossary, college-poetry-class knowledge of Neruda.

"I really don't know any of his stuff," he says to my relief. "But I just opened it to this poem and it made me think of you - and seeing you look at your work like that - I don't know. It's cool."

"What's the poem?"

"It's fitting. It's called..." He finds the page he was on and looks up again. "Sonnet XVII - what is that? Doesn't matter. Here's a stanza I think you'd like: I love you straightforwardly, without complexities or pride; so I love you because I know no other way than this: where I does not exist, nor you, so close that your hand on my chest is my hand, so close that your eyes close as I fall asleep." He looks up at me from the book and says, "That's what it's like to sleep next to you at night."

Having poetry read to you - even very famous poetry - feels like a dream. It feels like something that happens in movies, not real life. Yet here we were in a bookstore. My hands held the book I ghost wrote with the sexy scenes inspired by my feelings for Jon. Jon stood like an open heart reading Neruda like it was bleeding out of his chest. They were the feelings of another person in love, sure, but lover is so ubiquitous. We all feel like it's *so* strong, too strong for our own words, that we love to rely on the words of others.

I have no words in that moment. There's nothing I could say that would possibly compare. I put my arms around him and kissed with a passion that would make Neruda blush.

Maybe I was more like Jamie than I originally thought.

TWENTY-FOUR

It's time. It's time to help Howard.

Howard knows what we want to do and he hasn't been coming around to see me. I can feel his presence, but he won't appear the way he used to. He doesn't hang out with me like he did before. It isn't because of Jon, either. It's all because he doesn't want us to help him go to the other side.

So we have to force it.

Jon and I do our best to replicate what Betty did when we held a seance in my kitchen. We light tall white candles that I bought at the botanica nearby. I bought fresh ones just in case the used ones would be less powerful in the spirit world. We need all the help we can get to make Howard reappear.

Jon and I sit across from each other at the table. We hold hands and close our eyes. I decide to say almost exactly what Betty said before. I don't want to chance it. We have to try to help Howard and we have to try to do that now. I take a deep breath in and I can feel Jon breathe with me across the table. The room smells like candle wax and incense. It's now or never.

"We gather here tonight hoping for a sign of your presence. We are a friendly circle, a safe space for you to join us whenever you feel ready. Please, spirit, join us tonight."

And just like that, I feel that familiar change in the air. I don't see him yet, but I can feel him.

"If you are with us, Howard, please make yourself known. Please appear."

Howard appears. Who knew I had this power to ask to come and go? It felt commanding!

He doesn't look happy to see us. He looks scared.

"Hello," he mutters.

"Howard! Where have you been?"

"Here and there."

I release my hands from Jon and stand to meet Howard's chalky apparition. "Why have you been hiding?"

"I don't want you two to help me."

"But it might be better!" I say.

"It might. Might be worse, too."

"You won't know until you try," Jon chimes in.

For a moment I worry that Howard might be offended by Jon helping, as if he would feel territorial about me the way a good friend can be about meeting a friend's new boyfriend. He isn't. He's fairly welcoming.

"We have no idea," Howard explains. "I know what this is. Let me stay where I know."

"Howard, please don't talk like that. You can't be here forever."

"Why not?"

"Do you really want that?" I ask.

He is quiet for a moment. "I like being around you."

Jon and I look at each other. It's sweet, but it can't be enough.

"She might not be here forever," Jon says to ease our sadness.

To our surprise Howard calmly responds by saying, "Good. I hope she's not."

"I hope that for you, too, Howard."

I extend my hand. It's more of a gesture than anything. I don't think he can feel it. I certainly can't.

But his hand actually does meet mine. It's remarkable. It looks like a chalky, translucent light in the perfect shape of a hand with lines and knuckles and everything place directly on mine. We are holding hands, but we can't feel anything. I can't, anyway. But I pretend.

"Let us help you," I plead.

He looks between me and Jon. He's scared, desperate like a wild animal. All I want is to bring him close to me like a mother nurturing her child, but I can't hug him. I can't feel him. All I can do is go through the motions of comfort.

"Promise me," Howard says very seriously. "Promise me you'll move on, too. Don't be stuck here like me."

I nod. "I promise."

He squeezes my hand and I feel it. I *actually* feel it. With that squeeze we are transported into the in-between. Everything is black and cold out of nowhere. It is such a sudden shift that it feels like this is the way it's always been. The other reality now feels like a dream. We can no longer hear anything. His hand feels real.

I can't stop staring at his hands. They are real. I see and feel the flesh of his hands, small and stocky like paws. I look up at him in awe. He squeezes again to let me know he feels it.

Jon pats us both on the shoulders and points behind us. We turn and see what he was talking about: a faint light in the distant as if there was a door cracked open down an exceedingly long hallway. It's just barely a light, but it's there and it might be the way out.

I nod at Howard. *It's time,* I think. I want to say that out loud, but I think it hoping he can feel my intentions.

He lowers his eyes and steps forward. The two of us now walk hand-in-hand toward that light. Jon walks beside me on my left. I look over at him, this supportive partner helping my ghost find his way out. I reach out and grab his hand, too. We all walk together in harmony as the light grows larger and larger. With each step, it's more visible. It's definitely a light and it's definitely a door that's been left ajar. It was exactly what it looked like from a distance. How about that?

When we finally get to it, we all look up. It's huge. It's an enormous door like it belongs to a medieval fortress. But it's just a large black door - the same black as everything else - that seems to open to light.

We all look at each other. Do we open it...?

Jon reaches forward and for a moment I'm terrified the light might be dangerous. What if it's hot like fire and it burns his hands? What if it sucks him in? What if it means that he dies in real life? I reach out to stop his hand, horrified by the idea of losing Jon. I shake my head and turn to Howard. Howard should open it. I think he's the one who can.

Howard breathes in deeply. It's time.

He reaches his fingers through the crack of light and bends his fingers around the door. He pulls it open and the light washes over all of us. I squint. It's too much to take in all at once. Our eyes adjust and she's standing there. It's *her*. It's Rebecca.

"Papa," she says. "I've been waiting *so* long."

Howard crumbles. He's all tears and smiles simultaneously as he stretches his arms open and embraces his daughter. He doesn't think twice about it. He never looks back at us. He goes to her, into the light, and the next thing we know he's gone. They're both gone. It's all gone. They were swallowed up by the light until it became too bright for our eyes. The light overwhelms our eyes, so we defensively shut them. When we open them again, we're back in my apartment.

Just like that, it's over.

"Howard?" I call out.

Nothing. We look around and wait. I call out again, but there's no response.

"I think..." Jon starts to say.

"Yeah." I know what he's going to say. I know because I can feel it. We're actually alone for the first time since I moved in. "He's gone."

TWENTY-FIVE

"Is that the last of the books?" Jon asked me as he tapes up a cardboard box of paperback books I lugged from place to place. I'm not sure why I keep these books, but to have a life without books seems cold.

"That should be it," I say as I hand him the packing tape. He tapes up the box and puts the tape to the side. He picks up the sharpie and labels the box 'Glad's Books'. Glad's. That's funny to me for some reason. No one has ever shortened my already shortened name that much, but he does it. He sometimes sings a small pillowtalk song to me that goes 'Glad makes me feel so glad'. I know it's nothing extraordinary. It's not poetry and it's not a Grammy-worthy song, but it's from him. It's between us. That's what makes it mean the world to me.

He picks up the box and kisses me on the forehead before heading out the apartment door to carry it down to the truck we borrowed from Brandon (of all people) for this move. We're moving in together. I'm going to move my things into the place he lives in. I've slowly brought things over in the past few months: clothes, toiletries, hair ties. I kept filling his place with my things like a bird dropping seeds. I did this all to prepare for the eventual move.

This place hasn't felt the same since Howard left. I didn't realize how much I came to appreciate his presence. When he was gone, it felt so empty. It felt like a good friend or a lover leaving you. Now what?

Now what is this? This moment. This next adventure. I scan the apartment that looks emptier and emptier. Bookshelves are gone. The couch is gone. I sold my bed. The few pictures I hung up on the wall have been packed away, leaving behind little light shadows where they hung. You don't realize how much color and dust the walls gather around them.

It feels so weird to erase the tracks of myself in this space. All of my personality has been packed away into boxes to be scattered around a different place with another person. I wonder about what my things even mean to me. They are reflections of me, but when I'm gone is that it? When all of this is packed away, am I also? Do I pack myself and move from this space? Or will parts of me stay behind like Howard did?

I know the answer because when the ghost was gone, he was really gone. I have memories, but those don't sustain a person. We all know that.

I pick up my broom and sweep a little, attempting to return this empty apartment to what it was before so that a new person can come in and enjoy. I've done more cleaning today than I ever did when I lived here and it's such a shame. This place is so cute spotless. Oh well. That just means it's a beautiful blank canvas for another renter.

I won't haunt this space and neither will Howard. They will have a place that has been swept of memories and they can create their own. We never really know what was left before us because it ultimately doesn't really matter.

That's why I don't ask questions about Jon's place. He's

lived in his kitschy apartment for a long time, so there is no doubt there have been girlfriends and lovers sharing that bed. There have been difficult moments, arguments, nightmares and passionate lovemaking strewn throughout that place over the years. I'm sure of it. But I can't think about it because what came before me doesn't really matter.

Besides, I'm coming with my own bag of bullshit from my past. It's not really up to him to unpack it.

I look around and see the only thing left is the pink mid-century lamp. The vintage one I bought with Jacob. I really love that lamp, but the lamp doesn't have a life of its own to me. It is connected to things that are okay to leave in the past. I decide that it's okay to leave that lamp here. The new tenants can have its light.

I put the broom down and explore a little bit of my emptied out place. I open the fridge to nothing. Standing in the kitchen, I remember the seance. The way the wind burst through the place and blew out the candles. The fear. The excitement. God, that feels like a lifetime ago and in this empty kitchen it's impossible to believe we really did that. It really happened here.

I'm excited to move in together and move forward. I want us to create newness and loving energies and if god forbid one of us was left behind to haunt, it would be filled with sweet energy. The haunting would smell like cinnamon and make people feel warm. That's what I hope anyway.

It's scary to move on, but I promised Howard and myself that I would. I'm taking a risk for love and is that not the best kind? Anyway, what's the worst that can happen? It ends? One of us moves out? One of us dies? The whole thing does?

So what. We get through it until we don't.

The End.

DEPARTURES

BY JEFFREY DOKA

DEPARTURES

Jared died on Monday and dashed for the office on Tuesday fifteen minutes before our big presentation. This town-hall meeting defined a turning point for both of our careers. He could at least show up on time. As I waited, I exhaled my frustration and hoped Jared wouldn't let his death ruin our shot at moving up.

Outside, Jared's lanky and now-translucent form juked between hurrying techies and the snoozing homeless sprawled across the sidewalk. He probably didn't need air anymore, but his sunken chest still heaved. A few feet from the entrance, he let out a shocked squeal and dove inside in a blur.

Good. I'd been worried that being flattened by an Uber driver might mellow Jared's workplace drive. He panted, clutching his knee with one hand, but with the other he held up a USB drive with a little carved wooden cat dangling off the end. It looked like something from a souvenir store.

Nervously glancing over his shoulder at something outside, Jared coughed out a few words, "I... I just got the presentation done this morning."

"I needed it by nine last night, dude."

"T... that was right after the accident."

"And?" This presentation was our chance to remake ourselves at DataFirst Marketing. When we'd started three years ago, we'd gotten stuck on the worst team in the company's history. This was our path out and up.

"Well, it's finished now." He waved the USB stick.

I grabbed for it. Unfortunately, when your co-worker is translucent, it's hard to gauge distance. My fingers missed the drive and plunged into his forearm.

My hand locked up like I'd dunked it in liquid nitrogen. A sticky sense of closeness to Jared rushed over me. Was that his cold breath on the back of my neck? I yelped and yanked my hand free.

Dripping ectoplasm soaked my forearm, stained my best navy suit jacket and soaked through to my Brooks Brothers button down.

Cursing, I wiped the goop on a random coat at the rack by the door, and then checked my sharply combed hair. Not a strand out of place. Okay, I could still salvage this.

I held out my hand for the USB this time.

"Sorry, Pablo. Sorry. I'm new to this too." Guilt widened Jared's bug eyes, as he dropped the USB into my open palm. "Still buddies?"

"Yeah, whatever."

Jared grinned way too widely for someone who'd died in the last twenty-four hours. Still smiling, he marched for the stairs to DataFirst's offices on the third floor. I waved him back. "Dude, I am not presenting your slides blind."

He stumbled to a stop. "You... presenting *my* slides?"

"You're translucent. The audience can't see you."

"I want the VPs to hear my results from me."

"Good results don't matter if you present them badly."

Jared held my gaze for a few moments before looking at his shoes. "But... my Facebook ads got twice as many clicks as the old ads."

"What? Do you know what this means? We'll be free of Ted and this trash team! We might even get promoted!" I shuddered with relish at the prospect of being able to rub my advancement in the faces of everyone who'd doubted and back stabbed me. I needed this presentation to be flawless.

"So, can I present my campaigns? Please?"

"Uh what?"

Jared bent his head. "It'd mean a lot... if I could present my slides... considering..."

Of course Jared would ask me if he could present his own slides. But why did it have to be today? I groaned. "Fine, but don't screw this up for me."

My portion of the presentation flowed smoothly. Jared faded into the background, impossible to see in the low light as I talked through my pitch conversations with our client. I only faltered when I noticed a pack of older folks in suits that I didn't recognize. Were those prospective clients? Here in our Town Hall? Weird.

As I passed the microphone to Jared, the speakers squealed. Wincing, Jared stepped forward. A few people raised eyebrows when they saw that he'd died and become a Returned. Ted, our manager, smirked, folded his hands over his gut, and muttered a joke to the people he liked on the team. The rest of the audience just leaned forward, struggling to see Jared's hazy form.

As he talked, Jared got flustered and forgot to use the laser pointer. He motioned to the pictures of the advertisements he'd designed with his hands, but the projector drowned out his arm, making it impossible to understand what he was saying.

He realized he was losing the crowd, got more flustered, and started talking even faster. Feedback squealed louder over the microphone, and the crowd's eyes started rolling up with boredom.

I grabbed the microphone. Speaking in a clear, firm voice, I highlighted the legendary results his advertisement creative drove.

The crowd warmed back up immediately. Even the COO, the VP of Marketing, and the new people in suits sat forward in their seats.

After the presentation, Jared collapsed into one of the seats for presenters. He looked exhausted.

As the marketing team headed to their desks, Trellis, a girl from the support team, sat next to Jared. She had a runner's legs, dark hair, and nothing to do with the Marketing Department or Jared. So why were they muttering together like conspirators?

Ted's hand clapped my shoulder. "Yo, yo, thanks for stopping that goo-boy from embarrassing us."

"HR will kill you if they hear you call him that."

"I'm so sorry, Mr. Politically Correct Police. I forgot you're such a good little cadet." Ted raised his hands in a fake salute, laughing. "But what is Number Five doing with that goo... person."

Ted, along with the more annoying marketers on our less-than-stellar team, liked to refer to the office women by their attractiveness rankings. Apparently, Trellis was ranked five because she didn't have the pencil thin legs and... the other features of the higher ranked girls. I thought they were underestimating her. With intelligent eyes, a sharp wit, and a gentleness that always warmed a room, she should at least be ranked three.

I gave Ted a conspiratorial wink, knowing he was too stupid to recognize the sarcasm in it. "I'll investigate and report back."

Ted gave me a thumbs-up and crept back to our marketing pod with an exaggerated sneaking walk. Moron. Still, I did want to find out why Trellis talked to Jared of all people.

I gathered the leftover slide printouts on the chairs near enough to the stage to catch Trellis's voice.

"At least you can rest now... go to the Rising and start your Pilgrimage, right? Get out of here..." Wait, was she crying?

Jared mumbled something.

She shoved her sleeve against her running nose. "Yeah, you... you too."

I just caught a snatch of Jared's reply. "Outside... huge..."

Trellis jerked upright; tears streaked her cheeks. "What do you mean can't?"

Jared muttered something, then I heard him say, "Don't tell anyone."

Anxiety tightened the lines on Trellis's forehead and her hands shook. I thought back on how weird he'd been acting before the meeting. Was the little guy in trouble?

Trellis kneeled to meet his downcast eyes. "Listen, it doesn't matter what's out there, if you don't go to the rising--"

A hand coiled around my wrist and I yelped in a higher pitch than I'd have preferred.

Claudia, the VP of Marketing, tightened her vice grip on my arm and towed me to her office at the corner of the marketing bull pen. Had I accidentally said something offensive to the VPs? Had I inadvertently voiced an out-of-taste political opinion? Hell, had I looked at someone the wrong way?

Her office's glass windows boasted a pristine view of the bent heads of the fifteen marketing teams she managed. Our dysfunctional team sat in desks right beside her window—all the easier to watch us.

She dumped me into a stiff seat facing her glass desk and studied me. She looked like a watchful raven in a neat black dress; her pointed features twitched into a scowl before she sat across from me. "It's good you were there today to... salvage your presentation. A very important client joined us today."

My face heated up. "Salvage? It went well... those numbers are hard to argue with."

"It went well after you took over from that thing."

"Well, I'm always happy to help. Wait... what thing?"

"The Returned."

"Jared?"

"I suppose." She waved a hand. "Unfortunately, your good performance has presented me with a problem."

"P-problem?"

"Yes, WeightWin's senior team saw your creative and liked it."

I rocked back in my chair. "No way. WeightWin? A contract with them has to be worth like a hundred million."

Claudia lifted a red-tipped nail. "One hundred and fifty million. And they've requested your team, Ted's team, to prepare a demonstration for them."

"Oh... oh no."

Claudia leaned forward across her desk, her shoulders shifting like a panther's. "One of the most valuable clients ever to walk through our doors has requested mock-ups from the lowest performing team in DataFirst's history. Oh no indeed."

The amount of work to build mock-ups for a company of that size was staggering, and Jared was the only person on that team that hadn't fully wedged his head in his own... rectum. But he was a Returned now, and there was no guarantee he could perform like normal. Hell, with whatever Trellis was freaking out about, there was no guarantee he could perform at all. "Ted will be terrified."

"Ted won't have a chance. While his friendship with the CEO makes him difficult to remove, I'll be transferring him." She folded her arms and smiled. "I'm taking a gamble and promoting the innovator who came up with those amazing campaigns to team lead."

"Wait... you mean me?"

"Congratulations, Pablo."

"Wow... thank you so much. And Jared, he's getting promoted too, right? That was his creative."

"Oh, you know how inconsistent *they* are."

I gave a noncommittal shrug and tried to keep my grin going.

"He'll be leaving for the Rising to start his Pilgrimage with the rest of those creatures before long."

Creature? My face got hot. "He's really reliable. You really--"

"He *was* reliable. I won't promote one of them only to have it quit a week later."

I pinched the bridge of my nose, thinking. No one living really knew what the Rising was, but it sounded like an over-hyped start to a boring undead stroll through memory lane. Jared wouldn't sacrifice all our work for that, and from what I'd overheard, he might not even be able to. And this was Jared. He wouldn't ditch the team now; he was a career-first guy to the bone.

I met Claudia's gaze. "Me and Jared, we slaved under Ted for years to get this chance. Jared is loyal. Just trust me on--"

"There's one position open." Her smile faltered, and her voice came out sharp. My childhood had taught me what to do with someone angry and talking over me. I bowed my head. Her smirk returned. "The promotion will go to the *human* that made those campaigns successful. Now, how significant was your creative input?"

My mouth opened and closed. I hated the fact that, on reflex, I was already making myself look smaller for Claudia. I took a breath and forced myself to sit up.

Claudia was a jerk, but that didn't mean she was wrong. Given the option, maybe Jared would desert the team for this Rising thing. Besides, Maura and I had a trip to Cabo planned and reservations at two Michelin Star Restaurants. Team leads got a thirty percent raise. Now that Jared was dead, how much cash did he really need? "I uh... I gave him lots of notes. Feedback on the camp--"

"Yes, yes, I'm glad you understand." She stood and rushed me out of her office. "I'll make the announcement Friday."

I signed the forms at five, and it was almost seven before I'd made a dent in the prep work for my new management role. Then, Maura's texts hit me in a flood.

Maura: Where the hell are you?!!??!!

Maura: How dare you stand me up? I look like an idiot.

Maura: You even listening?!? You'll pay for this...

I sprinted out of the office before more texts could come, wording my reply to spark her curiosity: "Sorry, sorry, sorry, one of my co-workers died, but good news. Promotion!"

I got to the Foreign Cinema Restaurant in under five minutes. Maura lounged at a table close to the screen in the big atrium. Donning a curvy red dress, she tapped at her rhinestone encrusted iPhone, looking bored. It might have seemed, to the untrained eye, that nibbling on her kale salad starter was exactly what she intended to do while her date was in the bathroom.

I knew the truth: she was humiliated and raging pissed.

Dodging between tables, I leapt into the seat across from her.

She didn't look up from her Instagram but just flicked a strand of black hair away from her lips.

"I... How's the salad?"

Expression neutral, she spun her phone toward me. Pictures of a stunning apartment in the Lower Haight glowed in my face. "I love the marble counters, and those floors: amazing. You'll need to buy some carpets, of course."

I took a slow breath. "We have marble counters in our apartment right now."

"Our place has bad lighting."

"Come on, I can't afford a place like that. How about I take you to ice cream and we call it even?"

"Didn't you get a promotion?" She raised an eyebrow. "A promotion worth so much more than being on time for dinner with me?"

My fist tightened around my steak knife. "All right, we'll go to the open-house."

"Good!" She clapped her hands and resumed pecking at her kale salad while surfing on her phone. Minutes later, she glanced up at me. "And your day?"

"Fine, fine..." What was I saying? My day hadn't been fine at all. "Jared, my teammate, died yesterday. He's a Returned now, so I still get to see him, but it's weird, you know? I'm not sure if he's leaving or if something is wrong or... I don't know."

I stared at my hands. "We rose through the ranks together and now that we've finally earned a shot at manager, he can't..."

One finger swiped up on her phone, she nodded absently.

I frowned. "I'm cheating on you with your stepdad."

She kept nodding. Fine then. I tugged out my cell and wrote a few more work emails while we ate, but I still couldn't get my mind off Jared. He'd seemed so... off after town hall, not to mention the fact that I'd just stolen his promotion.

After dinner, Maura called in my offer for ice cream. I turned up Mission toward downtown. Maura frowned and hooked a thumb over her shoulder. "The sugar-free, organic fro-yo spot is that way."

"There's another location... downtown." I gave her a winsome smile. "A walk would burn dinner calories."

Also, the Rising would take place in Union Square at the very center of downtown. That was where all the Returned of San Francisco gathered to begin their journey to... wherever. I knew better than to mention to Maura that Jared might be there tonight. If he showed up, I'd be pissed that Claudia was right and that he'd ditched me. Best case: If he was there, I could convince him to stay. Worst case: He was my buddy and didn't have any family here, and I could give him a nice little sendoff.

"A walk downtown?" Maura folded her arms.

I shrugged. "We could get some photos of you at that Rising thing. We've never been."

Her ruby lips quirked. "Now you're speaking my language."

The tang of sweat hovered around the hundreds of people squeezed into Union Square. Families packed the nearby side-walks, and at the square's center, the Returned seethed around the Dewey Monument's main pillar.

A few Returned dallied on the staircases up, giving last embraces and final charges to their families, but they soon joined the rest of the Returned converging around the monument.

I craned my neck, looking for Jared, when the all the Returned square started grasping at the air, reaching for something hidden from living eyes. Then, in one silver mass, they rose into the foggy San Francisco air like a great gray cloud.

I turned to Maura, but she was already posing in front of the main stairway to the Rising, her phone clamped to one of the banisters, ready to rapid-fire a gigabyte's worth of pictures once the action started.

They wandered, laughing, enthralled by unseen movements. Each Returned drifted outward in a different direction, expanding into a wide circle as the entire group rose into the skyline, forming a glowing halo over San Francisco.

Then, one by one, in sparks of luminescent color, in red and blue and gold light, the gray figures vanished into the night air. The crowd applauded, and for a moment I thought I smelled the popcorn my Grandpa Terry used to make and rain over the desert and the chlorine of my friend Ian's pool, aromas from all the good places I used to go to escape home. The aromas mixed together into something sharp that I missed desperately, and the flash of multi-colored lights overhead grew so bright it hurt.

Then, all the Returned were gone.

Foggy blackness remained. No one spoke. Families and lovers and friends trudged back into the City, disappearing into the bustling streets of the living.

Maura packed up her phone, and for the first time tonight she grinned. Breathless, she gasped, "What a fantastic idea. The lighting. The colors. My shots are going to be amazing."

* * *

Jared hadn't gone to the Rising. The next day and the days after, I found him working at his desk. He only exchanged quick "good mornings" with me, and I wondered if he'd heard about my promotion. I thought about telling him the real story about my promotion all week and even asking about his conversation with Trellis. Before I could find the words, Claudia's meeting to make the official announcement arrived.

At the end of a long list of projects and to-dos, she outlined that Ted would be moving to another team and that I'd be their new manager. Everyone clapped. Everyone except Jared. He didn't look sad or angry. Confusion furrowed his brow, and for a moment, a faint red glow smoldered at the center of his chest.

I should have told him.

He would have expected me to share this with him. As weird as the guy was, whenever I got a leg up on a unicorn client or me and Maura got in a fight, he was the only person I told. He'd actually listen while everyone else on this crappy team would fake a smile and either try to steal my client or my girl.

I'd grown up in Shitholesville, Texas and Jared hailed from the charming town of TrailerTrash, Colorado. We understood each other. DataFirst was our shot at never going back, never working at the local hardware store or the damn cotton gin, and never having to deal with our families again. We were going to live the city life! Even if he was a nerd and hanging out with him wasn't great for my career, we were in it together. Keyword being were.

I should have told him.

After the team filed out of the conference room, Claudia shoved a bundle of papers into my arms: the creative brief for WeightWin. They wanted carousel ads, ten different types of weight loss creative, and a whole blog series on health tips. And the sales numbers they asked us to hit... insane. The papers shook in my hands. I guess they really could ask for the impossible when their contract was worth millions.

Jared was the only creative guy on the team who had the chops to get close to the numbers they wanted. But something had been off about him since his death, and after watching me get his promotion, nothing was stopping him from bouncing and leaving for the Rising.

If I wanted his help, I'd need to play this smart.

His desk was in the far corner of the marketing bullpen. Next to his laptop, an old pine carving of a pouncing cat was the only decoration. Maybe the guy thought it was a conversation starter.

As I got closer, I found Trellis leaning over Jared's crappy IKEA chair. She whispered to him in a blur of words, "There's not much info, but deadandwhatnow.com has a few testimonials about what you're seeing."

Jared murmured something in reply.

Trellis clasped her hands together. "I know it's terrifying, but I'm here today. I'll walk out with you... We should try now..."

She trailed off as I walked up to Jared's desk and sat next to his keyboard. Trellis glowered at me. What the hell did I do to her? I gave her a smile. "Uh... just wanted to talk to Jared."

"I'm sure." She turned her back to me and continued whispering to Jared. "Look, I think it's simpler than it sounds... Today's my last day, and you know how crazy security is here. I won't get another chance."

I raised my eyebrows. Trellis leaving?

That red light glowed in Jared's center again and he shook his head. "I can't with work... It's crunch time."

"It's *always* crunch time. That's just something they say." She pinched the bridge of her nose. "I know you're scared, but you need to take this seriously. These people don't care about--"

"Not scared. And it's... it's time for me and Pablo's Friday lunch. " He let out a nervous breath and looked up at me with a distant smile. "Are we still doing that now that you're... in leadership?"

A strained smile tightened my lips as I glanced between Trellis and Jared. I still couldn't guess what she was so stressed about and what Jared seemed to be avoiding, but Jared very obviously wanted me to bail him out of this conversation. "Of course! Besides, I got a new brief for the WeightWin contract. The whopper."

I started towards the lunch tables. Trellis's jaw clenched tight with anger, but Jared looked at his shoes and whispered something to her before following me.

Trellis remained standing over Jared's desk, her hands balled into fists, her shoulders shaking. I opened my mouth to ask Jared what had happened, but he mumbled. "We were going to go on a date last weekend, just before the accident. She actually asked *me* to a picnic in Dolores Park with her nephews. Can you believe it?"

He was dodging the real question I had, but for now, I had to play along. I forced myself to laugh. "Her nephews? Real romantic."

"I know, right? She knows I never got to... well, do stuff like parks with how things were when I was little."

It had been the same for me. Parks were a great place for jackass parents to give themselves the wrong kind of publicity. My pops avoided them. "And how did it go?"

"I uh... had work..."

"Dude, seriously?"

"She'd just end up hating me. If she listened to me for too long, she'd realize something is wrong with me... that I'm not..." He sat down at our lunch table and met my eyes with that fixed stare that got him branded as a weirdo in the first week. "I don't understand... how normal people do well... anything. My dad never explained, and whenever I asked, he never..."

I focused real hard on the delicious salami flavor of my sandwich for the next few minutes. During our lunches, Jared sometimes went on a roll about his family as if he were unique to have an asshole for a dad and a mom that skittered around the house avoiding notice. I didn't need the reminder of home and the memories of my scumbag old man yelling over every word I said.

Jared was in the middle of talking about a family trip to someplace called Cloudcroft when he suddenly winced and stopped talking. Maybe the memories of home sucked for him too.

A moment later he barked out a nervous laugh. "Sorry... I..."

With him flustered, I risked asking a direct question. "Trellis is trying to convince you to leave. Why?"

"She's just stressed about... stuff. And she's sad." He stared out past the lunchroom for a moment before turning to me and grinning. "But we'd never have landed the WeightWin contract if I hadn't skipped a date or two. Besides, you and me, we're in this together. I can't leave now."

"Speaking of..." I told him about the creative brief and the revenue goals WeightWin had sent us. Jared's shoulders sunk.

"I... It's impossible." He mumbled.

A stress headache began slamming against my skull. Maura had seen the new apartment last night and insisted we sign a two-year lease on the spot. If I didn't land this contract, I'd lose my promotion. Without my promotion, I'd go broke paying rent on that apartment. "Look buddy, I need you to work a miracle for me."

"I might have some ideas, but..." Jared's skull shone faintly through his translucent skin, and his jawbone twitched. "Could I ask you one favor? Something to help?"

Ugh. Of course. Did he want the next spot as team lead or one of the coveted window seats?

"Could you take care of Nibbles?"

"What? Uh... who's Nibbles?"

"Oh... he's my gerbil. Just with all the work to do... I won't have time to make arrangements." He slid a key to his apartment across the table to me, being careful not to touch my skin.

"So, working nights then?"

He shifted his feet. "Something like that."

If Maura's reaction that night was any indication, I might have thought Jared gave me Nibbles solely to piss her off. She hated the sawdust, the smell, the squeals, and the creak of the wheel turning and turning. She didn't stop shouting until I stuffed the damn thing's cage in our guest room and shut the door.

It was a few days later when I discovered the real reason he'd asked me to watch his gerbil.

He worked around the clock. Apparently that whole "sleep when you're dead" thing isn't true, but what really threw me off was the fact that he stayed in the office the whole time. Why not work from home? Why not pull a few hours at a twenty-four-hour Starbucks? I didn't doubt it had something to do with whatever Trellis was so frustrated about or maybe why he hadn't gone to the Rising.

I resolved to find out before the project wrapped, but to my surprise, I wound up learning the truth at the next happy hour.

* * *

The San Francisco skyline glimmered in sunlight outside of our floor's wrap-around windows. The air over the marketing pods thickened into a warm fog of body odor despite the cool fall weather outside. Sure, we had a lot of work left on Weight-Win's brief, but it was so damn hot, I had to get outdoors.

I waved to my team and pantomimed guzzling a beer. Laptops snapped shut at record speed, and the marketing professionals under my purview bolted for the door as if it were a race to flirt with the cute bartender at Zeitgeist.

The other, better ranked, marketing teams didn't budge, and beside them, alone in our pod, sat Jared.

Ignoring the little carved cat that stared at me from his desk, I peered over Jared's shoulder. The ad he was making filled the screen with vibrant color. Elegant lines of bright neon blues and pinks circled WeightWin's signature Wi-Fi enabled scale where an elegant girl that reminded me of Trellis hung a few inches in the air. The ad read "Nothing is Lighter than Light."

Stunning. That ad alone might land us the contract.

I waved my hand in front of Jared's face, careful not to touch him. "Team's heading to Zeitgeist for drinks to celebrate WeightWin accepting our first drafts."

"Oh, do you mean my first drafts? I thought everyone else was working on something for a casino."

"Yeah, so um... you're the guest of honor. So, let's go. The Barcelona game starts in twenty."

Jared winced. "I don't... I don't like soccer."

"Maura's meeting us there, she hasn't seen you in ages."

"I don't... I don't think she likes me very much." Jared turned back to his computer and started typing. "Besides, I have work."

"Trust me, Jared, I love hearing that, but we need the whole team at happy hour to meet Claudia's inclusion quota for the Death Togetherness Initiative." He gave me a blank stare. I leaned forward and hissed, "We need equal representation for all stages of living and undeath. If our team fails, do you know how bad that would make her look? Claudia would kill me."

Jared cast a nervous glance at the stairs to the bottom floor. He seemed freaked out, but whether it was because of whatever Trellis had been talking about or his generally extreme levels of social anxiety, I couldn't guess.

That's when Ted and his new team of under-performers marched for the exit. Ted stopped and gave me a nudge. "Heard about your happy hour, bro. Fireball shots on your company card, right?"

"Claudia said I could spend one grand max."

"I can hit that number." Ted leaned in and gave me a wink. "Is that fox you're dating going to join?"

"Maura?" I pasted on a fake smile. "Dude, you're married."

"Yo, looking isn't a crime." He fist bumped and followed his team out. They roved like a pack of hyenas, eyeballing the pretty office girls so overtly that even the girls they weren't leering at tugged down their skirts.

I spun Jared's chair away from his desk, easy to do when the occupant has no mass. "You're coming with."

"I... These designs are due Tuesday."

"Dude, please don't make me spend happy hour making small talk with Ted." I leaned forward and whispered, "I'll cover the extra work. Come on, buddy."

At the word "buddy", Jared's eyes widened. He knew I was useless with Photoshop, but he hesitantly stood anyway. "I... I could try. Maybe it won't..."

As we marched through the marketing pods, Jared's hands shook. He'd lost weight, and his polo shirt drooped over his bony shoulders, making him look like a soggy scarecrow cringing and moping across the marketing floor.

"You all right?" I struggled to keep annoyance out of my voice. Sure, Jared had stuff going on. Who didn't? Why couldn't he just get it together and back me up against Ted?

He didn't answer.

When we reached the entryway, Jared cringed backward,

staring out the glass doors opening onto the street. "Oh no... It... it's still there..."

I followed Jared's gaze. Cars drifted down Market street outside. A pack of techies wearing matching backpacks and conference name tags marched past some homeless men dozing on the corner. Nothing out of the ordinary. Nothing threatening.

Jared hyperventilated and inched back toward the stairs to our floor. I waved at the window. "All right, what's all this about?"

"I... can't." Jared shook his head and started scurrying back to the office.

"No, you don't," I snarled and seized his wrist.

Mistake.

The pressing sense of intimate closeness that I'd felt when I'd first touched Jared lifted the hairs on my neck. My hand didn't go numb this time, so when my fingers gripped the warm bone in the center of his arm, I felt it. Heat spread up my hand.

The room dimmed, and sharp chords of neon light glowed in from outside. An ache, a yearning tightened in my gut. I longed to drift, wander, feel. The air smelled rich, like a freshly opened Zinfandel.

Something huge moved outside the window.

Dread tightened my throat; my muscles froze up. The sweet aroma in the air turned so putrid, that sour bile rose in back of my throat.

For a breath, I saw it: a tiger as large as a city bus, corded out of sharp red and white neon. It opened its mouth to roar, and its jaw unsocketed like a snake, exposing rows upon rows of teeth. A bone-shaking wall of sound issued from the animal, but before the noise flattened me, my fingers left Jared's arm, and the room returned to normal.

Jared stumbled backward, reeling from the roar I'd avoided.

I gawked at the window as ectoplasm dripped off my hand. The receptionist frowned at me like I had worms wriggling out of my face. It took a moment for my mouth to work. "What... what was that, Jared?"

He pressed his lips shut and hugged himself as if speaking of that glowing tiger would give it the strength to burst through the glass and eviscerate him.

My eyes shot open as it all snapped into focus. "Is that why you haven't gone to the Rising? It's not because you like the work or Trellis so much. And it's not because you really have my back. You're just scared of that thing outside."

He finally met my eyes. Tears streamed down his translucent cheeks. "This... this is my business. It's not about you."

He hurried back upstairs.

That hurt, but I still started to follow him to see if he was okay. I was halfway up the stairs when I saw the time. Happy hour was already half-over. I'd miss it if I waited any longer. I shifted from foot to foot. Jared's back still faced me as he drifted toward his desk. He didn't want to talk to me, and I had a responsibility to the team just as much as I had to him. Biting my lip, I turned around, sprinted for Zeitgeist, and let Jared walk back to his desk alone.

Jared avoided me for the rest of the week. He only emailed to notify me that he'd turned in the "Lighter than Light" campaign, but every time I tried to bring up what I'd seen or anything other than work, he ghosted me.

I finally cornered him at our Friday lunch. For a second, I didn't see him as I entered the cafeteria. Would he really break tradition and miss our lunch? Hell, we'd had our fair share of disagreements in the past, but we never skipped lunch.

As the light shifted, Jared's hazy form grew visible. He sat at our table, waiting dutifully. I let out a relieved breath, sat down, and unwrapped my sandwich. He never ate anything, though he'd grown so gaunt after Trellis left, you'd think he might want to give it a try.

I dusted some stray bits of lettuce off the table and gave him the best disappointed manager look I could muster. The little guy melted. His head bent so low that his forehead almost touched the table, Jared mumbled, "I'm... sorry about Tuesday."

"Sorry won't cut it." I folded my arms. "What the hell is going on?"

"It won't influence my work."

"It already has!" My voice came out louder than I expected. I had to take a breath.

"I'm sorry, Pablo. Please don't be mad."

"Look, buddy. I'm just worried about you." Jared gave me a skeptical look before I lifted my hands. "Yes, and I'm worried about the WeightWin project too. I won't BS you, but you gotta talk to me."

"It's embarrassing," he muttered. "Abnormal."

"Who am I going to tell?"

"I know, but... almost no Returned experience this. Trellis only found one mention of it in her research." Jared tugged his smart phone out of his ephemeral slacks pocket. He held the phone out to me.

It displayed a two-year-old post in an obscure research forum that read: "The phenomenon of a guardian in a Returned's anamnesis is a rarity due to the generally positive nature of an anamnestic episode. The presence of a guardian constitutes an indicator of significant trauma or a perceived failing in the subject's unconscious. The neurosis causing this phenomenon is usually unacknowledged by the subject and resolution surrounds a confrontation and integration. In the rare occurrence of a guardian, it usually takes the shape of a stray cat (typified as a guardian of the afterlife in eastern traditions) or another small animal reminiscent of the trauma."

"Do I look like a college professor to you?" I pushed the paper back to Jared. "What's that mean in English?"

"It's embarrassing."

"And..."

Jared pocketed his phone and fidgeted. "It says my subconscious believes I failed in life somehow, but I'm too afraid to admit it, so an animal appears."

"That thing out there is no kitten." I massaged my temples. "Isn't it supposed to be a small?"

"Maybe I failed more than normal... maybe I'm just that stupid... so stupid..." Jared's hands balled into fists and a red glow flared up in the center of his chest.

"Whoa... look at your campaigns and tell me if that's a stupid person's work."

"That's not what I mean." He hunched forward and his thin shoulders shook. Quiet sobs broke the monotonous noise of the lunchroom.

Yikes. Was he crying? I glanced around for any VPs. A general malaise on any team was acceptable, but I was expected to maintain morale well above despair. "Come on, buddy. Do some research this week and we'll find a way for you to go to your Rising or do whatever you Returned do... after this project is done, of course."

"It's just..." Jared sniffed. "Trellis was so worried when we spoke last..."

Spoke last? Had he and Trellis been out of contact? "Dude. You're freaking out. Wasn't there some website where she got all this? Just do some research yourself."

Teary eyed, Jared nodded. His shoulders still shook with the occasional sob, and he was starting to draw looks. "Bud? Hey bud. Nibbles is finishing his meals now. He's been way calmer, and Maura loves the guy."

That perked him up. Jared sniffed and leaned forward,

leaping at the chance to talk about his gerbil rather than the tiger outside. "She doesn't seem the type to like... well... something like Nibbles."

"She'll surprise you," I lied.

Earlier in the relationship he'd discouraged me from dating her, but in the end, he'd stopped his objections, assuming I was happy. He sighed wistfully. "You two really are a special couple."

"Well, we were compatible on over fifty dimensions of DateHarmony's algorithm, so... it makes sense." I shrugged, relieved that he was finally calming down. "It still surprises me sometimes what Maura and I have in common."

Jared folded his hands on the table and nodded for me to go on. He always was a great listener. "Well, we both love putting a movie on and surfing Instagram, and... um... cat photos. Both of us love those... and our new apartment.

"And we also both like..." I frowned. There had to be more. I suspected Jared was egging me on just to change the subject, but still, the guy looked at me with genuine interest. "Um, your gerbil? And..."

A riot of cheers rose up from the marketing floor. Both Jared and I jumped up from our desks. Sudden happy roars were as rare as explosions, and Jared and I stared at each other, unsure whether we should run toward or away from the noise.

We peered through the kitchen doors. Confetti flickered through the air, analysts danced between the desks, and drinks flowed.

A champagne bottle popped over the marketing pod. Fizzing booze spilled onto a laptop, which crackled, sparked, and died, but no one noticed.

Some liquor spilled on Jared's desk. He yelped and hurried to mitigate the damage that might be done to his work.

Every team, even the heads-down, workhorses jumped

around clapping each other on the backs. As I went further into the pod, I heard the words "Lighter than Light" chanted like a spell.

Ted gave me a too-hard "playful" gut-punch and blathered that he never thought a prissy little needle-dick like me could ever land a real cash whale. Then, it clicked. We'd gotten WeightWin! I'd led the worst team in the company to land our biggest client yet.

A blur of handshakes and congratulations laced with thinly veiled jealousy swept me across the marketing floor. I didn't care; I floated in a cloud of motion, laughter, and confetti.

I'd done it.

I wrestled myself free and pushed my way through the other marketing teams toward Jared. Once he'd reached his desk, it looked like he'd immediately sat down to start emailing WeightWin's launch team.

That guy... he should be celebrating more than anyone. "Jared! Get over here!"

He didn't hear me.

I edged through another marketing pod packed with people. I cupped my hands over my mouth. "Jared, dude! Come celeb--"

A heavy hand clapped me on the shoulder, followed by the musky aroma of expensive cologne. "Got a minute, son?"

"Sure, in just one..." The COO, David Fillbert himself, had pulled me aside. He wore a tailored Italian suit and had a short, salt-and-pepper beard trimmed with similar precision. The crowd parted in his wake and I spun to face him, turning my back on Jared. "Sir, of course. Happy to chat."

Envious mutterings rose around me as David led me into his corner office.

The view of the San Francisco skyline framing his marble-topped desk was so perfect that if the clouds drifting past the skyscrapers hadn't moved, I'd have thought someone had taped up a photo. David kicked back in a plush chair and gave me an appraising look. "That's one hell of a contract you just landed."

"Thanks... uh... sir."

"Just call me David."

"Sure, David... sir."

He ran his thumb along the even stubble of his beard. "That was no easy proposal to deliver."

"Well, the WeightWin's crew was great, and my team gave a stellar performance as always." There wasn't a chair on the other side of David's desk, so I awkwardly stood .

"Don't lie, son." David folded his arms. "Your team was an embarrassment to the company until Claudia put you in charge. I wonder exactly how you turned them around."

I folded my shaking hands and forced a smile. "Isn't being a caring and compassionate manager enough?"

The COO laughed and stood. "Well, I hope your caring management style serves you when you take over Riley's team."

My mouth dropped open. "But, they're the best ranked--"

"You'll need them. I'm giving you a special project." David circled his desk to stand beside me. "The WeightWin contract gives us a chance at something big if you take my meaning."

I didn't. I raised my eyebrows with the air of understanding and hoped he'd elaborate.

Unfortunately, he only nodded as if I'd passed some unspoken examination. "As you can expect, we'll need a much nicer office to make that possibility an option. An office to rival the best New York agencies."

"We're moving?" My mind leapt to my lunch chat with Jared. What would he do if he couldn't leave? Jared's tiger had just become a much bigger problem. I cleared my throat, hoping David hadn't noticed my shock. "We're moving. When?"

"With this momentum, as soon as possible. I want you to

lead the PR, press, and advertising for the transition to the new office." He gave me a nod. "Your team's work made this possible after all."

"Wait, I get to interview with TechCrunch, talk to press, everything? Me? But that's Claudia's job, she'll be--"

"She's starting extended maternity leave in a week, and well, her decision making has always been..." He seesawed his hand.

No kidding. How could Claudia make the mistake of going on maternity for anything more than the two-week minimum during such a critical time? She'd leave her position wide open for poachers.

"I have one request. I want Jared to join me on my new team. We've worked together for years, and--"

"Caring management style, huh? I was wondering about your little Returned friend."

My mouth went dry. "Um, he is a workhorse, but without my creative input well..."

"You can have him." He stared out of the glass doors opening onto the marketing bull pen. The celebration had pretty much wrapped up, and everyone had returned to their desks to continue working. Only the trampled confetti that littered the floor gave any indication of a celebration. "Does he really not sleep?"

"No. And he doesn't leave the office either, but I think that's probably unique to him."

"Amazing." He nodded, not turning from the window opening onto the marketing team. "If we could only guarantee they'd come back..."

"Um, sir?"

"Nothing. It's nothing." David blinked and waved me off. "Anyway, I've already had my assistant clear your calendar and book some PR calls for you this afternoon. Good luck."

I ducked out of his office and started marching to Jared's desk to give him the news. If he was going to move with us to the new office, he needed to figure out a way past that tiger fast. I hoped that when we did, he wouldn't turn around and ditch me for that Rising thing. My phone rang just before I reached him.

It was TechCrunch.

I swerved away from Jared and stuttered my name to the interviewer, hoping I didn't sound like a total idiot. That was only the beginning. David's assistant had booked me for back-to-back calls until seven, and by the time that was done, I had to sprint home to Maura.

Exhausted, I decided to game plan with Jared the next day before the news reached the team.

Unfortunately, the moment I got into the office, David called an emergency management off-site and I barely grabbed my coffee before I was whisked away to some boat ride in the bay with terrible cell reception. During our reflection breaks, I tried to call Jared, but phone calls were impossible.

When we finally got to shore, the flood of emails told me the company had learned about the move. Guilt twisted in my stomach. I'd wanted to tell Jared myself, to let him know it'd be okay.

That night, while lying in bed and reading emails, I noticed the discrepancy.

None of Jared's WeightWin mock-ups had come in. After weeks of on-time delivery, a whole new ad set was late. I sifted through my emails. Jared had been radio silent since the email announcement fired. I shifted beneath the sheets, trying to still a flutter of anxiety rising in my chest.

I barely slept for the rest of the night.

* * *

The next morning, I wanted to get to the office early and talk to Jared before the rest of the team showed up, but Maura insisted we get brunch at Plow. The stupid weather was gorgeous, so afterward she ended up having me take pictures of her all the way to the office in the "OMG so fabulous lighting."

I was so focused on rushing through a shot of her against the stone lion in front of our office, that I almost missed noticing Trellis. She was bent over the receptionist's desk inside, talking in an urgent whisper.

My curiosity won out. "I'll be right back... just hold that pose." Maura's phone still in my hands, I ducked inside.

As I approached, Trellis grumbled, "I'm not here to steal confidential information. I just need to talk to someone."

The receptionist gave her a bland look and pressed a few buttons on her desk, probably calling security. "I told you: without a form that he signed, I can't help you."

I walked up to the receptionist and held up my badge. "She's with me."

Trellis swung towards me. I prepared to block a punch. To my shock, she embraced me in a huge hug. "Oh thank, thank you."

The receptionist narrowed her eyes but waved her through.

Trellis hurried upstairs, holding a bundle of papers under one arm. I frowned, squinting to read the titles before she disappeared. Had she found a way to get Jared out? This could be huge. With him working under me at the new office, another promotion could be in order.

Maura's voice snapped me to attention, and I realized it probably hadn't looked like I was staring at Trellis's papers. "Friend of yours?"

"She uh... worked here." I cringed as the words came out of my mouth.

Maura raised a perfectly lined eyebrow and held out her

hand. I stared like an idiot for a moment before jumping in realization and returning her phone. "Sorry."

Maura scowled and turned toward the door.

"Still want that photo?"

She left without another word. Damn it, she'd make me pay for this... probably starting with first class tickets to an exotic location.

As I trudged to my desk, a stress headache pulsed in the back of my skull, but when I saw Trellis engaged in a quiet argument with Jared in front of the COO's office, it exploded into a full migraine. To make things worse, Trellis looked an inch away from either breaking down in tears or throwing something.

Trellis hissed a question to Jared, and he shook his head. His eyes were closed, and he hugged himself like he was freezing cold. Desperation drew lines beneath her eyes, Trellis clasped her hands and nearly shouted, "You don't have time for this. You don't..."

Jared shook his head again.

Resigned, she handed him the stack of papers and left. I couldn't tell if she was angry or sad on the way out, but Jared looked miserable.

I rushed up to him. A quick glance through the COO's empty office windows told me I was safe for now. I herded Jared away from the door. "Dude, are you trying to get us fired?"

"You shouldn't have let her in..."

"No kidding."

"Seeing her... The memories..." he continued as if I hadn't spoken. "Memory is different for me now. It's like fire... it burns."

With Trellis's papers in one hand, he still hugged himself. Jared's discussion with Trellis had drawn looks.

I waved Jared to a conference room and slumped into a chair. "Okay, what was she hollering about?"

"She brought me some information on my... condition."

"Well, that's awesome. Less research for you, but why was she mad?"

"She just won't listen, and she doesn't agree with what I'm doing about..." He nodded toward the front door. "That."

I nodded absently as I leaned over to read the titles on the documents Trellis had brought. The top one was titled *Guardian Driven Essence Deterioration in Returned Subjects.* Man, that lady liked her scholarly journals.

"She said the creature is cutting me off from sustenance." He glanced out the window. "She's worried I'll starve and eventually fade."

I looked him up and down. "I mean you've already kind of faded. And the kitchen is stocked if--"

"Not food: memory." He flipped open one of the documents Trellis had printed out and read a line or two. "Until I get free, I need people who know me and hear me to stay close."

"Well that's easy. Everybody here knows you, and you've had lots of chats with people on every floor. Even the guys in the co-working space hung out with you at our happy hours." I rubbed my hands together. "So, you're telling me that as long as we get some people who know you to the new office before you arrive, you'll be fine."

Jared's translucent shoulder twitched a half-shrug.

"Then, the only problem now is that thing outside." I leaned over Trellis's papers. "Did she give you any tips on how to get past it?"

Jared pulled the papers closer to his chest. A red glow flared in his chest. "No."

"Come on, dude."

He lifted his chin and that red light in his center burned a little brighter.

"Fine, I believe you." I gave the stack of papers a closer look, and I could just see the pen-marks of handwritten notes. Was it something personal she'd uncovered? Something secret? Jared jerked Trellis's notes out of my view, and I frowned at him. "At least explain to me why she wanted to talk to the COO?"

"Trellis?"

"Why else did she drag you to his office?"

"Drag me? No. I was waiting for David when Trellis walked up to me. I'm going to convince him to stop the move."

"What?" I inhaled sharply, choked on some of my own saliva, and coughed. "Dude, that off-site I went to yesterday. It was just six hours of David repeating that the move was critical and that those who fell behind would be left behind. I have an interview with Gizmodo right now talking about how critical the new location is for us."

Jared let out a nervous whimper and started glancing around the conference room as if looking for a way out. "There has to be a--"

"Six hours of meetings, Jared. I don't see the COO changing his mind."

"Maybe he'll leave a team here."

I tried not to think about the press meetings—all about the move—that I had booked over the next few hours. My shoulder blades tightened. "Jared, buddy, he won't have to leave anybody here because you're figuring out a way past that tiger and coming with us, remember?"

"And what if I just go to the Rising once I'm out?"

"You wouldn't because you've got my back, buddy."

"You know me pretty well, don't you?" A sad smile tugged at Jared's cheeks. He lowered Trellis's papers below the conference table. "But if I can't get out, I'll need your help. I don't want to lose my job, Pablo. I don't want to lose..."

"You won't lose your job, dude." That damn migraine was coming back. "Just find another couple of Returned, get some ghostly weapons, and kill that damn tiger."

Jared cringed and whispered as if the tiger might overhear, "It doesn't work like that. We... we all see something different. It's like the article said: the anamnesis--"

"I believe you; I believe you." I stood and marched toward the door, mentally phrasing an apology for my tardiness to the Gizmodo interviewer. "Look, if you don't move with us, they'll let you go no matter what I say. There's no way the COO will let you keep a team here."

"Not for me maybe, but for his rising star..." He held my gaze.

"No."

"Pablo, please."

"David hates being questioned. I can't."

I couldn't look at him as I reached for the door handle, but Jared leapt forward blocking my exit. Tears sprouted in the corners of his eyes. "Please Pablo, just talk to David. See if there's anything he can do."

I wavered at the door. I was running later and later for the call with Gizmodo, but this was Jared. We'd started here together, and he'd stuck it out for me countless times.

I had to say no. But how could I do it without sounding like a total a-hole?

A gear turned in my mind. An impossible task. I'd tell him to hit some crazy goal for WeightWin, and voila. He'd have to actually deal with the tiger, rather than weaseling out of it by making me talk to the COO. And I wouldn't have to put my damn career on the line because Jared's scared of a big cat. Win-win.

I raised a finger. "I'll talk to David for you on one condition. The first WeightWin campaigns are coming due next week. They need to double domestic scale sales."

He gave me a determined nod, smiled excitedly, marched through the closed door. Jared didn't seem to realize that doubling scale sales with only a few days of iteration time was an absurd prospect.

I stared at the dribble of ectoplasm dripping from the door handle. I sighed and struggled to jimmy the door open without getting goo on my hands.

Jared was already back at his desk, and as I walked past him, he called, "I'll try to get the first drafts to you by tonight, all right?"

My stomach did a nasty little backflip, but I gave him a strained smile as I hustled to my desk. I should have told him to triple sales. I groaned and jumped on the meeting for my Gizmodo interview ten minutes late.

* * *

I turned over in bed. The noise of Netflix bored through my earplugs, and the snarky Gizmodo article played back in my mind on repeat. They had not appreciated my tardiness. I pulled the blankets higher and turned over to find that Maura wasn't even watching the TV.

Wearing her elegant silk nightgown, she lounged beside me, propped up on pillows. One of the straps had slipped off her shoulder, but she hadn't noticed. Motionless, she held her rhinestone encrusted phone. She didn't swipe. She didn't tap. She just stared.

That, more than the fight scene blaring from the TV, woke me up. I inched my way up the backboard, trying to not even ruffle the blankets. Maura didn't twitch.

I kept my eyes partly closed to feign sleep and leaned over to get a view of her screen.

Then, my own phone rang at max volume.

Maura and I both jumped, and she pressed her phone to her chest as she caught her breath. Glaring at me, she snapped, "Who the hell is calling you?"

Making an extra show of yawning, I checked my phone. "Uh... the office."

"Well, you better take that." She patted my shoulder with a vulpine smile. "Louis Vuitton's winter catalog is out."

"And?"

"You'll need a VP's salary."

She perched on the corner of the bed as I hoisted myself upright and answered the call. It was Jared, of course. I repressed a groan. "Hey buddy."

"The designs uh... did you see them?" For the first time since his death, Jared sounded exhausted.

Well, that's his fault for sending designs at two in the morning. I lumbered out of bed and grabbed my laptop.

When I flopped back onto the mattress, Maura still stared at something on her phone. As I opened up my email, I scooted closer to her. Was it an article? No. She wasn't into the news. Another blogger? An outfit she was trying to copy?

Pretending to reach for my laptop's charger, I bent double to get a better look. She was looking at an Instagram post. No surprise there, but it wasn't any model she normally followed. In fact, the people were packed into the corner of the picture, and a McDonald's play park took up the rest of the photo.

Sandwiched between two grinning kids, it took me a second to recognize Trellis. She wasn't wearing makeup, nor was she even facing the camera as she wrestle-hugged her two nephews. As a consequence, she only had a handful of likes on the photo, but she looked so happy in the picture that I doubted that the likes had ever entered her mind.

Maura let out a shuddering breath, snapped the phone off, and laid flat on her side of the bed.

Lightning fast, I turned back to my laptop and opened my email. Maura curled up, knees to chest, and I pretended not to notice. Had my acquaintance with Trellis bothered her? Or was it something else? I'd never seen Maura smile like that in her pictures.

Hell, I'd never smiled like that back home and barely did now either. I shuddered. The slate gray walls of my apartment suddenly felt confining. Maura and I sat hunched on the bed, her around her expensive phone and me around my top-of-the-line laptop. We may as well have been in separate rooms.

I started to set my laptop aside. I turned and reached out to hold her, but the ads loaded.

My mind emptied with horror, and I swung back towards my laptop staring at Jared's creative. The ads were flawless; they could ruin everything. "God... Jared... This is insane."

Two female forms coiled out of bright neon lifted up a third who hovered over the WeightWin Model Two Scale. The device radiated light blues and greens that stretched back out to the horizon line and formed the tagline, "Together we rise, weightless."

It matched the tone and branding from the last ads but added so much more. It showcased the WeightWin Model Two's community feature while managing to make the scale look stunning.

A swell of pride for Jared warmed my cheeks despite my shock. The guy had crawled up from the lowest of the low with me. He'd created something beautiful even under the confines of that Tiger.

Still, I had no doubt this ad could double sales. This ad

might force me to talk to the COO about Jared's predicament. It might ruin everything.

After I packed my laptop, Maura still hadn't moved from where she'd curled up on the bed. Her quick breathing made it obvious she wasn't asleep. As the night went on, recurring images of the COO firing me jolted me back to consciousness.

Neither of us slept well.

* * *

The ads went live, and my nightmare became reality. My fellow Americans bought more scales than three New Year's resolution spikes combined. Flabby middle-aged mamas who all wanted to be weightless unwittingly cornered me.

I tried to dodge talking to the COO. I pestered Jared daily, asking him if he'd stood in the entryway to acclimate himself with the tiger or formed a weapon or anything. He gave half-answers, implying he'd tried but that it was too difficult. Every day he didn't confront that monster outside was one day closer to me confronting David Fillbert.

Still, as hard as I pushed him, Jared gave me space. The accounting and finance teams moved to the new office, and Jared never checked on *my* progress. More than half the desks emptied, and Jared didn't tap on my shoulder to ask me when exactly I was planning on talking to the COO.

He put that much faith in me, and I still almost chickened out.

Then, the plan came to me: I could use the co-working space on the first floor. More than a few folks on my team believed that the commute to the new office would cut too deeply into their heads-down work time. It was only three extra blocks, but this team had productivity maximization to a science.

I could rent a few desks at the co-working space downstairs for Jared and whoever else wanted to shave off minutes from their commute. That way, Jared could stay inside, he could still do work for me, and the office would still have officially moved.

I finally sat down with David during our weekly one-on-one. It used to be Claudia's time slot. His sleek gray suit reminded me of something I saw on Shark Week. I took a slow breath and tried to warm him up by presenting the record sales numbers Jared's newest campaign had produced for WeightWin.

He didn't even look at my graphs. No, David just hammered away on his laptop while I presented to an empty room. As our meeting wrapped up, I fidgeted with the stickers on my laptop.

Taking a breath, I closed my slide deck and pulled up the leasing website for the co-working space downstairs. "The guy whose ads generated those amazing numbers, he and a few of the other high-skill folks on the crew... they really like this office since it's way closer to BART. It really cuts down their commute, so I was wondering--"

David didn't look up. "Mmm hmm, and how many reads did our expansion article in TechCrunch generate?"

"About fifty thousand, but... like I was saying, sir, this marketer, Jared." My voice sounded small in the cramped meeting room, and I smelled my sweat through the CK Eternity cologne I'd slathered on this morning. "He's one of the best, and he kind of needs..."

His eyes flicked up from his laptop. "The Returned? The one who can't leave?"

"How did... Um... That's right, sir." I took a deep breath. "He doesn't want to lose his job if he can't move with us, and he needs to have a few people who know him around. So, I figured letting him work with the guys on the first flo--"

"Our move will be a unified front."

"Yes, you've mentioned that, but there's the co-working space downstairs. We could lease a few desks and he could keep working at his amazing pace. We'd just need a couple to--"

"Did he ever tell you how he managed to come back?" David turned to me like a hawk fixing on its prey.

"No, but I don't see why that's impor--"

"And why he doesn't go to the Rising and his pilgrimage?" An edge of eagerness rose into his voice. I rolled my chair away from him.

I almost told him about the Tiger, Trellis's research, and the guardians as I understood them, but something in his look stopped me. "It just sounded like random chance to me. Poor guy's just really unlucky."

He stared at me. Did he catch my lie? Then, David grunted, sat back in his chair, and resumed typing on his laptop. His dispassionate tone returned as he said, "I want the links to all the press we've been featured in my email by tonight."

"I'll get right on that, but sir... Jared."

"I will not change our company's resolution on a whim." Without looking up from his email, he frowned.

My mouth went dry. "He's one of our top producers."

The COO slammed his laptop closed. "Tell me, Pedro, why do you think we're generating so much PR around a simple office move?"

I almost jumped out of my chair, ignoring the fact that he'd gotten my name wrong after our fourth time meeting together. "I... for recruiting, sir?"

A cold laugh escaped his lips. "And here I thought you actually grasped how this business works."

I started to object, but he held up a hand. I went silent.

"I'll explain just this once. Our WeightWin deal has positioned us for an acquisition, and if things go to plan, a Chinese conglomerate will purchase us in six months. This move's only purpose is to increase our sale value. Nothing more." He cast me a disdainful look. "Maybe if you'd figured out how to replicate what happened to your little friend, we wouldn't have needed to sell."

"Replicate?" My mind spun, trying to guess what he meant, but the idea of the coming acquisition and my failure to predict it drowned out all other thought. "I... what does an acquisition mean for the team. For me?"

"Someone who's VP material would figure that out for themselves." David gave me an appraising look. "Maybe I was wrong about you..."

My skin went cold from my fingertips down to my toes. "I... I mean obviously after any acquisition... they'll make changes..."

"They'll dissolve most of our staff and move advertising production offshore, leaving the new office for senior management only—those VP rank or higher." A cold smile thinned his bloodless lips.

My mouth opened and closed. Reaching VP this review cycle had become much, much more important, and here I was proving to the COO how little I knew about the business world. "But Jared... and the marketing team, surely they'll--"

"They'll move to Beijing or start looking for another job along with the rest of the low-levels at the company." He pushed open the door and whispered over his shoulder, "Figure your shit out before the next review cycle. Understand?"

I stumbled back to my desk in the marketing pod, avoiding my team's curious gazes. I was one of the lucky few who had one-on-ones with David Fillbert himself. Too bad I'd botched it. I'd written press releases for the move. How stupid must I be to not realize that David was grooming the company for an acquisition?

Seeing I'd come from talking with David, Jared sat up at his desk and raised his eyebrows. I brushed past him and sat down.

Shame oozed down my neck like hot tar, and with it came reality. Unless my team all got sudden, meteoric promotions to VP or above, they'd be gone in a few months. Jared would be trapped here, jailed by the neon tiger outside. And after that horrible conversation with David, I might well have lost my chance at VP and be joining them.

I wanted to blame Jared, but I couldn't. I led the most profitable team at DataFirst. If I couldn't protect them from layoffs, then that was no one's fault but my own. I should have been able to do something. I should have been able to stop this... I was just too weak.

Home. This felt like being home. I could only watch and shut my mouth, powerless to do anything, powerless to help. I could still picture my old man towering over me, shouting so loud it drowned out my own tiny voice. He called me stupid, weak, useless.

How right he was.

No matter how far I got from Shitholesville, Texas, my home followed me, black roots stretching across America from a rotten seed. I'd moved to San Francisco, gotten a beautiful girl, worked my ass off, risen, done really well, but some days the same weight fell on my back and the same knife twisted in my gut.

I grimaced and started hammering away at my email. What else could I do?

The poor idiot Jared stared at me from his desk, probably wondering how my meeting with David went. He gave me such a zealous thumbs up that he knocked over the little cat carving on his desk.

I let out a tired laugh and started to turn my chair to give him the news. Jared would listen, hell, he'd probably say something nice. In his weird way, he knew.

Then, I froze. I was a manager now. I couldn't go whining to my subordinates. What the hell had I been thinking? I was weak. God, this was just more evidence.

I spun back to my email. The layoffs were confidential, if I'd been stupid enough to say something to Jared, my chance at VP would definitely be forfeited. I'd get taken out with the rest of the trash, all because I was too soft on ol' Jared.

A hazy movement flicked past the corner of my eye and pulled me away from my work. Jared stood beside me and held a sandwich in his translucent hands. Ectoplasm dripped off the wrappings. Ew. His voice was faint as he said, "I wrapped up work and grabbed lunch for you."

Guilt, anger, and embarrassment roiled in my stomach. I didn't look up from my computer, so Jared shuffled from foot to foot. "You look like you have a lot going on right now, but we're never too busy for our lunchtime chow-downs, right?"

He meant I looked pissed and stressed, but it was just like Jared to go around pretending that everything was fine. He sounded like all the other suck-ups in this place, trying to get an angle on me, trying to make me talk.

I fought to keep anger out of my voice. "Can't today."

"Oh okay, sure, yeah..." He set the sandwich on my desk, and his damned ectoplasm dripped on my interview questions from the Washington Post.

I shoved the sandwich off the documents. It splattered on the floor, breaking the butcher paper wrapping and spilling lettuce across the carpet. I glared at Jared as he scurried back to his desk like a spooked mouse.

That night, I worked late from home, hoping to make up for my fumble in front of the COO. I'd set up my laptop on our kitchen table beside Nibbles's current home. Jared's hamster seemed happy to be free of the guest room, and he stayed quiet as I worked. I made good progress scheduling press and interviews for the next week until Maura leaned over the couch and snapped, "Uh, why did I just get a cancellation email from the Four Seasons Oahu?"

"Postponed our trip... work stuff."

She jolted off the couch, upsetting the bowl of buttery-smelling popcorn she'd microwaved for herself. "Tell me you're joking."

A headache began hammering at the back of my skull, and I massaged my temples. "I'm just being careful. Hawaii will still be there."

"No, it won't." She stomped toward me while mashing the spilled popcorn into the rug. Seeing a heap of delicious food, Nibbles squealed and kicked up his stinking sawdust. I groaned; I'd be the one vacuuming all this up later. "I already posted a countdown on my Instagram. I'm expected in Hawaii."

"Babe, stuff went down at work today. Stuff that might slow down my track to VP and well, other things." The headache spread down my neck and to the bridge of my nose. "I'm going to need to put a lot more hours in at the office for optics alone."

"I see." She folded her arms. "And your sudden desire to work more has nothing to do with that Trellis girl skulking around with her cute little nephews."

"She doesn't even work at DataFirst and I've never even met her nephews. Maura, what the hell is up with you right n--"

"I just... It's just... I can't let down my followers." She shifted from foot to foot, and for a breath, a shadow of pain tightened the lines between her flawlessly plucked eyebrows.

Maura paced like a caged peacock. Her breath came in desperate gasps, and she squeezed her phone so tightly her knuckles went white.

It was probably the exhaustion or the day I'd had, but for a moment, I wondered, if I extended my hand, would it hit a glass barrier like the ones between animals at the circus? I knew I should stand up, embrace Maura, and let her head rest on my shoulder, but as the squeals of the popcorn crazed hamster crescendoed, I despaired of ever breaking through the glass and holding my fellow inmate.

Half-dazed, I watched her march back and forth across our apartment for a minute before finally mumbling, "Babe, could you just Photoshop some pictures like you're in Hawaii?"

"You would think that, wouldn't you?" She spun on me. "You'd want me to lie like a marketer."

My face got hot at that remark, and my impulse to hug her dissolved. I woke up enough to sit forward. "Well, you sure don't have a problem using Photoshop to tighten your waistline."

"Everybody does that, but lying about a trip?" She recoiled with disgust. "I will not let you humiliate me in front of my followers."

"Maura, I don't know if I'll have the cash. I might not even be getting promoted anymore." A lead blanket of exhaustion pressed down on my back and almost smothered the headache pressing against the back of my eyes. Almost. "If your fans care so much, maybe they'll pay for the hotel."

"That's not how it works. I've got to at least reach fifty thousand followers on Instagram and Twitter before I start monetizing."

Nibbles's desperate squeals grew shrill. A mix between a wince and sarcastic smile yanked my lips taut. "Well, you've been stuck at two-thousand for the last six months. Maybe that could pay for what... one night? An afternoon? Oh wait, it can't? You know Starbucks is taking applications."

Even beneath the layers of makeup, her cheeks turned pink. Guilt crashed into me, but after all that had happened today, I was too tired to care. She stomped up to me and boomed, "How dare you. I order lattes from Starbucks, I sure as hell don't make them."

I stood to face her. My head felt dizzy, hot. Jared's stupid rat kept screaming in my ear, and the heat pressurizing my skull finally burst. Warm rage bloomed, spreading down my arms. I clenched my fists. "You know, you're right. With your vast experience sitting on couches and making microwave meals, you're a shoo-in for the next Apple CEO."

I thought she might cry, but a moment later, Maura roared with so much hatred it could hardly be classified as human. She threw knickknacks from the coffee table at me. She moved to knock over Nibbles's cage, but I shooed her back. She then resorted to throwing her jewelry. I didn't care. I'd bought all those pretty things for her after all. Her full lips curled, exposing her canines as she hurled insults at me and swore that "I would pay."

I flopped onto the couch as she, still raging, packed her things into a suitcase—also purchased by me. She was wrong about one thing: I'd already paid.

Work progressed as usual the next day. It wasn't until I got home to an empty apartment that the reality started to set in. I'd lost Maura. Sure, we'd never really been that close, but the constant roar of Netflix had insulated me against the eerie quiet that now saturated my oversized living room.

The sudden urge to hear a human voice gripped me. It wasn't that I was sad about Maura, I just needed to hear another voice, any voice. I opened up my phone's contact list and scrolled down. I flipped past my mom's cell, didn't even glance at dad's contact card, passed some old friends' numbers who I hadn't talked to in years, and avoided the jerks from work. Before I knew it, I'd reached the end. My stomach lurched. Did I not have anyone to call?

I almost called Jared's desk at the office. He'd listen to me ramble. He'd care. A wave of shame washed over me. I was one of the elites in my career, well known, on my way to becoming the youngest VP of a top marketing firm. No matter what my old man said, I could handle the hiccups in my personal life without having to go around whining like an infant.

I chucked my phone to the far side of the bed, rolled onto my back, and started counting the minutes until I could fall asleep.

The next day, the inevitable began. The marketing team started transitioning to the new office. HR contacted me and asked for a list of team members joining us at the new location, and when they realized Jared's name wasn't on it, they sent me a pack of departure documents.

I leafed through "Spectral Employee Dismissal Procedures" and "Exorcising a Disgruntled Team Member" until I found the Undead Termination Papers and the Afterlife Non-Disclosure Agreement. Once I handed these to Jared, it would all be over.

I massaged my temples, wondering whether the COO would give me the same set of documents when the general layoffs rolled around. It wasn't two minutes later when I got the email: my chance at redemption.

Hardly breathing, I read the project specifications written by David himself. If I pulled this off, this could get me VP in time. All my hard work at DataFirst might still pay off. An idea occurred to me, and I tucked Jared's departure papers into the top drawer of my desk.

The COO wanted to throw a Christmas Eve party like nothing before to celebrate the move. He envisioned something so amazing that it would dazzle Chinese investors worth millions. He implied that any chance I had at becoming VP and surviving the acquisition depended on this party being a success.

I delivered him a proposal that night. I pulled out all the stops. We'd have acrobats, local chefs with local ingredients, wines straight from Sonoma, and a drone light show. Now, I needed to plan it, hire all those people, and project manage the roll out. Yikes.

With the rest of the team packing their desks, maintaining client relationships through the move, and unloading boxes at the new office, I used my ace in the hole: Jared.

The next morning, I handed over all of the party planning to Jared. He slaved for weeks, calling vendors, verifying orders, managing time schedules and executive presentations and whining employees and alcohol deliveries.

He came through exceptionally.

To further reinforce the idea of the party celebrating a new beginning for DataFirst, David had ensured that Christmas Eve would be the last day on the old office's lease. The movers had hauled away the last of the boxes this morning, and all the party preparations were done.

I had one last thing to do before an evening of schmoozing with the COO, bowing deeply to Chinese investors, and exchanging business cards with both hands. Nausea roiled my stomach as I tugged Jared's departure papers out of my backpack and marched upstairs to the office.

Jared worked alone on our empty floor. His desk, chair, and computer sat adrift in a sea of freshly vacuumed carpet. Heaters off, the vacant office felt colder than the Alaskan tundra except the air smelled like Pine-Sol rather than pine trees.

As the marketing team moved out, Jared's form grew less distinct, but he'd stabilized a hair above translucent. His silvery back hunched over his keyboard. He was completing a last edit on the slides the COO would present at the relocation party tonight. I waited for Jared to save and upload his comments before stepping forward.

The slap of the papers on his desk tugged Jared's gaze away from his work. Fingers trembling, he read the forms, nodding in resignation. He met my eyes, his face pained, miserable, and I could see his eye sockets beneath the faded outline of his skin. My throat felt tight as I said, "I'm... I'm sorry buddy."

His voice was so faint I had to lean forward to hear him murmur, "Had to happen eventually."

I forced a smile.

"It's okay, Pablo. One of us might actually make VP," he said, smiling up at me. I looked for some sarcasm in his bland face, but the little guy honestly seemed happy for me.

"Thanks to you."

His grin widened. "Remember when we'd both just moved to the city? We were in such crappy apartments, but we'd made it here, you know? Now... your place... that gorgeous apartment... It's so nice to know you're living the dream."

"I guess." His content grin only faded when he turned back to his desk and saw the departure forms. As he took the pen and started signing them, I cleared my throat. "You know... my life isn't all that perfect..."

The tiny bones of Jared's fingertips slid the NDA forms aside so he could sign the termination agreement on the bottom. He blinked at me. "Come on, you're doing great. You're on your way to VP, and Maura makes you happy--"

"She broke up with me." I was almost as surprised as Jared when I blurted it out. I'd resolved not to talk to anyone about it.

"What happened?" He reached out a comforting hand but stopped himself before touching my skin. Then, with precise movements, he set aside the forms, turned to me, and waited, listening.

I didn't talk for a moment, and silence expanded between

us. It wasn't the same silence of my empty apartment; it was inviting, welcoming. It made the arctic office feel warm.

"I was angry about... well, I was angry and said some stupid things and..." My neck got hot as I mumbled, "And, she's going to be at the party tonight."

"She can't. She needs to be a plus one of someone in the company."

"She's going with Ted, even though the idiot is married. I complained about him so much, she probably thinks she's getting even with me." I shook my head and let out an empty laugh. "The weird part is, I should be angry or sad, but I just feel like... numb... tired... I don't know."

I blushed at my display of weakness. What if Jared was just playing me to get some dirt he could use to... No. That was stupid. Real attention and care shone from Jared's eyes as he nodded and kept his hands folded in his lap.

"I don't even miss her; the only thing I hate is coming home to an empty apartment every night." I let out a rueful laugh, trying not to think of how much time I'd spent talking to Nibbles the hamster in the evenings. "I'm sorry man. And here I am complaining when it's you that's... you know..."

"It's all right." He gave me a comforting smile, but resignation hung behind his eyes. "It's good to be sorry, while you still have time."

"Well, I don't have *that* much time. The party starts at seven, but the COO wanted to catch-up before, so..." I cleared my throat and motioned toward the documents.

"Oh... yes, yes." Jared cast a nervous glance toward the entrance before hurriedly signing the last form and handing me the stack.

I racked my brains for how to say goodbye, but I just wound up mumbling. "Um... a bunch of the guys in the co-working space still remember you, so you should be okay renting a desk there. Listen, I know how easy it is to just stay busy, Jared, but eventually you'll have to go out there." Jared didn't look up from his desk; he didn't even meet my eyes. I sighed and stuffed his forms in my pocket. "I gotta run, but maybe we'll catch up soon. You take care, all right?"

I marched towards the stairway to the entry hall, mentally reviewing the festivities I had scheduled with the COO. First, I'd show him to the refreshment center, then the disco hall, then I'd show him the ticketing that Ted's team managed. Ugh, Ted. I cringed as I started down the stairs and thanked my past self for stocking the party with enough whiskey to sink a freight liner.

A chill rippled up my neck; I spun. Jared loomed behind me, following. "Walking me out, eh?"

Jared just gave me a sad smile.

* * *

Store-bought wreaths and Christmas trees fresh from their boxes littered the marble entryway. Potpourri on the empty receptionist's desk clotted the air with an artificial holiday cinnamon aroma.

"Going to miss you bud." I strode towards the door. Cold afternoon light streamed through the front windows and washed out Jared's outline. The fading sunlight drowned out the faint skin and bone hiding the source of that glow in the center of Jared's chest, and I finally got a good look at it. Pulsing with red luminescence, a rough-cut ruby hung in the center of his rib cage.

Jared's thoughtful expression finally gave way to a resolute frown. He extended his hand toward me. "I understand... I think... what it's like for you."

I jumped and gave him a strained smile. Was I staring at that weird jewel too long? "What's that?"

His hand stretched closer to me. "I'm sorry. I didn't see before... that we're both trapped where no one hears, but your cage was so different, I didn't notice until..."

Embarrassment warmed my ears. Was I really getting this from the guy who'd spent his life like his death: bent over his computer? Was Jared of all people making fun of me?

He wasn't laughing. Grief tightened the lines around his eyes. Maybe that was worse. I hated that weird little Jared apparently felt sorry for *me*.

Annoyance strained my voice, "Late for the COO. Gotta run. Sorry, bud."

He started to reply, but his head snapped to the window, tracking unseen movement. I followed his gaze. Market Street looked like Market Street: trolleys, cars, businesspeople marching past the homeless. Was that tiger still stalking him? I guess the poor guy had never figured a way past the damn thing.

"You okay?"

He stayed silent.

"Keep in touch, all right?" I closed my eyes, preparing for an evening of brown-nosing, awkward conversations, and seeing Maura. At least the noise of the party would be nice, but the prospect of my empty apartment waiting to enfold me in silence sent a shudder down my back. It would be fine. I would be fine. I set my jaw and reached for the door.

Jared seized my hand. I couldn't even feel the warm bones beneath his flesh.

Not bone, not flesh, not touch, but the light insistence of Jared's fading will, a thought made manifest drew my hand away from the exit and toward the pulsing ruby of rugged stone in his chest. My heart pounded, but I didn't resist as my fingers passed through his spectral polo shirt, his skin, his ribcage, until they finally closed around that smoldering gem.

It burned hotter than a sauna stone. I gasped, and my arm spasmed.

Fire.

Scorching heat crawled up my arm, my shoulders, my neck, like an ember eating through a napkin. The fire inched toward my eyes, and I bit my tongue, tasting copper. I stared at Jared, horrified, but he only distantly gazed through the big window.

Then, the searing heat circled my eyes. I screamed.

As the fire crept down my optic nerve and into my skull, the city faded, giving way to the neon world I'd glimpsed months ago.

Buildings faded to gray outlines, and the people marching along the sidewalks vanished, leaving only shadows behind to mark their passage. Freshly cut grass replaced the road's asphalt, and the aroma of new leather, summer nights, and fresh vegetation filled the air.

Neon forms twisted to life along the sidewalks. An orange python rippled down the shadow of Market Street. A ballet dancer carved from yellow and turquoise light rose in a pirouette and spun and spun. A few doors down, a circle of green neon kids played jacks while another child that looked like Jared watched from a few feet back.

"See, buddy? I understand too," he muttered softly, his eyes downcast. "I never knew what to say. How to make them hear me."

"These... are these your..."

"Memories..." He turned his head to stare at the glowing expanse in front of us. "And dreams..."

A road forged from molten gold yanked my gaze down Third Street and toward the Financial District, toward the Rising, and the Pilgrimage beyond. That shining path twisted upward from Union Square through the city's glowing skyline and into a spinning sea of starlight far above.

Standing like sentinels among the skyline, a pack of neon giants loomed over the city. The form of a man twice as tall as the Transamerica Pyramid scowled down on Jared and me with so much silent disapproval, I wanted to sprint out and apologize. He had Jared's chin, or maybe it was the other way around.

This brilliant city of memory, all this light, all these people staggered me. After all these years, after how much Jared had listened to me, I'd hardly heard a word of his story.

Another giant stood beside the frowning man: Trellis. Thousands of delicate neon threads twined together to form the shape of her. Clothed in brilliance, she beckoned Jared forward. Maura had never smiled with such gentleness. That's when it sunk in: the Rising and the Pilgrimage weren't just some solemn march of the dead. They were a final sweet breath of life.

Jared's shoulder shrunk. "Dreams that never were."

A moment later, fear crept into the neon in Trellis's eyes, and she waved Jared forward more urgently. Tingling fear rippled up my back. Distantly, I heard my own voice shouting, "Go quickly. Go now! Go!"

Jared leaned forward, straining toward the door, confronting the stern father and falling into Trellis's embrace. He crouched, finally about to sprint for freedom.

A lurid red glow blurred past the exit. Too late. Jared yelped and reeled backward. Even the giants looming over the city recoiled.

The tiger lunged right up to the entryway's glass windows. Its neon flanks rose higher than a souped-up Escalade, and its shoulder blades shifted with the surety of raw power.

Its mouth opened, exposing endless ranks of white neon

teeth. Then, the roar poured out from the monster's sharp innards.

The sound rocked me to my heels, and every shameful memory of my cowardice, my petty selfishness, my weakness, and my loneliness snapped into sharp relief in my mind. A moment later, I crouched in the dingy halls of my middle school, crying because I couldn't find the words to talk to Susan, the ballet dancer. Then, I was in my college dorm, whittling to distract myself, trying not to picture the game night I'd missed because... well what did you say to people?

I shook my head, wait... I'd never carved anything in my life.

The roar's echo resonated in my skull, a headache's needles. Then, I was ten. I looked down, and in my hands was the first thing I was ever proud of: a tiger I'd carved. I'd seen something like it at a corner-store in Cloudcroft, and with my very own Swiss Army knife and a piece of pine I'd found on my hike with mom, I'd whittled one myself.

The soccer game on TV blared in the background. My dad crouched over his hardware store's checkbook balancing the month's numbers, working in silence. I stood behind him, holding the pine tiger I'd carved, waiting as he switched between his adding machine and balance sheet. The sun sank low in the sky, lengthening the orange squares of light crawling across our living room's ugly carpet. I brainstormed ten different ways to ask what he thought, but never said one of them. Minutes passed. Then an hour. I still waited, unable to tap his shoulder and bear his quiet annoyance, unwilling to confirm that he was too busy to listen, too busy to care.

I shook my head, and the hulking neon tiger snapped back into focus. Those weren't my memories. My dad worked for the town's cotton gin, not some hardware store, and he never stopped shouting long enough to balance his checkbook. But if

Jared had just zapped me a picture of his childhood, then why the hell did the gut-twisting hollowness of home feel so damn familiar?

Tears, faint but visible shimmered at the corners of Jared's eyes. He'd never told me about his carving, probably guessing that with an apartment, a promotion, Maura, and happy hours on my mind, I wouldn't have listened. He'd have been right.

I began to understand the risk he'd just taken. What would have been his agony if, after seeing all, I still hadn't cared? My indifference could have been the final cruelty. He'd taken a horrible gamble to show me his silent pain. No—our pain.

A sob shook Jared's shoulders. He extended an arm toward Trellis's glowing form, but his hand drooped, exhausted. The tiger that he'd never found the courage to face prowled in front of us, blocking Jared from the golden path that would lift him high enough to finally embrace the gorgeous woman and ask his distant father the simplest question in the world.

Jared turned away from the prowling monster outside, and my fingertips slipped off that burning ruby at his center.

The world shuddered back into a dull evening in San Francisco. The neon streets, the towering giants, the tiger, all of it vanished. The air reeked of fake cinnamon again, and the chattering pedestrians and honking Teslas swelled to their normal volumes.

Jared glanced back at the stairs to the office and murmured, "My work... my campaigns... were they good?"

I coughed out a tight breath. "Best I've ever seen. Half of America is still quoting that 'Lighter than Light' thing."

"They really loved my work, didn't they?"

The greasy city stretched out before us, so many empty offices on Christmas Eve. Everyone else had flown back home to Texas or Nevada, back to their families, everyone except Jared and me.

Jared reached into his pocket and pulled out the little carved cat that always sat on his desk. He weighed it in his translucent hands for a moment before handing it to me. "Merry Christmas."

"You don't have..." I was about to pass the cat back when I realized what it was. It wasn't a cat. It was a tiger, worn down by time and constant handling. "I... Jared, I can't accept this."

He met my eyes. "Merry Christmas, buddy."

I bowed my head and told my friend the most honest thing I'd said in months, "I'm really going to miss you."

He flinched at some unseen movement from outside. I couldn't do anything about his tiger now, and I was running horribly late for my meeting with the COO.

Still, I laid a comforting arm on Jared's shoulder while he stared wide-eyed out the window. Ectoplasm be damned.

We stood like that for a while.

The sun dipped beneath the skyline, and brake lights turned the foggy streets deep red. I stayed as long as I could for my friend, knowing that time would run out eventually. I'd have to beg for forgiveness from the COO, bear the indignity of seeing Maura, and go home to my cold apartment. Then, I'd have to do it all over again year after year.

Still, for a few more minutes, I refused to let Jared face that tiger alone.

Some while later, I let my arm fall. The launch party had started half an hour ago. I hoped one of my crew had clued in the COO during my absence. I sighed. They'd be eager for the chance to demonstrate to David that they could do my job if I wasn't around. I swallowed a twisting sense of dread as I stepped toward the door.

"Let's get lunch next Friday," I called to Jared over my shoulder. "Keep the tradition going."

He gave me a sad smile. "Yeah, sure."

His form seemed fainter now, only a hint of his outline remained. Even that red light at his center dimmed to a smoldering glow.

I ducked out into the movement and bustle of downtown San Francisco. Cool air rushed into my lungs and the tension squeezing my shoulder blades loosened.

I jogged across Market. An Uber honked at me as it sped past, forcing me to dive for the far side of the road. Jerk.

Making good time toward the new office, I turned down Third Street. As the office shrunk behind me, my relief at being outdoors crumbled. A horrible sense that I'd forgotten something shortened my breath. I slapped my pockets: wallet, phone, keys, Jared's carving. Everything there.

I looked back.

The office's lights had shut off after I left, turning the building into shadow against the skyline. I reminded myself that Jared would be fine. Trellis's own notes had said that he wouldn't fade as long as someone who knew him was around.

Honestly, I should be more worried about myself. Images of the party and the steamy press of young professionals waiting for me there came to mind. My teammates would lean sticky arms on my shoulders and bullshit about how great of a manager I was. I wondered how many of them would still suck up or pretend to listen to my replies if they realized all their jobs would be shipped to China in a few months.

Icy fog slipped down my back. I pulled my button down tighter around my shoulders. Bars of dark skyscrapers surrounded me, the skyline nothing but claws slashing at the black fog.

With the upcoming acquisition, the party I'd planned was another stupid game of make-believe, marionettes glad-handing and promising non-existent promotions to keep our team working until the very end. I'd created a diversion, nothing more.

There, standing in the blend of traffic, businesspeople, homeless, and tech workers, I realized I was completely alone. No one cared. No one knew… No one except Jared, the only substantial thing among all the noise and lights and buzzing streets.

My mouth went dry. Jared. No one really knew Jared either. None of his acquaintances in the co-working space really understood him, his past, his family, his struggle to find words, his quiet isolation. I'd been the only one to talk to him, the only one to hear his story.

Realization struck me like a thunderbolt. It was me. I was the last person tying Jared to his fading, vibrant echo of life. Hell, after Trellis left, I'd probably been his only real tie.

I spun around so fast a few girls dressed up for clubbing squawked and hurried to the other side of the sidewalk. I dashed back down Third street toward Market. I shoved past pedestrians and tasted sweat as I rounded the corner to the office. The huge front windows swung into view, and I saw him.

Resignation and fear tightened the lines on his face. In the dim light, his outline was hardly visible. Jared, my personal workhorse, the one person who'd cared to listen to me even as I'd ignored him, Jared waited at the door even as his form shimmered and dissolved.

I screamed in frustration and juked between cars to cross the street. Back on the sidewalk, I cleared the remaining fifty yards to the office in ten seconds flat.

Skidding to a panting stop in front of its glass doors, I arrived in time to see my only friend's hazy form fade, and in a flash of red light, vanish.

COLD SPRING, MINNESOTA

BY RACHEL COYNE

"No matter how bad things get, you've got to go on living, even if it kills you."

— SHOLEM ALEICHEM

CHAPTER ONE

COLD SPRING, MINNESOTA, 2005

Deana recognized the veteran services officer from when she had retrieved her younger brother's body at the airport last month. Dwayne had left his card a few days later, tucked into the frame of the front screen door. The man was missing an arm, the cloth of his short-sleeved shirt pinned shut with safety pins. He was a thin man with thinning hair and slightly watery blue eyes. She guessed from his age Vietnam. Her brother had died in Afghanistan.

"There's nothing to be done? Kayla gets everything?" her mother said, staring at Dwayne from across the desk as if she were memorizing him. It reminded Deana of one of those memory puzzles she'd played with her father. As if the image of the nervous veteran services officer and his small office would disappear and she'd be asked to identify ten differences in the new image. The paperweight would move. The certificate would be on the left side of the wall not the right. The flag would be upside down.

No not that.

Deana remembered that an upside-down flag meant distress.

Tears poured down her mother Brandy's face.

Dwayne looked at his papers. "Before your son deployed, he filled out his will and insurance beneficiary paperwork," he explained. "It's all pretty clear."

"But I'm his mother," Brandy insisted. "He was nineteen when he died." Her voice quavered. Deana knew her mother's suddenly wandering hand was looking for her cigarettes. She gently took the purse away from her mom.

"And she's his wife," he said. "It's on all the paperwork."

"Kayla is seventeen! They shouldn't even have gotten married! It was stupid—he was shipping out, and she was still in high school! Her parents had to sign the marriage license! And now you're telling me she gets every goddamn cent!"

Deana saw it, the look of disgust, though the man tried to hide it. "I'm certain she's eighteen now," he said. "And it doesn't matter legally. They are married."

"My mother is a widow," Deana explained. "She cleans house for the Albright family. My father died three years ago. He worked at the chicken plant."

"Married," Brandy spat. She grabbed her purse back from Deana and started rummaging for her cigarettes. "She bought herself a pickup! A seventeen-year-old girl with all that money! Already everyone says they see her out in the bars. Don't goddamn tell me there's nothing we can do!"

Dwayne stood and gathered his papers. "I'm sorry for your loss," he said, though there wasn't any pity in his voice. Deana had begged her mom to remain calm for this very reason. Dwayne abruptly left the room.

Deana didn't bother to tell her mother smoking wasn't allowed. She watched her mother take a long vicious draw off the cigarette. Deana looked down at her stomach and silently apologized to the small, hidden baby growing there.

* * *

When Deana got home, her younger sister Casey stood in the driveway. They lived off the busy county road. Casey had her arms crossed, watched down the highway, swayed from one foot to another as she waited. *Reedy,* Deana thought with a wave of tenderness for her seventeen-year-old sister, *she's reedy like the cattails on the water.* The thought brought to mind fishing with her father, the smell of the lake.

"Waiting for Boo?" Deana asked.

Casey nodded, then looked around Deana into the car. The passenger seat was empty.

"Mom wanted to go to the Albrights," she explained. "She only had a half-day off, I guess."

Casey rolled her eyes. She still wore her work uniform from the drive-in, minus the shoes. Grasshoppers in the driveway leapt around her bare feet.

The rattling of a truck made them both turn. Cleary, his mom Arletta, and the baby he shared with Casey rolled into the dirt driveway. The bumper sticker on the truck read *White Earth Nation Pride.* The truck had a magical rattle that always put the baby to sleep. When the first tooth had come in last month, they'd called Cleary's mom, and at midnight, she drove over to go cruising with them all—Casey, Deana, Cleary all hovered anxiously over the fussy little one.

"We should go to the doctor," Cleary had said.

"Just a tooth," Arletta had told them calmly.

"Pure magic," Casey said, leaning into the window to look at the sleeping baby. "Please never get rid of this truck, Mrs.

Reynolds." Cleary climbed out and stood beside her. Casey didn't look at him.

"Did he eat good?" Casey asked.

"Like a little piggy." Arletta laughed. She opened the door and gently drew out the baby. She smiled as she passed the tiny one over to Casey.

"Thanks for watching him," Casey said to Arletta.

"Not me," said Arletta. "The father is learning to change diapers just fine."

"How was your shift?" Cleary asked. Casey grunted a little and scowled angrily, and Cleary got out the baby bag and shouldered it. "Do you want me to get Boo in the crib? We could hang out for a while."

Arletta pursed her lips. Cleary had been grounded ever since she had found out about the baby. Only school and football practice. Only tutors over. Baby. School. Practice. Work. Baby. Sometimes, Deana even felt sorry for the kid.

"I can handle it," Casey said, tugging at the bag. "Thanks again, Mrs. Reynolds," she called over her shoulder.

Without a backward look at Cleary, Casey went into the house.

Arletta winked at Deana as Cleary, suddenly looking sullen, climbed into the car.

"How is your mother?" Arletta asked her.

"It's rough," Deana said. "She's not getting over things." Arletta patted her shoulder and climbed back into the truck. "Love that little baby," she said. "Kiss him goodnight for me."

Deana watched them pull away and once again felt her own stomach. She went into the house. The basement door was open; Casey was downstairs already rummaging through the freezer for dinner.

She came up holding a package of fish wrapped tight in

white paper. Their father had marked every fish he caught. Deana took it from Casey, who juggled the baby and dinner.

"What's wrong?" Deana asked. "What happened at the drive-in?"

Casey shrugged. "Saw Mr. Callister. Wouldn't say a word to me. Looked right through me."

Casey's teacher and chess coach had been like a father to her after their own dad died. At least until she got pregnant junior year. The fight had been bitter. Casey still wouldn't repeat what he'd said. Deana winced. "Sorry," she said. "People are assholes."

Casey blinked and Deana had the idea she might cry. "Yeah, what are you going to do?" Casey carefully looked her sister over. "What's wrong with you?"

"I reached up to grab a package of toilet paper for Vera Johnson at the grocery store today and she saw my stomach," Deana replied.

"You sure she noticed? You're not just paranoid?" Her little sister's face was suddenly pale, frightened.

Deana let out a long slow breath. "Yeah, I think she did."

Casey jiggled the sleepy baby. "What are you going to do?"

Deana looked down at the wrapped fish. *Sauk River*, it read. *Walleye*, written in her father's square handwriting with a date two weeks before he died. "I guess I'll make some dinner."

Casey followed her into the kitchen, the baby sleeping on her shoulder, his face all squashed up and delicious.

CHAPTER TWO

Manny Albright dropped Brandy off well after dinner. Deana's father-in-law waved to her as he backed down the driveway. He was a handsome man, tanned year-round in equal measure from the tanning bed, the golf course, and weekends on his boat. His teeth flashed like a signal flag—*man in the water*, she thought. *Danger*. Brandy pushed past Deana into the house. Evening was falling, a late spring evening that brought the chill with it.

"Courtney's dress has real crystals in the shoulder straps," Brandy breathed as she heated up her leftover dinner in the microwave. "It will be so fun to sit in the stands and see her walk across the stage. Like a princess!"

"The dress is all covered up by the graduation gown," Deana said, glancing at Casey washing the dishes.

"I know, but it comes out for the party," Brandy happily chirped. "That's why I had to stay so late! LaDonna and I went over to the car dealership to make sure the decorations match the car for the big surprise."

A dish crashed in the sink. Deana winced.

Casey pushed past. Minutes later, across the house, her door slammed. The baby cried.

Deana turned off the water at the sink. "Could you let up just once?" she asked.

Brandy set her food down on the table. She shrugged. "All I said was it will be nice to go to the graduation."

"You didn't go to Casey's graduation."

"I mean a *real* graduation," Brandy said, poking at the walleye. "Fish," she sighed under her breath.

"It was a *real* graduation," Deana pressed, gritting her teeth. "The girls there worked hard. They had gowns and caps and their babies right there. They worked harder than any of those kids at the high school. Casey graduated six months early even."

"Well, it was during when I worked," she said, pushing the fish away at last and taking out a cigarette.

"The Albrights would have given you the time off."

"Well, it was embarrassing to ask to go. An unwed mother's graduation."

"You think Courtney Albright is like a virgin queen or something?"

Her mother clicked her cigarette lighter and pursed her lips.

"Why do you always act like those Albright kids shit gold? Just like you always put Lucas on a

pedestal and look where that got me—in the goddamn hospital."

Her mother scowled. "You're still angry about that? It's been months, and it was an accident. They didn't even press charges. And he's redeployed now anyway."

"*I* didn't press charges," Deana clarified. "The cops were willing to."

Her mother looked away. "Well, anyway, Manny is

building you a house. I watched them put the foundation in last week. Right on the edge of the Albright property, by the pond. When Lucas gets home from Afghanistan... well, you can all start over. Have you even been over there to look at the house?"

"No."

"Well, LaDonna thinks you're ungrateful."

Deana stared at her. She remembered Dwayne from this morning, his empty shirt sleeve where his arm should be, his look of disgust. She had felt such shame for her mother. Now she felt his revulsion. She looked down at her hands. They were clenched.

"Next time, thaw out some chicken," her mother added, still not meeting her eye. "I'm sick of fish. It's all I ever ate with your father."

The phone rang, breaking the silence. Neither went to answer it, but moments later, Casey returned to the kitchen. She looked puffy-eyed, wearing her pajamas and holding up a pair of keys. "I forgot to leave the keys for the closer at the drive-in."

Deana nodded and took the keys. "I'll drive us," Brandy said, rising.

Deana and Casey exchanged a glance. "Why?"

"Because I want to get out," she irritably said. "I've been working all day. This goddamn tiny house is too much." She was already at the door and Deana trudged behind her. "Besides, if you go out alone, you'll stay out all night."

"Have fun," Casey murmured, disappearing into her room.

* * *

The drive from one end of town never took them long. Some bars, the grocery, a drug store, and a smattering of shops. The bars were open, and in the cool night air, people stood in the parking lot, smoking. At the drive-in, Deana ran the keys into Hoppy, the night manager. Deana wasn't surprised when Brandy didn't turn back toward the house right away. It also didn't take long for her mother to find what she was looking for: The County Line Bar and a big shiny electric blue pickup truck parked in front. Kayla's new truck. There was an American flag painted across the hood. Deana closed her eyes and shook her head. Though brand new, the truck already had a busted front light and a sizable dent on the door.

"You didn't do that, did you, Mom?" Deana asked, pointing at the dent.

"Don't be ridiculous," she said, taking out a cigarette.

"I'm tired," Deana said. "Let's go home."

"No."

"Do you want to talk about the meeting with veteran services?"

"Fuckers."

"They said it doesn't matter what Kayla does with the money. It's her money now."

"It's Jim Jr.'s. And I'm his mother."

There was no point in arguing with her. They had argued all month. Deana settled back into the car seat, closing her eyes. The music from the bar thumped, and a fight spilled out the front door. Deana cracked open an eye. No sign of Kayla, the merry widow. That was a relief.

"Are you going inside?" Deana asked.

"No," said her mom, lighting a cigarette. Deana hastily cracked open the car window. "We wait. I want to see who she's with."

"Why?" Deana demanded.

Cigarette smoke curled into the dark of the car. No answer.

* * *

Deana stiffly woke and realized she was still in the car. This wasn't the first time this had happened. She groaned. They were now outside a motel on the far edge of town. It was a low, cinder block building with each of the doors painted pink. Deana looked around and found her mother sleeping in the back seat. She looked at the clock on the dash. She had to be at work in half an hour. She slid across to the driver's seat and started the car.

Kayla's truck was nowhere to be seen at the hotel. Deana cruised homeward and then around her own neighborhood. A few blocks over, the truck was parked at Kayla's parent's house. Kayla should have been graduating with Courtney and Casey this year. They had all been in Brownies together.

Deana turned toward home and left her mom sleeping in the car in the driveway. She quietly opened the front door, then went and peeked silently in at the baby and Casey. The baby lay on Casey's chest. Casey looked at her with bleary eyes. "Rough night?" Deana whispered.

"More teeth coming in."

Deana nodded and went to take a shower. At least she had gotten more sleep than the new mom.

Casey entered the bathroom where Deana was brushing her teeth. She had a towel around her body and another wrapped in her wet hair. Casey's eyes moved over the scars on Deana's collarbone and chest. Self-consciously, Deana shrugged on her T-shirt.

"What are we going to do about Kayla?" she asked.

Deana shrugged. "Can't change nothing. That's what they said. It's Kayla's money. Kayla's ashes. Kayla's everything. She decided not to have a funeral."

"And Mom?"

Deana shrugged.

"I think she's like fixed on this because she doesn't want to face grieving for Jim Jr. You know, so she can repress her feelings," Casey said.

"Dr. Phil?"

"Oprah," Casey corrected.

Deana shrugged. "I miss my brother. I know you miss him. I'd do anything to have him back, but..." she shook her head, "you know I always felt like any one of us could drop off the face of the earth and as long as Courtney and Lucas Albright were fine, she wouldn't even notice."

"Ouch," Casey said.

Deana felt guilty. "I'm sorry," she said. "But I don't know how to help Mom grieve for a kid she didn't give a shit about. Hell, I blame her. He only joined the army to be more like Lucas. I know he did."

"Is that why you married Lucas?"

"Ouch."

Casey looked contrite. "Yeah, I should go check on Boo."

Casey left, and Deana could have kicked herself. She dressed hastily and was glad to find Brandy had already woken up and put herself in her own room. Walking out to her car, she looked over at the trash can on the curb. It was already full to bursting; sometime last night, Casey had gathered up all of her chess trophies. All the ones she'd won under Mr. Callister's coaching. Even the huge national one poked out of the trash. Half the town had fundraised to send her there.

"Oh hell," Deana said, looking back at the house. It seemed to tiredly gaze back at her.

Though it made her late for work, Deana gathered up all the trophies, wrapped them in a blanket, and hid them in the trunk of her car. She would have to figure this one out later.

CHAPTER THREE

Small towns have their ghosts. But no one needs to die to haunt you. Not really. When Deana finally rushed to her place at the supermarket register, the first person in line was Kayla. Kayla pretended not to notice her as she unloaded her cart, but eventually, she made an unconvincing look of surprise and beamed. Then perhaps to get more attention, she squealed. "Sissy! Good to see you!"

Deana reached over and hugged her.

"I haven't seen you in so long," she gushed.

"Yeah, you know, not since we retrieved my brother's body," Deana said.

Kayla nodded. On the conveyor belt below her, a package of condoms flowed past. She went pink. Deana scanned them and put them in the bag without a word. "You should come 'round and see my mom some night," Deana suggested. "She was hoping to pick out a gravestone soon."

Kayla's eyes went flat. "I'm not ready for that."

"But you're ready to fuck other men."

Kayla's eyes narrowed to near slits. "Aren't you supposed to keep people's purchases quiet? Isn't that the law or something?" She looked around. "Maybe I should talk to your manager." Kayla leaned in. "Besides," she said in a loud whisper. "Don't you know? Everyone already knows about your...um little problem." She looked at Deana's stomach.

Deana blinked. Kayla maliciously smiled and took her bag of groceries. "Have a good day," she chirped and was gone.

Deana felt dizzy; she looked at the long line of people standing behind Kayla, and suddenly, their faces seemed to bubble. "Shit," she murmured. Then, for the first time in her life, she fainted.

* * *

Casey placed a cool towel on her forehead "Are you sure you're okay?" she asked.

They sat side by side on the tattered and sagging sofa in the living room. She and Jim Jr. had made forts out of the pillows for Casey when she was little. The night before their brother deployed, they'd even made one for old times.

Deana started to cry. "I'm four months pregnant, and my husband, the local war hero, has been deployed in Afghanistan since Christmas six months ago. How do you think I feel?"

Casey pulled her into her arms. Deana started to shake. "What did the doctor say about you fainting?"

"It's just dehydration," she warbled into Casey's chest.

Casey held her closer. "You remember Tanya Eckard?"

"From dance class?" Deana looked up.

"Yes."

"The one who copied your art project in the fifth grade? And then stole yours and tore it apart?"

"Yes."

"The one who put pig shit in your locker when you told everyone you were pregnant?"

"Yes."

"What about her?"

Casey picked at a loose thread on the brown cushions. "Cleary started dating her."

Deana rose up. "Oh, this shit is on," she said. She picked up Boo from his playpen. "Let's make some dinner and talk this out."

* * *

Casey and Deana dug through the freezer in the basement. With Dad at the plant until 2 a.m. and Brandy at the Albrights, the basement freezer had always been their surrogate parent. It even hummed its own mechanical lullaby. Inside, everything was wrapped in white butcher paper and silvery freezer tape. Chicken from the plant, hamburger from a good sale at the grocery, venison dad had hunted—these were all anonymously wrapped. Picking one meant dinner could be a meat surprise. But the fish, these were all meticulously labeled: Perch -caught by Deana, Horseshoe Lake; Sunnies -caught by Casey Cedar Island Lake; Smelt -Fire Dept Trip, Knife River; Perch - Jim Jr., Lake Knaus.

"Things are looking thin." Casey frowned as Deana rummaged through the packages.

"Hamburger?" Deana asked, holding up a squarish package.

Casey squinted at the shape. "Your guess is as good as mine."

The soft whomp of the freezer closing behind them was a homey sound.

Deana used the chicken they discovered in the package to

make Chicken-Chip Bake. The recipe called for a dash of paprika, but as the family's cook, she had long ago dispensed with that. Casey crumpled up the chip topping in a Ziplock bag using the back of a spoon. Deana smiled. In her mind's eye, a much younger Casey performed the same task.

Brandy only cooked on Sundays. She brought home turkey loaf or meat loaf from the grocery store and added frozen peas and carrots. The rest of the days, she was at the Albrights. She made LaDonna's brood dinner and came home. When Deana first started dating Lucas Albright, she was amazed when the food started to come out to the big dining room table. For the first time in her life, she realized that her mother was a terrific cook.

"Oh," Courtney had moaned, heaping her plate, "these mashed potatoes are my favorite."

"I hope she made cake, too," Lucas added. "Your mom's pineapple smile cake is amazing."

Deana couldn't remember Brandy making a single cake—even on their birthdays, it was something from the store. Deana rummaged around in the cabinet. There was a box that had been there for years, left over from a Girl Scout project. She held it out to Casey. "Should we try and make a cake?" she asked.

"How hard did you hit your head when you fainted?" Casey asked.

"How are we going to trash talk Tanya without cake?"

Casey smiled for the first time that night.

Deana grabbed down the big mixing bowl, and Casey put the casserole in the oven. "So, tell me why you and Cleary broke up," she said.

"Nothing big." Casey frowned.

"Tell me."

She sighed. "Cleary wants to go to college. Together. And I just don't see it. "

Deana was surprised. "You're brilliant. Why wouldn't you go to college?"

Casey made a gesture of impatience. "I'm a seventeen-year-old single mother," she said as if Deana were being stupid on purpose.

"And a chess champion," Deana added. "You can figure this out."

"It's in Morris. In Minnesota."

"You can't stay in this small town forever."

"I need you. I need help."

Deana felt a lump in her throat and looked down at her stomach. "You know sure as hell Lucas is going to kill me when he comes home."

She heard a little strange choking noise and looked up to see Casey was crying.

Deana sighed. "I guess I shouldn't have said that out loud. Sorry." She drew Casey into her arms. Casey started to cry in earnest now, her shoulders shaking. With her one free arm, Deana put away the cake mix.

"I'm so afraid for you." Casey sobbed. "He almost killed you at Christmas."

She hugged her sister closer. "Yes," she said. "He almost did."

"I hate myself so much for how much I used to like him," her sister said. "When did you...when did you find out that he was such a monster?"

Deana broke away and rubbed her stomach. "Almost right from the beginning, I think," she replied. "It just gets harder and harder to get out. Then with the Army tours...it almost starts to feel normal when he's gone. Like it wasn't so bad. But, when he comes home... it's good for a week or two, then some buddy comes over, and they start the drugs and then I get knocked down." She took a shuddering breath. "Usually, it's not as bad as it was at Christmas."

"Christmas was bad," Casey said, and she started crying a little more.

"Yeah, it was," Deana agreed. She put the big mixing bowl away now. "Momma cried for a week, thinking LaDonna might find out and fire her."

Casey looked like Deana had slapped her. "You're making a joke?"

Deana shrugged. "What else am I supposed to do?"

"What about the father?" Casey asked. "Will he help?"

Deana bit her lip. "I haven't even thought about it." Casey still stared at her, so she turned away. "I rescued your chess trophies, by the way. They're in the trunk of the car."

She felt Casey still watching her, but the baby started crying in the next room. "Oh, that's a

hungry cry," Deana said. "Better go." Casey hesitated, but then she went.

Deana looked down at her belly. "You know what," she said. "Let's make a fucking cake." She took the box and the bowl back out. She opened the dusty box of cake mix and poured the bright pink powder out into the bowl. The unnatural sweetness of artificial strawberries hit her nostrils. She felt wrenchingly, pregnantly sick. The cloying smell sent her to the bathroom where she heaved up the green bile-stained contents of her near-empty stomach.

CHAPTER FOUR

Cleary neared the end of his shift at the grocery store when Tanya showed up. He was stacking paper towels, and as Deana came back from her break, she heard him say, "This weekend is my time with the baby."

"You mean with *her*," Tanya said, her voice shrill enough for people in the aisle to turn.

"I mean with my baby," he repeated.

"That's all you care about."

Silence.

"I gotta go," he muttered.

Good boy, Deana thought, then sighed because she had to pee again. She turned back to the meat aisle, and there was Vera Johnson watching her. This time, she was with Joleen Crisp. They both stared at her then slowly leaned in and whispered to one another. Deana felt herself flush. After Christmas, she'd walked about for weeks with a matching pair of black eyes. No one had said a thing, just politely averted their gaze. She fled to the bathroom only to find it was out of toilet paper.

She felt slightly feverish by the time her shift was over.

"You okay?" Cleary asked, walking her to her car.

She leaned into him a bit, and he helped her outside. "Fresh air is good," she said. On the street, a bright blue pickup truck with an American flag on the front hood buzzed past. "Or maybe not," she muttered.

They watched the truck stop at the light, then fire all engines as it rushed ahead.

"I miss Jim Jr.," Cleary said. "God, he was so damn funny. When Casey would sit around and watch replays of old chess matches all weekend, Jimmy would make up fake commentary in this fake Russian voice." He laughed. "God, that would drive her crazy. For years, all he had to say was Grand Master Boris Spassky, and I'd wet myself."

Deana hugged him a little and he smiled.

The moment passed and she frowned at Cleary. He was like a little brother to her. "Why'd you break up with my sister?"

He looked abashed. "We all gotta move forward," he said. "I may not be a chess genius like my girl, but I know that."

"But Tanya?" she pressed.

He looked away. "Has it pissed Casey off?"

"Incredibly."

He reached into his wallet and took out three twenties. "I helped my uncle tear down an old barn out by Little Sauk. He finally paid me for the job." He handed Deana the money. "Make sure Casey and the baby have what they need. I gave her my paycheck on Friday, but it was a day short, because I took off for my SATs."

"You have gas money to get home?" I asked.

He shrugged, heading back inside. "My dad is picking me up."

* * *

The big packages of diapers for Boo dragged a little on the ground when Deana carried them to the house. Casey met her at the door, looking pale. She had Boo in her arms with a tight grip.

"What's wrong?" Deana immediately demanded.

Casey shook her head, too choked up to talk.

"Is something wrong with Mom?" Deana asked, following Casey into the house, then the kitchen. On the counter was a wrapped piece of fish from the freezer. *Jim—Walleye, Mille Lacs Lake*, it read.

Deana stared at her sister in confusion.

"It's the last one," Casey said. "It's the last piece of fish in the whole freezer. I looked everywhere."

"Can't be." Deana gaped. Her stomach sank.

But it was. They moved everything in the freezer from one side to the other, examining everything. Wrapped venison, chicken, hamburger. But no more fish. No more handwriting.

They cooked the fish that night with ceremonial solemnity. Deana heated up the butter flavored Crisco slowly. Casey mashed the cornflakes into crumbs. Deana mixed up the eggs and milk and then they dipped and fried, dipped and fried. The fish emerged golden brown, the way their father had always liked it.

"Jim Jr. liked fish potpie best," Casey said as she and Boo watched Deana cook.

"There isn't enough for that," Deana softly said. "Can you take out some frozen corn for the side?"

When they sat at last, Casey took a tiny piece and mashed it. She fed a little to Boo who slurped and smiled. They ate the rest of it in silence.

When they finished, they could only stare at each other.

Tears ran down Casey's face. Deana wiped her dripping nose on her sleeve. It felt awful.

"Daddy wouldn't want you to stay here," Casey blurted out, breaking the silence. "He'd want you to be safe. To be better."

"Daddy would have wanted you to go to college." Deana said as she reached across the table and took her sister's hand. "We can't let him down. He took care of us our whole lives. Hell, he's been taking care of us, even though he died. We owe him better." Deana was crying, too. "We have to do better, Casey. It's only us. We have to make each other. We'll do better."

Casey took a deep breath and gripped her hand. "I know," she said.

Boo looked between them both and with a serious face loudly farted, startling himself. Deana laughed and took the baby, while Casey washed the dishes.

* * *

Manny dropped Brandy off at nine. Deana waved him down in the driveway, and he hesitated, then put the car in park. "I made you spaghetti," she told Brandy, who nodded and ducked inside. Brandy had a cigarette in one hand and a clutch of Polaroids in the other and was equally engrossed with each.

Deana didn't watch her go, but listened to Brandy's feet crunch on the gravel, the noise of the screen door opening and closing. Manny shifted a little in the car. "I was going to run back to the plant," he said. "Maybe you could come over for dinner on Sunday, honey?" he said. "I know LaDonna misses you. We don't see you nearly enough now that Lucas is deployed."

Manny glanced hopefully at the front door, but Brandy didn't come back. "Has your mom told you all about the progress on the house? Lucas and LaDonna, they talk every day on the phone. Got the foundation in."

When she was a kid, Manny Albright seemed like the coolest dad in the world. He was handsome, never tired and smelly like her dad after a day on the line. He didn't talk endlessly about fish. He owned the Northern Pride chicken processing plant where her father worked. The parking lot was festooned with yellow ribbons each time Lucas came home. Half the t-ball teams in town wore uniforms that said, "Manny's Northern Pride."

"I'm pregnant," Deana told him. "You're the father."

* * *

The concussion Lucas had given Deana at Christmas lingered for months. It made her head feel like her skull was too tight for her brain somehow. Like she wore a very tight hat that she couldn't take off. The worst part was the numbness she felt in her extremities, her hands, and her legs.

She felt like that again now. Deana stumbled back into the house and slowly sat down next to her mother on the couch. Brandy was watching the news, shuffling through her Polaroids. "Courtney changed her mind about the dress," she said. "They said I could keep the pictures we took in the new ones!" Brandy announced this like keeping the pictures was a winning lottery ticket. "I liked her in this blue one best."

Deana didn't look. Her mother didn't notice. The television promised better weather tomorrow. Deana put her tingling hand on her belly and closed her eyes.

CHAPTER FIVE

The next morning, Casey dropped her mother off at the Albrights' front door for work. She'd always thought the Albright place looked like an overgrown storage shed with Greek columns attached. The driveway was a circle of white gravel and the yard a flat treeless expanse. The bushes tried to make the whole thing look presentable, but it was too much ground to cover. She watched Brandy let herself in the house and let her eyes drift over around the driveway. Manny was already at work, of course. LaDonna's baby blue Cadillac remained, and there was Lucas's bright red truck, unused during his deployment. Today, it was attached to a trailer with a float for the graduation parade.

She felt her stomach give a sick flutter. She had forgot that was today. In all the past years, she'd helped one club or another decorate a float for graduating kids. One for the choir, one for the art club, the football team, the chess club. The float sitting in the driveway was red and white with the school's colors and little cardboard cameras all over it for the yearbook club. Courtney and her friends ran the yearbook with an iron fist, making sure there was maximum exposure for their own group and unflattering pictures of anyone who dared to cross them.

Casey was surprised to even feel anything when she thought of graduation. She felt like that was years ago. None of her friends from school had visited since the baby was born. She wondered what the chess club float would look like. She looked back at baby Boo in his car seat and gave him a bottle to hold. His chubby fists grasped it, and she smiled. She pulled out of the driveway and made her way back into town.

When she reached the high school building, Casey parked the car. She'd dropped Deana off at the supermarket before bringing Brandy to the Albrights. With Brandy in the car, there had been no chance to bargain. No chance to wheedle out of the promise she had made her sister just last night. The school parking lot was packed. The beds and back windows of trucks all over the lot were decorated for the parade as well. She looked back at Boo. She gripped the steering wheel and contemplated wading into the full building, the crowded and noisy halls, every other locker decorated with "Congrats Grads!"

"No way," she said. She turned around and went home.

* * *

At five o'clock, Deana helped set up the folding chairs on the sidewalk in front of the drive-in. Brandy, Arletta, her husband Ronnie, some of the Reynolds' uncles, aunts, and cousins waited for the parade. Deana held the baby on her lap. Casey, in her work uniform, stopped by and served everyone burgers and root beer. The youngest cousins had made a sign. It read "U R GR8 Cleary!" in glitter and glue.

The parade started with the police cars and then the fire

trucks. The baby happily wiggled in her lap. The float passed by for the honor club and the homecoming court. Behind them, the yearbook club waved from the float Casey had seen that morning. Manny was driving, and Deana had the impression that, though he saw them, he kept his eyes straight ahead. LaDonna leaned out the window and waved her red painted claws at Brandy. "Get lots of pictures!" she crowed. "It's just like when we were in school, isn't it, Brandy?"

Brandy hustled right up to the float and called Courtney's name, brandishing her camera. Courtney waved, looking mortified, then turned her back and waved at the other side of the street. Manny rolled up the windows on the truck so LaDonna would stop talking. Some of the dizziness Deana had felt the night before returned. Worried, she handed the baby to Arletta. The silver foil on the sides of the float glittered like fast moving water.

She remembered Manny at the hospital. "Look," he said, "we told LaDonna it was an ATV accident down by the creek. You know how she is about the kids, about Lucas—her little prince. This would kill her if she found out. I'll take care of everything. Lucas will re-up in the Army. LaDonna has always said he needs the structure."

Brandy snapped pictures until the float was out of sight. She contentedly settled down and said, "Too bad Manny wouldn't get Courtney the car early. She wanted to pull the float in the parade."

Deana rolled her eyes at Casey, who she realized watched her in concern. The soccer team, then the baseball team ran past, handing out candy. The choir sang, "Sunshine on My Shoulders," to a recorded band as they rolled by.

She remembered Manny driving her home from the hospital. She had to work the next day, and only painkillers kept her upright. No matter how she moved or sat, it felt like a hot metal pole poked her spine. Manny helped her out of the car, and when she couldn't walk, he simply picked her up in his arms and carried her in the house, right back to her childhood bedroom. It was the only place she had left to go. Lucas had destroyed their rental. Before he left, Manny bent down and kissed her forehead.

"If I can help with anything, Deana," he said. "Anything at all, just call me. Call me at my office. You know," he said. "So LaDonna doesn't know."

Deana felt a warm hand on her shoulder, pulling her away from her memories. Deana looked up into Arletta's calm, concerned face. The older woman met her eye. "Breathe, honey," she said. "You look pale. Do you need me to drive you home?"

Before she could answer, the noise of Lee Greenwood's "God Bless the USA" filled the street, and people rose for the flag, startling her. Hitched to the ROTC float, festooned with a great big yellow ribbon on the front hood was Kayla's electric blue truck. She waved from inside, pausing in front of them while all the kids in their uniforms jumped on and off to hand out recruitment flyers. Arletta let the baby hold the paper, but Brandy quickly took it away.

When they pulled away, Brandy took out a cigarette with a shaking hand. Deana reached over to squeeze her mother's hand, but she pushed her away. "What's wrong with you?" she rasped.

Finally, the football float arrived and the crowd cheered. Cleary stood there, pumping his fists with the other players. They did a goofy line dance. The Reynolds' aunts, uncles, and cousins roared with laughter and clapped. The little cousins waved their signs. Arletta handed the baby back to Casey who held him up to see Daddy. Cleary caught sight of them and jumped down. He plucked a pinwheel from off the side of the float and ran it over to his son.

"There's my guy," he said. He gave the baby the pinwheel and kissed his chubby face. He winked at Casey and then ran to catch up with his friends.

Seconds later, Deana felt a glare like a heat ray and turned to find Cleary's girlfriend Tanya walking behind the float, handing out red rosettes. Her hateful gaze lingered on Casey, the baby, and the pinwheel.

"Someone looks as mad as she was in the third grade when you got the angel part in the Christmas pageant," Deana said.

Casey half-grinned. "Remember she tried to steal my wings? And Jim Jr. called her a bitch and got his mouth washed out with soap by his Sunday school teacher."

"Watch your language," Brandy scolded as she stood and began to fold up her lawn chair. It snapped together with an angry click. The football float was always the finale to the parade. "Let's go home," she said to Deana, her face still pinched with anger from Kayla and the ROTC float.

Casey gave her a look that said "good luck" before kissing the baby and returning him to Arletta. She was just about to say goodbye when another familiar face passed by on the sidewalk. Mr. Callister with his small daughter, holding an overflowing bucket of candy. He stopped in surprise at the sight of his former student and prodigy. He nodded tersely at the family, then picked up his own little girl and walked away. Casey quickly returned to work.

"I guess Casey hasn't talked to him yet," Deana murmured, watching her sister flee.

"What?" her mother said.

"Just talking to myself," Deana said. She eyed her mother nervously. "What are you thinking of doing?" Brandy was almost vibrating with anger now.

The look on her mother's face told Deana that maybe she didn't want to know.

* * *

Brandy paced the whole evening, muttering to herself. Ronnie and Cleary dropped Casey and the baby off after work. Casey pretended to be tired and wouldn't meet Deana's eye. She didn't want to talk about Mr. Callister. Finally, they both went to their rooms before a fight or worse broke out.

"Just me then," Deana muttered to herself, turning on her small television and sitting on her bed. "Sorry," she said, looking down at her stomach. "I know you're there." She turned on the late show. "Do you want some popcorn?"

Half an hour later, Brandy was slamming doors, her face set with anger, almost frightening. Brandy grabbed the car keys. Deana followed her outside, barefoot, clutching the bowl of popcorn she had made.

Brandy was already in the car and rolling out of the driveway by the time Deana got there. The rear lights disappeared down the county road. She looked down at the popcorn. "This doesn't look good," she said. She munched a little popcorn and looked up at the stars. "Daddy, Jim Jr.," she said, "if you're up there, you might want to talk Mom out of whatever she thinks she's doing."

CHAPTER SIX

Deana woke cradling the popcorn bowl, half slumped over on the couch. She blinked into the early morning light. Her mother was at the kitchen counter, drinking a cup of coffee. Her hair was done, ready for work. She had on her maid's uniform. Her mother had maintained her figure through a diet of coffee and cigarettes her whole life. Her hair was the same blonde in a bottle she had chosen at sixteen. She had aged well, despite the smoking. The woman standing at the counter could have been Deana's mother at 5 or 10 or 18. She hadn't changed much.

"I didn't hear you come in last night," Deana said, picking popcorn out of her hair.

Her mother fixed her with an angry, bleary eye. But said nothing. She poured another cup of coffee.

"What bar was Kayla at last night?" she asked. When her mother gulped down another cup, Deana sighed and stood up. "You know this isn't good for you, Mom. You heard what they said at the veteran's office. It's her money. She's the wife. She keeps the ashes. She keeps the flag. If she doesn't want a funeral, there's nothing we can do."

Her mother set down her coffee cup with an angry crash, gathered up her purse, and walked out.

Deana followed her. "Hey, I need my car for today," she called out. "I have to work."

Brandy was already driving away.

"What's going on?" Casey asked from the hallway. "Did she blow up Kayla's truck yet?"

"No idea. Hope not."

"She was in my room this morning," Casey said. "She thought I was sleeping. Kept my eyes closed." She shrugged. "Thought she just needed to borrow some socks."

"Really?" Deana said in surprise. They both looked back at her bedroom.

* * *

Casey had reassembled her trophy collection. That's where they found it. A small metal urn nestled in among the smaller trophies. Deana sighed and picked up her brother's ashes.

"When you and Kayla went to the airport and met the body," Casey asked, her voice low, "did they let you see him?"

Deana shook her head. "The casket was sealed. You know that. It was an IED—one of those explosive things. He died instantly."

Casey nodded. The doorbell rang, and they both jumped in surprise. Deana almost dropped the urn. Casey took it from her and gingerly put it back among the plaques, trophies, and prizes. In an odd way, it blended in; she could see why her mother had chosen the hiding spot. Sometimes, the best hiding spaces were in plain sight; she'd learned that with her marriage to Lucas.

Deana opened the door. She looked quickly behind her, relieved that Casey hadn't followed. Manny stood at the end of the driveway, leaning against the car. He looked handsome in his well-tailored suit.

The spring air was still cold. She reached in for a jacket on the coat rack, one of her Dad's old plaids for fishing. She shut the door and went down to meet him.

For a long time, they didn't say anything. She leaned against the car next to him. The cars moved past on the highway. She guessed anybody cruising by would think he was picking up Brandy, his maid of twenty or more years. She thought a minute about Brandy and LaDonna. Their odd friendship. They'd been best friends in high school. She never wondered before how they managed their situation. Maid and employer. LaDonna—always hysterical, helpless, ridiculous. Brandy—always angry, jealous, enthralled.

Eventually, Deana said, "If you want to know if I regret it, I don't."

He looked away. "I'm a son of a bitch. I've never, never been able to keep it in my pants. My mom..." He shook his head. "She was a saint. I think maybe I should have begged her to slap me a little more."

"Does LaDonna know? About ...about it all?"

He laughed; it was a bitter barking noise. "About the others? Yes. Hell, she doesn't care. She finds out, I buy her a new car. It stopped mattering a long time ago."

"How about Courtney?"

He grimaced. "I love her, but she's as dumb as bricks. She walked in on me with the babysitter

once and she still thinks I'm some sort of hero for giving her babysitter CPR."

"About me?"

He shook his head quickly. "About you? Christ, no."

They said nothing. More cars passed. A few trucks still had flags streaming behind them from yesterday's parade. "It was a stupid thing to do," he said. "I take responsibility for it. For being an idiot."

Deana shrugged. "You came to the hospital every day," she said. "You and Casey were the only people who stood by me. I thought you cared."

"I did care," he insisted. "I do care. It's just with me, caring always leads to the same thing."

She half-smiled. "I guess I had a crush on you when I was little. My dad, he came home smelling like the plant. You always looked so handsome—at the VFW, the Rotary. Your suits. I guess I wanted to know what it was like."

"What was like?"

"Being with someone who made me feel good."

He looked away. "He's my son, you know."

It was her turn to laugh. "God, I know that."

"I always blamed LaDonna. She let him do whatever he wanted."

"Yep."

"But I did it, too, didn't I? I was always out chasing something else. Someone else. I just let LaDonna raise the kids. Happened pretty fast."

He reached in the car and pulled out a duffle bag. "I didn't..." he said, then paused, struggling for words. "I didn't mean for any of this to happen this way. But," he added grimacing, "I guess I didn't do anything else to stop it." He offered her the bag.

Deana took the bag and frowned, confused.

Manny didn't explain. Instead, he bent in and kissed her forehead. "This will be our secret, all right?" he whispered.

The door behind them opened, and Casey stood on the step, baby on her hip. Manny jerked back, looking guilty. He looked from Casey to Deana, then back again. "I should go to work," he quickly said. He climbed into his car and was gone.

"What was that all about?" Casey asked.

Deana shook her head. The bag was heavy. She set it on the ground, unzipped it, and looked inside. She heard Casey gasp, or maybe it was her. There must have been over 10,000 dollars in there.

"Holy shit," she said.

Casey quickly grabbed the bag. "Let's get that in the house."

They all but ran for it, but as they reached the front step a car crunched into the driveway. "Don't let mom see the money," Deana hastily said.

But when they turned, it wasn't Brandy, but a police squad. Deana quickly rezipped the duffle bag.

"God, do you think Manny robbed a liquor store?" Casey whispered. "I've never seen that much money in one place."

Another squad, this one from the Sheriff's office, also pulled into the drive.

"Don't be ridiculous," Deana whispered back. "He's got a ton of money. And he's the baby's father."

Casey's jaw dropped. Her knees gave way a little, and she clutched the door frame.

The pair of law enforcement officers approached. Deana knew the man from the Sheriff's office. He was a lean, light skinned African-American man. He coached track at the high school in his spare time.

"Hi, Nash," Casey said, her voice sounding high and strained. Deana mentally rolled her eyes.

"Are you working today?" he asked, smiling genuinely. "I was thinking of coming by for a burger and onions."

"No, it's my day off," she said. "Today and tomorrow. Two

days in a row. Who-hoo!" Casey babbled. Deana stepped on her foot.

Nash had been the only one who pressed Deana to file charges against Lucas. He'd visited twice when she was at the hospital. One more visit than Brandy had bothered with.

Deana was more familiar with the local cop in blue, Grady Lewis. He was ruddy and pale. Irish stock. He'd been friends with Jim Jr. since pee wee hockey. He looked like a chubby kid in his uniform—like her brother when he joined the army.

Grady was more direct. "You know why we're here, right?" he said.

In almost perfectly practiced innocence, Casey and Deana shook their heads.

"The Peterson family says their residence was broken into last night," Nash said.

"Jim Jr.'s ashes are missing," Grady added. "Can you think of anyone else who would steal them?"

Deana shrugged. "Local kids? Like a prank?"

Grady gave her a look of unvarnished skepticism. "Is Brandy home?"

"No."

"Do you think she took the urn?"

"Did Kayla see my mother take the urn?" Casey asked.

"Nope," Grady said, shaking his head. "She woke up this morning and saw someone had used a hammer on the front lock."

"How'd she miss that?"

"Her parents are out of town. She said she was sleeping pretty heavily, so she—"

"She was drunk," Casey interrupted.

"Would your mother have any reason to take the urn?" Nash asked.

"Other than it contains her only son's ashes? And that his

widow keeps it on the nightstand while she sleeps with other men?" Deana said. "No, I can't think of any reason for her to do that."

"Look," Grady uncomfortably said, "I know how hard this has been on you all, but Brandy has to know she can't take the law into her own hands."

"You said Kayla didn't see her."

Grady looked torn. "We'll need to look in the house."

Casey and Deana looked at one another and then stepped aside. Both men took their hats off and went inside the house. Casey looked down at the duffle bag.

"You go take care of Boo," Deana said. "I'll put it in my trunk."

"Your car's not here," she whispered.

"We're awful at this," Deana whispered back.

In the end, they put the duffle bag right in plain sight, on the bench by the coat rack, mixed in with all the boots and hats from winter. Deana shucked off her father's fishing jacket and casually put it over the bag.

Casey scrambled into the back room and picked the still sleeping Boo up out of the crib. She came and stood by her sister in the kitchen. "They were in my room," she whispered. "They looked right at it."

Deana felt her heart in her throat. They stood there, listening hard while both officers searched the back of the house. They spent a lot of time in Brandy's room.

Eventually, the officers gave up. They came back out into the kitchen, and Deana handed them coffee.

"Where is Brandy at?" Grady asked.

"At the Albrights' house," Deana replied. "If you wanna go down there and haul her off, I'm sure the Albrights will appreciate that."

Nash and Grady looked at each other nervously. The

Albrights heavily sponsored the annual law enforcement dance. The thought made Deana like Nash more. He had really pressed her to file charges.

Casey felt bad for them. "You know she's always been crazy," she said. "She took my sister's car this morning, too."

Nash stopped his cup halfway to his mouth. "Do you want to file a police report?"

"No," Deana said. "I was more hoping Grady would drop me off at work."

Jim Jr.'s oldest friend gave her an exasperated look.

* * *

Casey was alone in the house, nursing the baby when the next knock came at the door. She didn't like the feel of the house after the police had left, even though she had known both men. It felt odd, like there was a coating of dust all over everything. Somehow, the house looked dirty. Nervously, she eyed the bag of money still sitting in the duffle beside the coat rack. She looked through the peephole in the door to see Cleary standing there. Casey let out a sigh of relief.

Casey opened the door. To the side, outside of her view from the peephole, stood Tanya.

Tanya looked at her and crossed her arms.

"No," Casey said.

"She wanted to come along for family time. What am I supposed to do?" Cleary asked.

"No," Casey said again.

"Come on," he plaintively said, "we can all go to the park."

She slammed the door in his face. She waited and listened to the truck pull out of the driveway. She then put the baby into the stroller and started pushing him down the street; she wasn't going far. She pulled the hood up over the stroller to keep the sun out of Boo's eyes.

She knew exactly where she was going. Pool parties after the chess season. Same houses, same sidewalk. Her legs felt like a machine. Though it was a cool spring day, she felt hot. The air rippled around her like a heat mirage. She had never been so angry in her life.

She got to his door and picked the baby up out of the stroller.

She rang the doorbell. Mr. Callister answered, wearing shorts and a polo shirt. He hesitated when he saw her, holding half a peanut butter sandwich. She hitched the baby up on her hip and stuck out her chin.

"All right," she said. "You were right. You win. Now, I need that recommendation letter. For college."

Mr. Callister began to smile.

CHAPTER SEVEN

Casey was walking back home when she recognized Arletta's truck returning. Just Cleary in the cab this time, he slowed and paced her. "I'm alone now," he said. "Wanna have family time?" She kept walking, pushing the baby, not looking at him.

"Come on," he said. "Lot of traffic out here for the stroller. It's dangerous. Let me at least give the baby a ride home."

She stopped, and then he stopped the truck and got out. He kissed Boo and put him in the car seat. Cleary gave him his toy. Casey climbed in the passenger side as Cleary folded up the stroller and threw it in the back.

"Where is she?" she asked. "Tanya."

"Drove her home," he calmly said.

"Was she happy about that?"

"Not at all."

She handed him the letter. "I asked Mr. Callister for the recommendation you said I needed. For the college application," she said.

He paused as he reached for the ignition, took the letter, and opened it up.

"You're a damn fool," she said while he read.

"Why is that?" he mildly asked.

"Tanya," she said. "You sleeping with her? She's always wanted what I got. You're going to end up with another baby by next spring. That will work out fine for your plans."

Cleary tucked the letter carefully into the truck's sun visor. "My plans are working out fine," he said, checking his son in the rearview mirror.

"What do you mean by that?" she snapped.

"Mom and I drove out to campus to look at the family housing. You'll like it."

"What about Tanya?" she demanded.

"Already broke up with her. Never slept with her." He reached across the seat and took her hand. He kissed it and smiled. "You think just cause I'm the jock and you're the chess queen, I haven't been listening to you talk about your matches these years?"

She frowned at him.

"Sicilian Defense," he said. "Just like Boris Spassky. I had to get you to open up your position. And you hate Tanya."

"You think that's funny?"

He shrugged. "I think I was right not to let you name the baby Boris. I think I'm right about college. I think our baby's going to get asthma if you keep living in Brandy's smoky house. I think your mom's a bitch. I think your father was an amazing fisherman, and that if he were alive, he'd tell you to go to college with me, too. Anything else I should know?"

She blinked. "Deana's pregnant," she said. "And I'm pretty sure Manny Albright is the dad. And I think she's going to leave me."

Cleary looked stunned. "Yeah, I didn't know that," he said.

Casey started to cry. Cleary put his arms around her and held her tight.

* * *

That evening, Boo made it clear he was working on a new tooth. He screamed and fussed. Deana and Casey passed him back and forth all night. Brandy came home and went to her room, shutting the door firmly. The baby got fussier. Deana laid down for an hour, then got up while Casey laid down, but she couldn't sleep. He wasn't nursing. Arletta was working a double shift at the old folks' home, so Ronnie and Cleary came over in the magic truck. They all bundled in. They drove to the county line and back, but he was still fussy. Cleary checked his diaper in the men's room at the Gas & Bait. He came back frowning. "He's pulling on his ears a bit? Is that weird?"

Ronnie made a dramatic sigh. "Ear infection," he said. "Let's go to Urgent Care."

"Ear infection?" Cleary repeated, looking worried.

"Trust me, son, it was like you had one every week as a kid. Antibiotics will clear it up."

Cleary handed the crying baby back to Casey and they buckled the angry little guy into the back seat.

Deana sat in front so Cleary could be in back. The magic truck started up again, the heater filling the cab with soothing warm air, and Cleary crooned, "Don't worry, Boo, Grandpa knows what to do."

* * *

Right around dawn, when the antibiotics started to work, Boo dozed off. When Deana and Casey finally shuffled out to the kitchen for some breakfast, Brandy was awake, smoking and drinking her coffee. She nodded at a Saran wrapped bundle on the counter near her. "There's sweet rolls."

The sisters looked at one another, both suddenly remembering the police and the urn after a rough night.

"Something you want to tell us?" Deana asked.

"Manny brought these home yesterday," she continued, ignoring the question. "But both LaDonna and Courtney are trying to get skinny for graduation. Want any?"

She looked at them both, staring at her.

"What?' she irritably asked.

"Police came by yesterday," Casey tentatively said.

"They were looking for Jim Jr.'s ashes," Deana added.

"We kinda noticed you hid them in my room," Casey finished.

"Really?" she said, taking out another cigarette. "Are you going to have a roll or should I throw them out?"

They didn't move. For a long moment, no one said anything.

"Goddamnit!" Brandy swore and threw the rolls in the trash.

* * *

Deana called in sick to the grocery store. Casey drove their mother to the Albrights for work. Brandy wasn't speaking to either of them. The phone rang on and off for hours—Greg the manager mad that she hadn't come in, then Sue and Jane who were losing their day off. The two sisters counted, then recounted the money Manny had brought. Boo, tired from the night before, slept without stirring.

"Fifteen-thousand," Casey breathed when they were done. "Where will you go?"

"Someplace far enough away that no one can tell Lucas they saw me," Deana said. "What's a place far away?"

"From Cold Spring?" Casey shrugged. "Everywhere, I guess."

"Remember how Daddy talked about fishing in Montana?" Deana asked. "How peaceful he thought it was? Maybe I'll go there. See what it looks like."

"You'll let me know?" Casey's voice trembled, and Deana hugged her.

"Course I will. But you'll be too busy with college to miss me."

Casey didn't release her for a long while. "Why Lucas?" she asked. "Why did you pick him?"

"Everyone liked him," she reminded her sister. "Everyone still does. Daddy even liked him."

"He wouldn't have if you'd told him the truth."

"Yeah, probably not." Deana broke away from their hug and put the lid on the shoebox where they'd arranged the money. She'd have to get a bank account without Lucas' name on it, she thought.

"Why didn't you?" Casey asked. "Tell Daddy? Tell any of us?"

She shrugged. "It just never seemed important enough to bring up."

"You weren't important enough?"

Deana looked away.

"You didn't tell me," Casey said. "That's what hurts, you know. Like this was years, Deana, you hid it for years."

She touched her stomach. "Well, you know hiding is not really an option anymore."

Casey was about to reply when the front door opened and then slammed shut. Deana slid the shoe box under her bed and threw a blanket over her suitcase.

Brandy appeared in the doorframe. "Why is the car here?" she demanded. "Deana, why didn't you go to work?"

"I felt sick," Deana lied. "Why are you home?" She frowned. "How did you get home? Did you get a ride?"

"LaDonna sent me away," Brandy huffed, pulling out a cigarette. "Manny said I could borrow Lucas' truck to drive home. Everything's an uproar over there. Manny announced he wasn't going to buy Courtney a car for graduation. Courtney pitched a fit. She and LaDonna have had the car picked out for ages."

Casey and Deana exchanged a glance.

Brandy shook her head. "Don't know what he was thinking. But he's always been cheap. Even when they were dating. LaDonna was so upset she threw up. Hysterical. Threw everyone out of the house."

Brandy pressed a trembling hand to her temple. "I need to lay down." She left a little trail of smoke all the way to her bedroom.

"Guess that answers that question about the money," Casey murmured.

"I'm going to put my suitcase in the car," Deana murmured. They crept by Brandy's closed door, but only made it as far as the living room when a terrific pounding shook the front door. Then there was a scream of rage that was both female and otherworldly.

"What the hell?" Brandy said, coming out of her room. She walked past the suitcase without seeing it. Casey grabbed it and drug it behind the couch.

Brandy opened the front door to find LaDonna on the step, Courtney in her wake. LaDonna was not herself today. The whole of her had the air of someone who'd been to the mountaintop—her hair stood up with holy anger. "I need to talk to that daughter of yours!" she yelled, clawing at the air with her manicured fingernails.

Mother and daughter pushed their way into the house, past

the stunned looking Brandy. Deana felt their beady eyes land on her like a sniper's scope. She almost looked down for the red, telltale dot seen in movies.

"You bitch!" LaDonna yelled.

But Courtney was even louder. "You stole my car!" Courtney shrieked at Deana and lunged at her. Casey jumped between them as LaDonna just barely held her daughter back.

LaDonna fixed her daughter-in-law with an eye of pure hatred. "Manny had no right to give you that money!" she hissed. "It's my money as much as his. Give it back! He promised Courtney a car!"

"What are you talking about?" a deeply stunned Brandy demanded, looking from Deana to LaDonna.

"Don't act like you don't know what I'm talking about." LaDonna turned on her girlhood friend. "You know she has the money! I can't believe you lied to me today! Manny told me Casey wants to divorce Lucas, and he gave her the money to do it!"

Brandy turned to stare at Deana, and Deana felt herself go numb, her fingertips tingle. Her ears rang like in the hospital. Casey slid her hand into hers. Its warmth was reassuring.

Deana looked from her horrified mother to the almost comically enraged Courtney and LaDonna, then back again. "No," she said.

"Damn right," Casey added.

LaDonna's eyes flared. "You don't think I know what's going on here?" she raged. "When Lucas finds out about this, that little tap he gave you at Christmas won't seem like nothing!"

"You knew?" said a startled voice. They turned to see that Manny had arrived in the open doorway. He was looking at his wife aghast. "You knew about that?" he repeated.

Her eyes narrowed. "Of course, I'm his mother."

"You knew?" he repeated a third time. "We just went on with Christmas..." He shook his head like he'd been struck. "We went on with Christmas like nothing happened?" He heavily sat down in the battered armchair nearest the door. *That's my father's chair*, Deana thought.

"How much did you know about?" Manny asked. "The other times? All the other times?"

LaDonna dismissively shook her head. "What was I supposed to do? Get my own son arrested?"

He looked at her as if he'd never seen her before, in complete revulsion. "You could have told him to stop! That we'd get him help to stop!"

"Oh please," she snorted. "Then he'd never get his promotion in the Army."

It was like she'd slapped him. Manny seemed to regain his strength, and he roared out of the chair. "You spoiled him from day one!" He yelled so loudly that the commemorative duck plates hanging on the kitchen wall rattled. "You turned him rotten!"

"How would you know?" LaDonna yelled back, just as loud. "You were never there. Working *late at the office*. The whole town knows what kind of *work* you do *late at the office*. Don't act like some poor martyr, Manny."

LaDonna turned back to Deanna. "I'll call the police," she hissed. "I'll call them right now and say you stole the money."

"No," Deana gritted out.

"Give them the money," Brandy said. Deana gaped at her in surprise.

"You're taking their side?" Casey demanded. "Are you really taking their side?"

"Don't be ridiculous," Brandy said. "If Deana has the money, she's going to give it back to Courtney so she can get her car."

"The hell she's not!" Casey yelled.

"You bitch!" Courtney shrieked. "You stupid, slut bitch!"

LaDonna had her cell phone out, flipping it open, her jaw set as she punched in the numbers.

"If you call the police," Manny said, "I'll file a report myself. I'll tell them what Lucas did at Christmas. I'll report it to his commanding officer as well."

LaDonna's eyes narrowed. "You wouldn't dare."

"Try me."

"You shriveled old bitch," LaDonna yelled, turning viciously on Brandy. "You've always been jealous of my children! Because your kids are trash! And now you've ruined my family. Your whore daughter got herself knocked up!"

"Don't bring me into this," Casey said. "I'll knock you flat."

"Your other whore daughter," LaDonna sneered.

Everyone looked at Deana. Brandy looked like someone had hit her with a hammer. Oddly, even at that moment, Deana felt sorry for her mother. The way she sometimes felt sorry for Lucas when he hit her, afterwards, when he was sad. She felt dizzy again. Casey steadied her.

Courtney screamed. "What the hell is going on? What about my fucking car?"

"You don't think Vera Johnson at the store told me what she saw?" LaDonna raged. "You're pregnant, and it sure as hell isn't my son's baby!"

Brandy staggered. No one bothered to catch her. She sank onto the coffee table.

"I don't give a damn who's pregnant!" Courtney screamed, stepping over Brandy. "I want my fucking money! Where is it?" She pushed past Deana. "I want my car. I don't care if I have to tear this whole trash heap apart to find it!"

"Courtney," Manny roared. "Sit down. Sit your skinny ass down or your college fund is going to drive off with the car."

She stared at him. It was possible this was the first time in her life her father had said no to her. She gulped, then sat on the coffee table next to Brandy.

LaDonna was incandescent with rage. "Your own daughter...your own daughter, you talk to this way! This trash cheated on your son and..." She stopped midbreath. It was as if the truth came to her like a divine revelation, right there on the shag carpet, right there under the gaze of the commemorative duck plates.

"You bastard," she breathed. LaDonna looked between Deana and Manny. "You fucking bastard, how could you?" LaDonna gagged. She clamped her red-painted nails over her mouth and ran out of house.

"LaDonna, wait...let me explain!" Manny chased after her. They heard one car squeal out, then another.

In the silence of her parents' absence, Courtney regained herself. She ran out into the driveway. "What about me?" she shrieked. "What is happening? Get back here, you assholes! You fucking left me here!"

Brandy scrambled after her charge. Deana and Casey heard Courtney scream again and went to the door. "Get away from me! I hate you! I hate you. I want my fucking car! I earned it!" Courtney took off down the county road. Deana tried to follow her, but Courtney shoved her away. Deana and Casey gasped.

Slowly, Brandy staggered back into the house. "How could you do this to me?" she demanded of Deana. "How could you ruin everything?"

Deana and Casey stared at one another, and then they started to laugh.

"There's nothing funny about this!" Brandy roared.

It was impossible to stop now. They laughed harder.

"I want my car," Casey imitated Courtney's voice. "I

earned it."

Deana leaned against her sister for support, her sides hurt from laughing.

Brandy's lip trembled. "How could you do this to me?" she asked. "Jim Jr. is dead. Your dad is dead. The Albrights are all I have!"

"You have us," Casey said. Cars honked outside on the street; Courtney was crossing the highway.

Brandy didn't reply.

"Are you gonna run after her?" Casey said. "Like always?"

Brandy grabbed her purse. "Don't you dare speak to me like that. If your father were alive, he wouldn't have tolerated it."

She slammed the door behind her. One of the commemorative duck plates in the kitchen fell loose and broke on the floor. The baby started to cry. Casey ran and fetched him from his crib.

* * *

Brandy slowed down Lucas' borrowed truck beside Courtney walking on the highway. "Please get in the truck, sweetheart," Brandy begged. "We'll get this all figured out. I'll take you home."

Courtney kept walking. "Go away! I hate you!"

"Please!"

Courtney flipped Brandy the middle finger. She continued to mince her way along the highway in her high heels, Brandy following behind. Cars piled up behind them, honking. Courtney started to yell at them, bending down and picking up rocks. She hurled them at the honkers, looking deranged.

After half a mile, Courtney came to the bar. On a Saturday night, the lot was packed.

"You're too young to go in there!" Brandy pleaded.

"I'm going in there to call the cops and tell them you're following me!"

Brandy parked and was about to follow Courtney inside when a bright blue pickup with an American flag on the hood pulled into the lot. Dust whirled everywhere.

Kayla jumped out, leaving the engine running. "I know you did it!" Kayla screamed at Brandy. "I know you've got Jim Jr.'s fucking ashes."

The bar emptied with people gathering around to watch the shouting, first from Courtney, then from Kayla.

"You whore!" Brandy screamed back. "You took all the money. I can at least have the ashes!"

"Why?" Kayla demanded. "Jim Jr. hated you! I was his wife, goddamnit! You don't think he told me anything? He called you a mean old bitch! That's why I didn't give you a goddamn dime."

Brandy took a swing at her. It landed with a solid whack that made the crowd "oooh" in surprise.

Kayla spit a mouthful of blood in her mother-in-law's direction. It barely missed her. When Brandy was distracted, Kayla roundhouse punched her in the jaw. The women screamed and dove at each other. It took several minutes for the bouncers to tear them apart. With the men holding them back, they still screamed at each other.

"I'm going to your house right now to get his ashes back!"

"The hell you will!" Brandy screamed back.

Kayla shook herself loose from the bouncer and jumped in her truck. Everyone scrambled out of the way as Kayla whipped out of the lot, spraying rocks everywhere.

Brandy, still screaming, jumped into Lucas's borrowed truck and slammed it into reverse. There was a horrible thump and a scream. Everyone from the bar was yelling. Brandy jumped out of the truck again.

Courtney lay on the ground behind the truck, her eyes white and staring, her gaze empty.

She was unmistakably dead, her mouth gaped open.

The roar of voices all around Brandy was like a blackness, the screams, the shouting men, the panicked bar manager trying to revive Courtney. The noise of the sirens started in the distance.

Brandy looked at the girl at her feet. Courtney had been knocked clean out of her shoes. The older woman wanted to speak, but she couldn't. She just kept staring at the child she'd raised. She looked down the highway, the roof of her own house just visible in the distance. She'd gone to see Deana in the hospital just once. This was how Deana had looked, too, so still. Lucas had done that. Lucas whom she'd fed cake, who she had raised better than her own, had done that.

She pushed aside the bar manager and took Courtney in her arms. Cradling her to her chest. "Oh, baby," she moaned, "I didn't mean it," she sobbed.

She still held onto the girl for dear life when the police arrived.

* * *

Down the street, Deana held Boo while Casey heaved her suitcase, the box of money, and a few other things into the back of the car.

"Why did you have Boo?' Deana asked her sister. "You never thought of ... you know."

Casey shrugged. "I had lots of choices, didn't I?" she said. "But I knew right from the beginning, he was mine. I didn't want to give him up. I loved him too much." She thought about it. "Mom was so angry about me keeping the baby, but I knew I'd always have you to help me, no matter what."

"I'm sorry," Deana said. "I'm so sorry to leave you like this."

Sirens started to blare in the distance. They looked off down the highway.

"Busy night at the bar," Casey said.

"What will you do?" Deana asked her baby sister.

Casey took Boo back and kissed his soft head. He gurgled and smiled at his aunt. "I'll call Cleary to come pick me up. And then...I guess we'll find out what moving forward looks like," she said. "What should I tell all of them about where you've gone?"

"Why tell them anything?"

Casey nodded. "I put Jim Jr.'s ashes in your suitcase. When they ask, I'll tell them you took him out fishing."

Deana smiled even though she felt like crying. "Daddy would have liked that." She hugged her sister one last time and said, "I'll write."

"Course you will," Casey said, helping her close the car door.

The Sheriff's squad and then an ambulance roared by on the highway as Deana headed out of town. She reached down and patted her stomach. "Don't worry, we're headed in the opposite direction," Deana told the baby. "That ought to be good luck."

RECIPES FROM COLD SPRING, MINNESOTA

JIM SR.'S FAVORITE WALLEYE FRY

3-5 Walleye fillets
2 eggs
1 ½ cups milk
2 cups butter-flavored shortening (or oil)
2 cups crumbled corn flakes
1 TBS Schwartz's Deli Steak & Beef Spice or Montreal Steak Seasoning

Directions:
Carefully debone the Walleye fillets (check a bunch of times). Clean. Cut into strips. Crumble cornflakes in a gallon size Ziplock bag. Add seasoning to bag. Mix egg and milk in bowl. While shortening heats up, dip each walleye strip in milk and egg, add to Ziplock bag and shake until covered. Fry until light golden brown.

DEANA'S CHICKEN & VEGGIE CASSEROLE

Two bags frozen California Veggies
1 bag frozen Brussel sprouts
4 cooked chicken breasts (chopped)
One package mushrooms
2 cups shredded American cheese
1 can cream of mushroom
1 cup sour cream
1 TBS pepper
1 TBS salt
1 cup crushed potato chips
Dash paprika

Directions:
Preheat oven to 375 degrees. Place frozen veggies, mushrooms and chicken pieces in 13X9 casserole dish. Make cheese sauce on stovetop, mixing together cheese, soup, sour cream, salt and pepper until thick and gooey. Pour cheese sauce into the 13x9 casserole over veggies and chicken. Bake one hour. Crush potato chips in gallon sized Ziplock bag. Sprinkle over casserole, add a dash Paprika (don't actually do this) and cook ten more minutes until browned. Also good without chicken

BRANDY'S PINEAPPLE SMILE CAKE

2 packages strawberry cake (plus eggs, oil, water required on box)
1 can pineapple rings
1 cup coconut flavored rum
1 bottle maraschino cherries.
1/4 cup melted butter
1/2 cup brown sugar
2 package pineapple Jell-O (plus water according to package)
Large tub Cool Whip

Directions:
Soak pineapple rings in coconut flavored rum overnight. Preheat oven to 350 degrees. Mix up cake mix in one big bowl according to box directions. Pour melted butter into one 9-inch pan then sprinkle with brown sugar. On top of butter and sugar lay out pineapple rings with cherries in middle. However, reserve one pineapple ring and three cherries for later. Pour ½ cake mix over pineapple/cherries and the other ½ into an additional 9-inch round pan. Cook both cakes according to package directions until knife comes out clean. Cool, then poke both cakes with fork at 1-inch intervals. Mix Jell-O according to package and then pour over each cake, filling holes, dividing. Cool in refrigerator overnight. Invert cake without pineapple onto serving platter. Frost entire sides and top with Cool Whip. Invert second cake onto the first cake (so that fruit forms a middle layer with whipped cream). Frost again. Brandy uses the cherries and half a pineapple ring to make a "smiley face" for the Albright children on top of the cake. Deana finds this deeply creepy. Keep chilled until ready to serve.

JIM JR.'S FAVORITE SMELT POT PIE

1 lb smelt
6 medium potatoes, peeled and sliced
2 onions, sliced
1 clove garlic, minced
1 small bag frozen peas
6 slices bacon, cut into ½ inch pieces
2 cups milk
1 egg
2 TBS butter
2 premade pie crusts (lump kind to roll out)
1 egg yolk
2 TBS water

Directions:
Preheat oven to 275 degrees. Clean the smelt, cut off heads. In a greased 9X13 casserole dish arrange smelt, potato, peas, onions, garlic, bacon in alternating layers. Salt layers to taste. Mix milk and egg. Pour over fish and veggies. Add pats of butter throughout. Roll out pie crust to fit size of casserole. Seal edges. Cook for 5 hours. Mix egg yolk with water, spread on crust. Cook for another hour at 300 degrees. Jim Jr. preferred this pie made with walleye bits. If cooking with deboned walleye cook at 375 degrees for 45 minutes until casserole bubbles.

TRUTH AND CONSEQUENCES

BY KAITLYN RICH

TRUTH AND CONSEQUENCES

I wake up to the radio playing an old song my Mom used to like. Something about counting the cars on the New Jersey Turnpike, looking for America. Dad never liked them. He was more of a classic rock person. Zeppelin, I think. I can hear her humming to the tune. For a second I forget it's Connie's hum I hear.

"There is nothing out here," I say for what must be the twentieth time since we left Houston and made our way across the hill country of Texas, and then into the high desert of New Mexico. In my peripheral I see Connie glancing over at me, probably annoyed that my face is pressed against the passenger window and making it greasy. She used to say 'it's crazy right?' but that stopped a while ago. I think all she hears now is 'are we there yet?'

Our two-lane highway opens up on the right to a dust-filled ocean, nothing to break up the monotony of shrubs, sand, and in the distance, a bleak blue horizon. To the left, some more dust, dying plants, and a dead coyote who met an untimely end trying to cross the road. Out of context, he could be taking a nap curled up on the white line at the edge - the pavement ready to drape over him like a blanket and tuck him in. What poor luck. There are barely any cars out here. He must have picked a very inopportune time to try and cross from his barren wasteland on the left to the barren wasteland on the right. Unless he purposely timed his dart intending to end it all.

I try to think of a grass-is-always-greener joke but can't get there, so I continue staring out my passenger side window and looking for any signs of life as Connie barrels down the road. We've passed maybe three or four bombed-out abandoned buildings since Carlsbad so the structure I see coming up ahead is a fun anomaly. "And up ahead on the right," I say to Connie in my best tour guide voice. "We have," I pause and gesture to the building outside as we approach, holding an imaginary microphone with my other hand, "an old drive-thru burger place. A must-see along with the dead coyote."

Connie pretends not to hear me. She pretends to ignore me a lot these days. These days I wonder how much of our friendship is pretend. Pretend. A pre-end.

I'm doing it again. Swirling, Connie calls it.

The drive-thru's retro design long ago ran out of pieces it could slough off of itself. Its colors are bleached and muted. I always think of decay being worse on the East Coast with the winter, the water, and the humidity, but here everything seems to bake itself into ruin, hoarding more of the sun than it can handle. The last few plastic letters cling to the old backlit sign say:

Y U Can Hav
T S R
THE ND

I wonder how long it's been since someone updated the

sign. The missing letters swirl up in the wind from the car as we pass. I wonder who the hell works here. There are no houses or driveways anywhere nearby. The fry station guy must have driven three hours for his shift, but the last gas station was 150 miles ago. How did the employees even do the round trip to get to work? Who delivered supplies? I wonder who came here to enjoy themselves and sit around their cars and chat. I wonder who—

"Hey, can you check how far out we are?" Connie asks.

A top forty radio song plays in the background. Connie gets to choose the music because she's driving. And honestly, she's driven most of the way because I get too nervous behind the wheel, my mind elsewhere. I almost took us off the road earlier in the trip because I couldn't stop fretting over whether or not I locked the apartment door before we left.

Connie's playing with her hair again. Her dark eyes, the color of spilled motor oil, watch as she braids her equally dark hair with both hands while her knees hold the steering wheel. Connie is beautiful, but she works at it. The kind of girl who can apply a smokey eye while driving in rush hour. One eye on the road, one on her reflection. She's someone people say has 'a style.' She has clothes that I often borrow and often destroy. We've done this since high school, Connie's parents replace anything I ruin, and no one seems to notice. Or at least no one says anything to me. Though I can't remember the last time we shared anything willingly.

Unlike Connie, I'm disheveled with greasy unwashed hair pulled into a messy bun to keep me from twirling it nonstop. No makeup. I'm at the point where I'm flattered when people ask for my ID to buy booze. I know I look older than 30, that they're just being nice. I think how different the two of us look. But mostly I think how I wish she'd pay attention to driving. I can visualize the crash scene as if it's already happened. As if I'm watching our deaths covered on the local news traffic report. They'd have to dig up my senior year portrait for the newspaper. What social media eulogies would people post for me? People I haven't spoken to in the years since Mom's funeral. Strangers now. Trying to cope with the futility of their mortality. *Jean, gone too soon.* Something generic like that. Connie and I both play with our hair now, though mine is more destructive - I pull at it like an over-pruned bird. I can't remember when I took it down from the bun, but I can feel the oil on my fingers as I run my hands through it.

My racing thoughts seem to happen more often here in the desert than they did back home in Allentown, even on my medication. I stopped taking it before the trip, wanting to see the country, live a cross country road trip fantasy like *On the Road.* Or at least that's my most recent self rationalization. Everything feels vacant with the meds, like someone is telling me about my life, or that I'm watching it through a dirty pane of glass. I didn't want that for this experience but the trade-off is life accelerated, like when you're a kid and the cassette tape is being rewound too fast and the voices sound high-pitched, quick, and evil.

Connie and I are en route to White Sands National Park for a hike to break up the final day's drive. We've known each other since freshman year at our Catholic high school. Bonded because we both hated Catholic school. I remember the theology teachers telling us that Hollywood horror movies about exorcisms were scientifically and factually accurate. Connie and I used to joke about how ridiculous this was, but it's something I still think about. It's always women who are possessed in those movies. It's usually the consequence of hitting some invisible tripwire they shouldn't have gotten too close to. A punishment for curiosity, for asking the ouija board too many questions. Is the underlying message of the films that to question structure means you lose any control you had? There's a metaphor there. I know I fear losing control of myself more than anything.

Connie is moving from our apartment in Allentown, Pennsylvania to a new life in Phoenix, Arizona. Ostensibly it's for the 'job of her dreams' and not because she recently broke up with her long-term boyfriend, Jared. I know she's lying. Partially because the job is a cubicle job in sales for a software company, which is no little kid's dream. But I recognize this trip for the escape plan that it is because I imploded her life and the relationship for her. She knows, or at least heavily suspects her ex of cheating because of the silver turquoise ring Connie said she found in the bedroom when she returned home from a work trip. It obviously wasn't Connie's, but what she doesn't know is that it was, I mean that it *is* mine.

I still want it back and I have no idea what she did with it. I keep reaching for its ghost on my index finger trying to trace its flower design and oval shape. My stomach sinks and I resist almost kicking the dash as I remind myself it belonged to my mother, one of the only material things she could leave to me. I don't think she knows what it means.

I barely know what I said yes to or if I even did. All I have is waking up next to him, swathes of time redacted by the permanent marker of 15 plus drinks. I lock this away in my mind, tie another knot to close the trunk and then pull out my phone and stare into it, its bright light a beacon to halt my spiral and pretend to pause my life before she notices the look on my face.

Then I remind myself she never notices anything. Sometimes I don't leave my room for days and Connie doesn't acknowledge it. I often think if I died suddenly it would be one of those horror stories where I'd leak through the mattress and floor to the apartment below us before she thought to knock on my door. Both my parents are gone so no one else is going to look for me.

Wait, how long has it been since she asked how far out we were? One song, I think, maybe two.

Another old dad rock song crackles through the radio. Creedence Clearwater. Dad liked them, Mom didn't. Maybe it's been three songs.

"Umm I'll look it up but I don't think it's too much further to the park. Should we get gas?" I say trying to make it seem like I was plotting this out during the pause. "I think I see something that resembles civilization."

"Huh? Yeah, sure. Good idea." Connie looks up from her phone at the same time I retreat from mine.

My brain calculates the danger of her texting while driving, but decides against mentioning it since our odds of hitting anything more than a tumbleweed are slim. "Text from Jared?" I ask, trying to sound as disinterested as possible.

"No, Jean. It's my mom. My grammy isn't doing well." Connie stares ahead. "I should've seen her before I left."

I want to comfort her, but all my brain can muster is, "You weren't there for me with my mom," followed shortly by a less resentful and more sorrowful, "and there's no going back now." I don't think I say this out loud.

I clasp my hands. But my missing ring reminds me she's left her family, her grandma, and her life because of me. And I'm the only other person for miles and I can't even comfort her. I feel bad for both of us.

I play with the frayed ends of my denim cut-offs. Aware I

smell like stale beer and cigarettes. I was allowed one backpack since Connie's Subaru was packed to the brim with her life. After I filled my bag with a thirty rack of PBR, sunglasses, and a journal I haven't written in in years I was left with room for only two outfits. I've been in the same t-shirt and shorts since New Orleans, the pink stain of a split frozen hurricane still visible, making my yellow shirt look like a watercolor sunset.

Anyway, we're trying to go out with a bang today. We've hit two national parks already and it's only early afternoon. Both quick hikes at Carlsbad Caverns and Guadalupe National Park. If you saw us on those hikes you'd either think we were late to catch a train or that someone was stalking us. We speed walk through nature so we can hit another punchcard of life experience at the next park. White Sands will be our last stop before Phoenix, and it's the one we're most excited about. The dunes rise fifty to a hundred feet out of the nothingness of high desert on the site of a former, yet rumored to still be active, military testing facility. They tested the atomic bomb here. We've reminded ourselves of this Jeopardy-esque fact a few times now. This is right up our weird *Atlas Obscura* Americana alley. I think back to the times we used to watch episode after episode of Unsolved Mysteries together, always trying to solve it.

GPS says 20 more minutes.

"Can you look up some trails?" Connie asks once we establish our ETA, and with a quickness that suggests she's trying to change the subject away from her family in her mind, "something off the beaten track, with not as many tourists?"

After ten days on the road though, our conversations are always like this now: staccato, to the point, and with the ability to read between the lines. I know she means something different. More local than the overcrowded dunes Nature Trail option. Something memorable. More real. I pause at that word, real, knowing the betrayal that looms over our trip like a gathering storm. I start looking at hiking forums for more backwoods options.

Slaughter Canyon immediately catches my eye. The few pictures available in Google Maps show bleached-white dunes with beautiful green trees following a meandering path through the desert. Only a two-mile hike.

"Hell yeah," Connie agrees after I turn the phone to her, showing her the trailhead picture. "Put that shit in the GPS," she says and smiles, her malaise and thousand-mile stare disappear at the promise of something new.

Smiling along with Connie's approval I follow orders, but there's a part of me that's superstitious as I type in the name. It's the kind of superstition where my heart rate picks up and my mind races trying to suss out the danger, but also a part that finds the unsettling piece very funny. It sounds like something my Mom would do when she wouldn't want to share candy with me when I was little. How she'd call it her 'medicine' and say it was too important to spare me a Skittle. But she's gone so who else names an otherworldly beautiful hike, Slaughter Canyon? Someone who has a weird sense of humor or who wants to keep the hike to themselves.

"Oh, I think that's a gas station, right? Let's stop now. I don't want to double back," Connie says. Even though she phrased this as a question she's already putting the turn signal on.

"Yeah good idea," I chime in, almost in rhythm with the click of the blinker.

I strain my eyes to see through the desert haze and categorize the shape we're approaching as a gas station. The form I saw from way off a few minutes ago comes into a shaky focus. There's an old-timey Oregon-Trail-style large wheel wagon parked at one tank, a school bus with all flat tires at the other, and topping off the whole diorama is a 12-foot alien sculpture that ushers you into the parking lot like a crossing guard. Its eyes dark, pupilless, and unsmiling.

"Some interesting decorating going on here," I add as I take a photo with my phone. "Not sure what the wagon needs at the gas tank, but the one next to it is open."

"Yeah seems like our only option," Connie says, a twinge of annoyance in her voice.

I try to gauge the ways I am responsible for this, or if I even properly assess her tone.

"Can you see if they have any snacks or soda inside? I'm getting tired and hungry," she asks.

I can tell she wants me to drive, but I turn to the store and leave her to pump gas before she can add this request. Yeah, she's probably a little annoyed with me.

The only other car in the lot is a dusty wood-paneled, gold-colored 1948 Chrysler Town and Country. It's dusty but otherwise impeccable. I smile as I remember the make and model, thinking how proud my Dad would be that I retained some of the knowledge from sitting in his car shop as a little kid. Like most thoughts of my Dad though, the nostalgia bubble pops as I move to the next frame of the memory, re-remembering that we haven't spoken since my parent's divorce years ago. I tend to avoid thinking about him. Drinking helps to smooth the edges when it does come up. Maybe they'll have little travel alcohol bottles at this rest stop? I drank my last backup PBR this morning. Dulling the sharp sting of pain has also dimmed the good memories. The medicine comes with side effects. He exists now in a few facts I repeat only to myself - songs or cars. His form forever hunched over an engine with his face out of sight and his voice drowned out by the radio.

"Hi, welcome! Can I help you with anything?" says the grey-haired woman, hanging out of the storefront.

Her face is wrinkle-free, except around her eyes and

mouth. There, deep marks tell of many years of smiles or frowns like a map on her face. She at once looks both old and young. Her silver hair, which goes almost to her hips, and the near translucent paper-thin skin on her arms and hands seem to be fighting for resources from her. The hair is winning. The blue blood of her visible veins is the same shade as her eyes. She holds the door open, beckoning me inside. The brightest thing for miles are the flowers on her printed dress, gently swaying in the breeze.

"We don't get a lot of people at this stop since the interstate opened up, and that radio show came through and renamed the town. Well, 'town' is pretty loose now, I guess. Truth or Consequences, New Mexico is pretty amorphous," she says unprompted but genuinely pleased, it seems, to be talking to another human.

I pause trying to remember that name on any of the maps. "Yeah, my friend and I are headed to the national park." I jut my arm and thumb back in the direction of the car. "We're doing a cross-country road trip," I say with the same pride I do every time I get to repeat it to someone. Me and the woman smile at each other for a second, her face comfortable in the shared silence. I wish I had my sunglasses on so I didn't have to stare into her eyes. I feel like I need a barrier to diffuse the connection. I break first and start inside the store.

"So," I pause. "Um, I was wondering if you have any, um," why can't I remember what I was trying to say? "Oh soda and, holy shit, wow this place is huge." As my eyes adjust to the darkness of the store the sprawling rooms come into focus. The woman circles around in front of me framing a doorway that leads into another room and another room beyond that.

"Oh yeah, filled it with lots of knick-knacks and oddities over the years. Collecting is a hobby of mine, as you can probably tell from the stuff outside," she adds with a chuckle. "I don't have a theme. Anything's fair game."

"It's so," I look for the word, "impressive." My eyes go to a wall of taxidermied buffalo, hippo, and lion heads. In front of them sits a coin-operated animatronic gold prospector. He is forever frozen stroking his long beard in a tattered flannel. His gold pan sits empty. I wonder what he does when he's paid.

"Refreshments and snacks are in the next room over. Same room as the jewelry. Let me know if you like anything you see," the woman says with a wink as she turns to shuffle back to the antique register. She sinks into a well-worn leather recliner. As she plops into the seat I notice the leather is rimmed in a dark stain that matches her frame, like a chalk body outline, ready to absorb her.

I turn to go to the next room and glance back with a 'thank you' smile but her eyes are fixed on me like a spotlight. Her smile curdles around the edges. Maybe I lingered on the chair for too long. Did I just look at it again? She looks paler than earlier. The room sours and I speed up my pace, Connie's probably pissed I'm taking this long and waiting by the car. I add this to the list of ways I'm shitty to Connie and in my shame spiral and rush to grab the soda I crash head-on into a tall case of turquoise rings.

"Godamnit," I whisper to myself, worried this room's taxidermy will judge me. Their glassy eyes stare in all different directions, unfocused on anything except the distance, so it seems to have gone unnoticed. Despite their apathy, the crash is thundering so I pause waiting to hear the woman shuffle to me, but nothing stirs from that room. Okay, I can kind of put this back together. The case was plastic so thankfully nothing broke. I start pushing rings inside again as I calculate. I can shove the rings back in their box, grab the sodas and be back out in the car in under three minutes, and then we can be on the road... and... my breath catches in my throat as I hold on to one of the rings. My ring. Mom's ring. I know it by the weight in my hand without seeing it. It feels like an eternity before I open my fist and see the oval turquoise shape set in silver and framed by flowers.

I slip the ring on. It fits. All I can think is that it came back to me. I don't care what it costs, I need to have it. I grab the soda and rush to the register leaving its siblings scattered on the floor. I wonder a moment too late what those other rings looked like.

"Found something didn't you?" the woman says, now exhausted like a wind-up toy that's losing its propulsion. "Let's see it," she says, grabbing my wrist. "Oh, this is a family piece, my father made these." She squeezes my arm. "He was always trying to get one just right for my mother. Beautiful isn't it?" Her eyes stare off unfocused like the taxidermy on the wall. "He never did get it right though, impossible standards. Guess it's why I have so many."

Her dress looks faded now, I assume from the indoor light. "Yea I love it," I say standing on my tiptoes to try and catch her gaze. I realize she's staring somewhere above me. "It reminds me of one I lost actually." I stop short, not wanting to tell her more, and pull my hand back to my chest. "How much do I owe you?" I struggle to take the ring off so she can charge me for it. But the ring has other ideas. In protest, it's stuck on my finger.

"Well, looks like it chose you," she says, not blinking as she rises from her chair. "Sometimes the things we lost, or try to lose, have a way of finding us." Her eyes focus, like a cat's eyes going from darkness to light. "Take it. A gift from me to you."

"Oh, I can't do that. Please, what can I give you?" I say, still pulling at the ring, I know the strain is visible in my eyes. My muscles tense with the fight to remove the ring. It is making my brain think there's a danger we're flexing to fight. The commitment to manners and a polite exchange overrides my primal urge to run. An emotional specter of that night with Jared begins to form.

"Go. I only ask you to lead a good life. The life you want," the woman says as she ushers me to the door. "Maybe one day you'll come back this way and let me know how it went. Have a nice life, Jeanette," she adds, shutting the door behind her. The brightness of the sun outside blinds me momentarily before sucking the store back into darkness.

"Was it a Coke or Pepsi place?" Connie yells as she pumps the gas.

"What?" is all I can say even though I heard her. How is she still pumping gas? I never told the woman my name. It felt like I was inside for 20 minutes. I feel lightheaded and like my eyes can't adjust to the sun. Air traps in my chest as my thoughts swirl with the sand in the desert wind.

No one calls me Jeanette. Always Jean, J, or Genie if you are, or were, my mother. She and I both hated Jeanette. Mom wanted to name me Eugenia. An homage to the Greek myths she loved so much, but couldn't afford to go to college to study, so she read them to me as bedtime stories instead and spelled my name with a G. "Eugenia means well-born," she never failed to mention when she told me the story of her fights with Dad over the name. He thought it was too eccentric. I needed to fit in with Emilys, Annes, and Rebeccas. He planted Eugenia bushes, the same kind of shrub they use in mazes, around our half of the half-a-double house as a compromise - or in spite, depending who you asked. By the time Mom and I left, the bushes were either dead or gone feral.

Only he called me Jeanette.

The blindness of the sand swirl pauses when the mini derecho settles revealing the Chrysler. The tires. My thoughts stop. The tires are flat. Looking inside the dusty windows I notice the inside is gutted. It was perfect before.

"Yo, J, ya ready to go?" Connie replaces the pump. "I think I have to go inside to pay, there's no card reader here. Anything good in there?" she asks me while changing her volume mid-sentence to adjust for my distance as I run towards the car.

"Nah, pretty bare-bones. The lady said just leave the cash on the pump." I make up this lie not fully knowing why. "Just put a rock over the cash and let's get out of here," I add and jump into the car and lock my door, throwing the soda in the cupholder. Did I have that when I walked out of the store? I thought I just left with the ring. I try and remember the weight of my hands as I ran to the car. I know Connie's eyes linger on me.

"You okay? You look a little more frazzled than usual," she says, climbing back into the driver's seat, trying to get me to bite on the bait and banter with her.

What's usual? She turns the keys waiting for my response as I try to pull the directions up on the phone. I can't quite explain why I think the woman is still looking at us from the darkened door.

"I'm okay," I mutter. "Just ready to get going."

Connie finds this sufficient or at least gives up on pushing the subject and we continue down the road. Every minute further from the gas station reduces my heart rate a bit more. We ease back into our pre-stop slumps. I kick off my shoes and put my feet up on the dash trying to get comfortable and posture normalcy. My legs have gotten hairy. This normal thought is comforting. I turn the radio up for some background noise and a reminder of civilization.

"Did you just get one soda?"

I pretend not to hear her. Turning to my phone, I need to fact-check the woman and ground myself in reality. Still not seeing Truth or Consequences, New Mexico on Google Maps. It says the nearest interstate is I-25. Construction ended in 1957. How old was that woman? I don't see the gas station on the map either. I spin the ring around and around my finger, my thoughts slowing with each turn until they harmonize to the feel of the steel on my hand.

"Hey, can you check how far out we are?" Connie asks again.

How long has it been since we spoke?

Before I can repeat the direction prompt on the GPS, the radio goes static. Interrupting Robert Plant signing about tomorrow following today.

Connie reaches to turn it off, but just as she's about to hit the dial the radio static cuts to a clear laugh track underpinning an echoey 1940's transatlantic voice...

"HELLO THERE! WE'VE BEEN WAITING FOR YOU.... IT'S TIME TO PLAY TRUTH OR CONSEQUENCES!"

"What the fuck is this?" Connie half laughs, half shouts over the way too loud voice. The volume has more than doubled. We've picked up some weird broadcasts on our trip, a lot of weird doomsday make-your-peace-with-Jesus stuff being broadcast out of someone's basement, but never something like this.

"...I'm your host Ralph "Truth or Consequences" Edwards and boy do we have a show in store for you!"

It sounds like there's a studio audience, and the host knows what he's doing with his wordplay and how fast he's speaking. The laughter soundtrack swells. I can feel my pulse thump in my neck and my thoughts race again. Is this the old show that the woman mentioned? Where is it coming from? Are these people on the laugh track even alive anymore? I remember reading something once, that studios reuse decades-old laugh tracks for sitcoms, so technically you're listening to an audience of dead people cackle at jokes they never heard. The laughing is so loud it's painful.

"Thank you for the kind welcome folks! In just a moment we're going to meet a gentleman and a few other guests, but before we meet him I have a very lovely young lady by the name of Jean that I'd like to have you meet. Jeanie, can you come out here and stand beside me please?"

Without thinking my hand reaches up and turns off the radio. Swatting the dial like it's a bug that's flown too close to me.

Connie stares at me, her eyes look like she's about to laugh along with the audience, but concern is creeping in at the corners. "What's wrong? Why'd you turn that off?"

"Sorry, you want to listen to it?" I say, not attempting to turn the radio back on. That was my name. My Mom's nickname for me. It's just a coincidence though. Turning it off, I can feel my breath and pulse slow. I swallow a gulp of air and push the knob back in. The radio clicks back on, but there's nothing but static.

"I didn't change the station?" My brow furrows at my question. I turn the knob toward a station up and station down. Nothing. Just more crackling static.

"Oh well, that was kind of getting bizarre anyway. Any turns we need to make?" Connie pauses, "Oh, did you get a new ring?" She's looking at my eyes and not my hand.

My thumb spins the gem of the ring into my palm and I squeeze my hand around it. Does she know? Did she not hear my name? I hadn't looked at the GPS since before the radio show started. Somehow we missed the first turn. I tighten my fist, trying to absorb the ring.

"Ah shit, Connie, I'm sorry," I pause, not sure what I'll apologize for first. "I missed the turn but looks like it re-routed us up ahead. We'll just enter the park in a different way, but it looks like it will loop around. Just adds another twenty minutes or so to the drive."

Connie exhales like a car that can't turn its engine over.

"The right turn we need to make is just up ahead," I repeat the Google Maps instructions a second after the phone in hopes that it makes up for being so unhelpful. We turn off the highway and the road turns from asphalt to loose gravel. In another 100 feet, it turns to dust.

"Are you sure this is right?" This time the trepidation is in her voice.

Feeling the need to hide some of my insecurity to make her feel better, I work up some confidence, almost convincing myself that I didn't mess this up. "Yeah, I mean it's what the directions say, and we're still following the road for a bit. I can see where it loops back into the park up ahead on the map. Might just be dusty for a few more miles. The Subaru needed a wash anyway."

We settle in. I eye the radio for a second before I decide to scroll through the directions on my phone again just to double-check. A pulse of panic rises in my throat, the blue dot lets us know somewhere, some satellite following us has veered off the road on the map. We haven't turned. There hasn't even been a perceptible shift in the angle of the road. There's no service so the instructions aren't re-routing. "Shit, I think we need to turn around, it looks like we went off route somehow."

"How'd that happen, we've just been going straight on this road?" She sounds less agitated than unsure. She chews on her nails and spits out the chips of pink polish she takes off.

"I'm not sure," I say. "The GPS might be getting turned around, maybe let's just head back and take the main road, we'll just take a shorter hike to make up the time." We keep passing feigned confidence back and forth like a game of hot potato.

Connie nods and slows down and does about a 15-point turn to avoid going off the road and running over any cacti in our reverse. The last thing we want right now is a flat tire.

Back on track and I notice I'm fully hunched over my phone. My face is halfway to my lap while everything in me tenses, fighting to correct my posture. I force my shoulders back to the chair and suck in a few deep breaths. Everything is fine. We're fine and we'll be in the park with other people soon enough. A few minutes pass and I look back at the map hoping we've retraced our steps back to the road.

My stomach drops. The GPS blue dot has now passed south of the original two-lane road and we're again in the void of green and nothingness on the map.

"Connie, something's wrong," I say. "We lost the road. It says we're south again and not on the map. Did you see the gravel or asphalt?" I know we didn't pass either of those things, but I ask anyway.

"No, we haven't passed anything," she says. "Okay. It's okay," she tries to reassure herself. "We'll just keep going. It has to lead somewhere and maybe we just missed a turn somewhere on the map." Connie now assumes the role of calm, cool, and collected captain to offset my thinly veiled panic.

We continue driving for a few minutes, squinting at the horizon hoping to see a road perpendicular and intersecting our road or anything in the form of a landmark to say we're close to someone or something and can ask for directions. It's then that I notice what the phone GPS is doing.

"Connie, is your phone doing this too?" I hold the screen up to her.

Before today, the GPS hardly played a supporting role in our road trip. "W" it always read as we plotted onward toward Phoenix. But now it's a strobe light between "N", "SW", "E", "NW", with barely enough time for the letters to formalize before pivoting to another cardinal direction. We're still a blue dot pulsing through the void with nothing like a road anywhere nearby.

I look back to Connie. "Umm..." Her eyes widen with panic, both her hands grip the wheel.

Neither of us can pretend to be the soothsayer now. Our only choice is to keep following this road and ignoring the flickering of the GPS. We go on for what feels like 15 or 20 minutes. No service now, our phones' batteries die from the useless search for a signal and constant changing of direction. The clock ticks along, but the numbers look wrong. Tired, my head bobs down unconscious, giving up the struggle with gravity and then bounces back up fighting sleep. I notice the small bottle of whisky near the soda can. Where did that—

"Why couldn't we have just gone directly to Phoenix," Connie barks at me, her head whips in my direction. "I just wanted to get there and you insisted we do all these hikes. We haven't even seen anything we went too fast to pack it all in. And now this!" She almost slaps the phone out of my hand. "You have no idea where we are or where we're going," she says as she turns back ahead and slams the wheel with her hands.

"What are you looking for? Where have you been?" a quiet voice says.

"What?" I ask, surprised to feel compelled by the last question, "I don't know what I'm looking for. I'm lo—"

"What are you talking about? You're looking for the road," Connie snaps again. "Keep looking for it, Jean."

"Didn't you ask what I'm looking for?"

"No! No one asked that. I said you have no fucking idea

where we're going." Her eyes fierce, but her eyeliner runs down her cheek and betrays a stray tear. "I'm sick of you doing this. Falling apart all the fucking time. Never paying attention to anything." She stomps on the brake. The car slides for a second in the sand.

"Do you want to run? Where do you want to go?" the voice says a little louder now. It feels like it's coming from within my hands, my fists clenched together to smother the voice down.

"Me!?" I scream. "You never pay attention to anything! It's all about you and your perfect little life." Tears are coming and I hate myself for not being able to stay composed. "You weren't there when my Mom died. You did nothing. You did nothing when I started drinking, when I stopped..." I can't remember what I stopped doing. "When I stopped— everything! You did nothing. Why did you even ask me on this stup—"

"I was there Jean. But no one is ever enough for you. You're making your world so small. I asked you to come because I thought it would help." Connie pushes the words in like a sedative to my rant, "I thought you'd see there's more out there," she gestures at the whole desert. "I thought it would bring you back, like how things used to be. Make you try again, start —"

"How things used to be?" I laugh. "What does that even mean? What for one week or so before you leave me and start a whole new life without me on the other side of the country things can be how they used to be? Then?" I hold myself now, arms wrapped tight around my sides. "Who is this for then? Me or you?"

The ring burns in my hand like I just landed a punch. Like I'm ready to land another, and another, and another. "Do you know what it's like," I hesitate. "To want to sleep for years and wake up to a different life?"

"No, I," she hesitates. "J, there's help for that. You can change things," she says, her hand moves to my shoulder.

"How? With what money? With what job? I have nothing Connie. No one. Least of all you. At least Jared pretended to care about me. That's more than I have had in years. I'm famished."

Connie goes to speak but stops. She looks at me and tries again. Nothing. She turns back to the steering wheel, eyes cast down, calm as a metronome, she tries a third time. "J, I care about you. I know about you and Jar—"

"What are you owed?" the ring asks.

"I'm owed more. Better. I deserve better than all this, than you, than everything," I scream, wanting to fill the desert. Wanting any animal, human, or otherwise to turn and face me and nod in understanding and agreement. To make me hate myself a little less for putting all this on Connie's shoulders. I know it's not her fault, but she's my only target.

"Go, Genie." The ring jerks my hand to the doorknob.

Before Connie can stop me, my door swings open. No time to grab my bag or shoes. I run barefoot into the sand. I sway as I lose my footing and climb up the nearest dune. I know I look pathetic but I don't care. It's freeing to move, to stretch my legs after the claustrophobia of the car, surrounded by Connie and her belongings. The sand shifts beneath my feet. I don't think this dune was there a minute ago.

"Where are you going!" Connie sobs as she runs to the front of the car. "J, come back please we can figure this out. Plea—"

The wind cuts off her voice. The laugh track is back. I know it's in my head but I don't care. I keep running. My only thought is to get to the top of the dune. The sand grows whiter and brighter as I climb. I feel less heavy, faster, lighter, and clearer. At the top of the hill, I see a path open up. Flanked by Eugenia bushes. They would never grow in the desert. No water. Too much sun. This makes no sense. Wait. Is this Slaughter Canyon?

My forward motion is stopped by the ring. It feels like the weight of a dying star in my hand. I could throw it away. Toss it into the sand. Lose it for good. Leave this behind.

No, keep going.

The force and weight of the ring seem to pull me down and I'm laying on the ground, cheek to the sand. The warm sand feels like an embrace until the ring tugs again and pulls me headfirst into the grit. The dust rushes past me. It seems like it's ripping my clothes, my hair, even my skin away like I'm a table being sanded. I kick and fight as if I'm trying to avoid falling into a dream. I gasp at the effort. Instead of sand, I choke at the surprise of air. Even with my eyes closed, I know the light is blinding. The laughter is up close now. I open my eyes and see I'm surrounded by spotlights and behind them, a studio audience.

"Jeanie? Will you come out here and stand beside me please?"

I hear the man's voice from the radio speaking to me, but the light is still too bright to see him so I follow his voice. I wish I had grabbed my bag with my sunglasses. What did the host say his name was? Ralph, I think?

"Welcome to Truth or Consequences."

The audience breaks into applause. I can feel him stand next to me, arm around my waist. The fabric of his suit jacket feels old, a frames that long ago forgot its original owner.

"Now," says Ralph addressing the audience, "Jean here is a young woman on a road trip to nowhere. She is going to help us with a Consequence today that involves a secret message," he pauses as the audience inhales, "but first, let's get these sunglasses on her."

I go to speak but nothing comes out. The audience starts laughing at my attempt.

"Hold on Jeanie, one second, here you go," Ralph says as he gently places the sunglasses on my face.

The light dilutes, but not enough for me to see more than a couple of feet in front of me. The audience and the host are all silhouettes.

"Alright Jeanie, will you look this way, please. Tilt your head slightly. Nope a little higher. There. Can everyone see?"

Without question, I follow his directions and pause only when the audience approves. I feel my worth is directly tied to what they think of me.

"Alright so Jeanie, these sunglasses have a secret message written on the frame, a Truth. The goal of the game is to get the other contestant to notice the message. You'll have three chances. I won't tell you what it says so you can't cheat. You'll need the other person to read it first," he says like he's explained this a thousand times before.

I don't know where to look or turn.

"I'll ask questions to the other contestants and give them as long as we can to notice the message," he says to me before turning to the audience. "Alright, folks let's see how observant they are!"

I smell the whiskey before I see who's frame approaches me. It's Jared.

"Hello sir, please tell me and the audience your name and where you're from?"

"Hi, my name's Jared and I'm from Allentown, Pennsylvania. Excited to be here." He reaches for a side hug around me.

The spotlight is still too bright to make out anything more than his outline. I know I should try and look at him so he can read the message on the glasses but I don't want to. I'm so disgusted, but I can't tell if that disgust is with me or him.

If Ralph is annoyed at my refusal to play the game and look at Jared he shows no hint of it. "So Jared, how do you know Jeanie?"

"Well, we're really good friends. Close friends. She's a great girl. Not like other girls. She's one of the guys. Nothing ever seems to bother her, she doesn't really expect anything of you. Really cool like that." Jared sounds more proud of how he articulated his opinion than of me.

"Alright Jared thank you, I don't think we have any further questions."

I don't hear or see the outline of Jared walk away. He's just no longer there. For that, I'm grateful, regardless of what that means for him.

"Let's see if we have more luck with this next contestant. Jeanie, are you ready for try number two?" Ralph says, not expecting a response.

"Genie?"

"Mom?" I yell the word but nothing comes out.

I go to grab the shape next to me that makes up her outline but Ralph pulls me back. Without missing a beat he adds, "So ma'am how do you know Jeanie?"

"I'm her mother. Though it's been a few years since we've seen each other."

She sounds tired.

"A few years? Oh, well why is that? Have you been travel—"

"I killed myself. Pills. Genie was never sure about it. The doctors told her it may have been an accidental overdose from my pain meds," she says without inflection. "I guess she knows now."

I'm still reaching for her. Trying to grasp the shadow. I can see her hair's outline, how it's a little wavy but mostly frizzy and framing where her face should be. Her shadow looks so small and fainter than Jared or Ralph's.

"Sorry to hear that," Ralph speaks with the kind of sympathy someone uses when you get passed up for a job. "Well, how is it to see Jeanie now?"

"I wish she was happier. But I know how difficult the world can make that. I wish she knew how much potential she has. How she can make her life up any way she chooses. It's hard, but she can't give up." She holds my hand as she says this, the ring sits in the space between our skin. "How it might not feel like it, but it's okay to ask for hel—"

"Alright, thank you, ma'am. Round of applause for the lady, folks!" She disappears with the audience's claps.

I scream. I fall to my knees, head in my hands. I can't lose her again, I pant about to hyperventilate.

Ralph either ignores this or doesn't comment on it but he does something to make the audience laugh again before adding, "Alrighty, last chance. Everyone, let's hear it for our final contestant!"

From the ground, I can hear his tool belt jingling. Things I thought I'd forgotten come back to me. The sound of the wrenches and hammer hitting each other as he walks. The smell of motor oil and sawdust and how his boots strike with the heel first like he's marching somewhere.

"Hello sir, welcome to the show. How are you doing today?" Ralph asks over the applause.

Ignoring the question, I hear my father go into all the reasons my mom and I ruined his life like a rehearsed soliloquy. How we left him. How he worked so hard. How no one ever listens to him. How no one asked him how he was. The rant goes on and on. The shadow of him fluctuates while he speaks. He moves from the form of a young man, tall and strong, to an elderly man hunched over and then back again. I can see Ralph nodding along. The audience nods along too, everyone except for one. That one shadow rises from their seat. I notice the long hair and dress that outline her form.

"Help me!" the old woman from the gas station shouts. "That's the Truth clue. That's what the glasses say." She speaks like a teacher giving a lesson. "Everyone can see it. Anyone that's looking. Jeanette, it's your life. Not theirs. These mistakes aren't yours. Let them go. If you don't let it go soon—"

Static interrupts her. Ralph and Dad's shadows are gone. The audience and the woman are gone. I'm falling. I look down and I'm a shadow now too. The only color visible is the deep blue of the ring on my hand. The color of the sky in the desert at dawn and dusk. The color of her eyes.

My forehead on the glass is the first thing I feel. The radio is on again. Bob Dylan. Something about a vagabond rapping at the door and the dead left behind. Did they both like this song? The car's air conditioner feels colder now - frigid even. I hug my knees to my chest. I realize I haven't opened my eyes yet. Where have I been? Where am I going?

The dirt road opens up on the right to a dust-filled ocean, nothing to break up the monotony of shrubs, sand, and in the distance, a bleak blue horizon. To the left of the road, some more dust, dying plants, and the bones of a long-dead coyote. Bleached white in the sun. Up ahead I can make out the silhouette of a drive-thru sign, the building behind it leveled to the ground by years in the unrelenting desert. I've been here before. Only a foundation and debris remain. Is the gas station up ahead too? The sign's letters look recently filled in:

You Can Have

This Or You Can HAVE THE END

Everything around looks wavy, like light refracting on a hot highway in the distance, except it's all around me. It feels like one of those nightmares where the car is moving but I can't get to the steering wheel to control it. The end of what? The laugh track is back. I don't want to look to my left to see who's in the driver's seat. The host's voice comes through the radio and is clearer than anything around me. Everything, my perception, the car, the world, feels coated with a thin layer of sediment from the dusty dirt road, only my ring feels like it holds any weight. It begs me to acknowledge it.

"...And now it's everyone's favorite part of the program, our contestant's time to choose. What will it be? You get one guess to get it right, and then your choice of Truth or Consequences? WHAT WILL IT BE FOR OUR GUEST STAR?...."

The car continues, past the scant remains of the drive-thru, dirt swirls up and around the car. Across the road, another coyote sits and stares. Its deep blue eyes watch, looking at and through the car to me, daring me to make a choice.

BIOGRAPHIES

STEPHANIE WEBER

Stephanie Weber is a writer and a comedian from Chicago who is currently pursuing her MFA in dramatic writing from SCAD. Her work has been published in Slate, Mental Floss, Reductress, Atlas Obscura, Remezcla, and many more. Her debut novel Nothing Nice to Say was released in 2021 with Weasel Press.

JEFFREY DOKA

Jeff has written everything from short stories to screenplays to start-up blog posts to radio dramas. He designed narrative structure and wrote story content for "The Lost Library," a choice based narrative game. His short story "The Conference" has been published in the Wild Musette Journal, his short story "The Last Fare of M1S-3" was published in The Future Looms Magazine. You can find him at finalbossediting.com, and he streams his writing at twitch.tv/final_boss_editing if you ever want to stop in to say hi (or give feedback).

RACHEL COYNE

Rachel Coyne is a painter and writer from Lindstrom, MN. She is a devotee of Pablo Neruda, a collector of vintage editions of Jane Eyre and a lover of Don Williams songs. Her previous works include the novels Whiskey Heart and the Patron Saint of Lost Comfort Lake, along with a YA e-book trilogy the Antigone Ravynn Chronicles and a children's book Daughter, Have I Told You?

KAITLYN RICH

Kaitlyn Rich received an MA in English and Media Studies from Rutgers University. In addition to fiction, her creative work takes the form of award winning short films, academic conference papers, and creative non-fiction. She grew up in Northampton, Pennsylvania and after a decade in New York City now lives in Philadelphia.

Running Wild Press publishes stories that cross genres with great stories and writing. RIZE publishes great genre stories written by people of color and by authors who identify with other marginalized groups. Our team consists of:

Lisa Diane Kastner, Founder and Executive Editor
Mona Bethke, Acquisitions Editor, RIZE
Benjamin White, Acquisition Editor, Running Wild
Peter A. Wright, Acquisition Editor, Running Wild
Resa Alboher, Editor
Rebecca Dimyan, Editor
Andrew DiPrinzio, Editor
Abigail Efird, Editor
Henry L. Herz, Editor
Laura Huie, Editor
Cecilia Kennedy, Editor
Barbara Lockwood, Editor
Kelly Powers, Reader
Cody Sisco, Editor
Chih Wang, Editor
Pulp Art Studios, Cover Design
Standout Books, Interior Design
Polgarus Studios, Interior Design

Learn more about us and our stories at www.runningwild-press.com

Loved these stories and want more? Follow us at www.runningwildpress.com, www.facebook.com/running-wildpress, on Twitter @lisadkastner @RunWildBooks